WE THOUGHT WE KNEW YOU

LINDA COTTON JEFFRIES

For Amy,
best wishes!
Ld. C. Jeff.

FIFTH
AVENUE
PRESS

Fifth Avenue Press is a locally focused and publicly owned publishing imprint of the Ann Arbor District Library. It is dedicated to supporting the local writing community by promoting the production of original fiction, non-fiction and poetry written for children, teens and adults.

Printed in the United States of America

First Printing, 2018

ISBN: 978-1-947989-24-5 (hardcover), 978-1-947989-25-2 (paperback), 978-1-947989-26-9 (ebook)

Fifth Avenue Press

343 S Fifth Ave

Ann Arbor, MI 48104

www.fifthavenue.press

Cover and Layout Design

by AADL

for David, who brings the sweetness to my life

PROLOGUE

Jay Warren was surprised that he could actually feel the sound that the plane crash made, even from a distance. First, there'd been an ear-splitting squeal, followed by a thudding sound, all of it only slightly muffled by the humid air and dense foliage. Seconds later, a fireball appeared on the horizon behind them. The smell of diesel filled the air but it was hard to tell if it was coming from the crash or the piece-of-shit jeep they were riding in. Either way, he thought his driver showed remarkable training, looking neither left nor right, but focused instead on the rutted road into the village. As the jeep jolted over the washboard surface, Jay leaned back against the seat and smoothed the cuff of his expensive shirt, satisfied. That went well, he thought.

It hadn't taken much to get his father to agree to his plan. The notorious Walter Warren was a joke. His father didn't know half of what was going on, hadn't known since Jay had begun manipulating their business interests decades ago. In fact, duping him had become almost a hobby of Jay's. His father had thought this plane trip was one thing, while Jay had known full well it was another. He had persuaded the man with talk of a tropical resort where the two of them could relax and enjoy themselves while the FBI dicked around investigating their affairs in Pittsburgh. The crash would allow Jay time to finish shifting his affairs around to further solidify the FBI case against his father, while leaving him free to carry on with his own enterprises.

The directions that Jay had given to their pilot were Boston to Dallas to Bogota, then a turn back north to a small airstrip outside of Caracas where the plane would "unexpectedly" need to refuel. Once they landed, Jay planned to part company with the plane. The FBI would be all over the crash and he was counting on the scene to take weeks or even months to decipher.

When the time came, his father only looked up briefly as the pilot announced that they needed to make an unexpected stop at an airstrip outside of Caracas. "The delay should be minimal, sir, I apologize. I will oversee the refueling myself."

Once they'd landed, the older man stood and reached his hands up over his head. "I think I'd like to get out and stretch my legs for a minute. You?"

Jay shook his head and returned to his newspaper. He saw his father walk down the steps and enter the small building, the pilot following after. On the plane, Jay folded his paper and the thin jacket he'd worn and placed them in the small duffle bag he'd shoved under his seat. The briefcase, he left sitting open on the seat beside him. When it came time for take-off, they had agreed that the pilot would make sure his father thought he was resting in the rear of the plane. Jay patted his pockets for his passport and wallet, grabbed the duffle and left the plane, darting to the left at the bottom of the stairs instead of into the building. He found the jeep running just fifty yards away.

The diesel smell was overpowering now, so Jay rolled the window closed in spite of the heat.

"Ten minutes to the pick-up point, sir."

"And the mechanic?

"Already taken care of, sir."

2

Jay nodded. The first step in protecting his fortune was done. The accounts as well as the accountant had all been taken care of. He had been working for months to separate himself from his father's old-fashioned enterprises so that the FBI investigation would finish along with his old man. Now, he just needed a few more days to see the loose ends wrapped up. Once the air had cleared, so to speak, he'd be back in Pittsburgh, looking the dutifully bereaved son. But more importantly, he'd be the one in charge. He was done with his father's penny-ante bullshit like numbers running. It was patently clear that the real money was in export/import, whether it was guns, drugs or women. And, it was time to move up to a more global scale. The connections he needed were already beginning to fall into place. He smiled to himself, satisfied to see his careful plans coming together.

CHAPTER ONE

"Sabbatical, what? You can't take a sabbatical from a marriage. This isn't Harvard. I'm your husband."

Marybeth and her husband, Ken, were in the kitchen, the most normal of places in their house for the most abnormal conversation they'd ever had. Glass jars filled with flour and sugar stood as they always did at the end of the counter. The coffee maker still held remnants from breakfast and an empty cup sat on the counter, waiting to be put into the dishwasher. The aroma from the pan of lasagna she'd baked and left in the freezer still hovered in the air. Wet boots sat near the door. It was as ordinary a scene as anyone could imagine. But the conversation wasn't.

Marybeth tried to roll her suitcase out of his line of sight, but it didn't help. He was angry, hurt and bewildered all at the same time. She watched as his six-foot frame paced uncertainly in front of the sink. He ran his hand through his short, graying hair in a gesture that hurt with its familiarity. She forced an air of calm that she didn't feel, sat down across from him at the kitchen island and waited. She didn't blame him. She couldn't answer all of his questions, at least not yet.

The leather stool under her turned slowly as she released her breath and worked to maintain a calm demeanor. He couldn't see that her hands were clenched in her lap, the knuckles white as she talked. "Look, I'm not walking out. A sabbatical is a very specific word. Usually colleges grant them for people to go and do research. That's what I'm doing. A few weeks of research, then I'll come back. I promise. We've got our trip with the boys planned for mid-July. I'll definitely be back before that."

Ken exploded, slamming his hands on the counter, making the tops of the wide jars rattle. "Our trip? Are you crazy? You're going to walk out of here today and come back for a vacation?"

"Yes, I just need to get away to do a little research."

"Research on what? You're a special ed teacher, what the hell do you need to research, chalk?" He slapped the cabinet door behind him so hard that it popped back open again. "Jesus, June, what are you talking about?"

She willed herself to stay still, although even now, the butterflies were starting. "Ken, please, don't be ridiculous, no one even uses chalk anymore. I'm being upfront with you. I'm not sneaking out the door in the middle of the night. I'm asking you for a few weeks, that's all. You can give our friends whatever explanation you like. I won't contest it. You want to say mean and ugly things about me, then that's your right. I just ask that you not say anything mean to our boys. Please, be mad at me but don't take it out on them." Marybeth pulled her hands apart, flexing them to restore feeling, then touched the back of her hair. The short ends lying flat against her neck still surprised her. After years of suburban, shoulder-length hair, she'd had it cut short on the day school got out. She hadn't made up her mind whether she thought the new cut made her hair look more or less gray but she decided that she didn't really care. It was easy and therefore perfect for someone traveling.

Ken was shaking his head and seemed to be struggling to understand what she was saying. She knew he loved her, needed her on a daily basis. "But June, you *are* sneaking out, you're not saying where you're going or why, what am I supposed to think? I thought we had a good marriage." He paused, then resumed in a sadder tone. "I thought we'd gotten past all of this secrecy. I thought we were happy."

"We are, Ken, we are, that's why I'm not leaving our marriage, I just want to take a short break from it."

"But for all I know, you're meeting some guy and spending a month in Greece skinny dipping in the Mediterranean. No one takes a 'sabbatical' like this."

He had resorted to air quotes so she knew he was upset. He despised air quotes and most of the people who used them. She answered slowly and deliberately as she stood and shouldered her pack. "I swear to God, Ken, there is no man, there is no sex, there is nothing salacious about this trip at all. Now, I have to go. The bills are set up to pay automatically so you don't have to worry about that. There's food for several days in the fridge and a few more items in the freezer. After that, you'll have to take over the cooking. I'm sure you'll be fine."

She headed for the door, her suitcase trailing behind, then stopped and turned, her hand on the front doorknob. "And please, stop calling me June. I hate that nickname. My name is Marybeth. It's a good name. I chose it for a reason and I'm sick of being called something else."

She opened the front door and pulled her suitcase over the threshold behind her. She wanted so much to kiss him good-bye, to have him put his arms around her and pull her close before she left, but she couldn't risk losing her nerve. She kept moving forward. She heard him pulling on his boots and following behind her, but he seemed to pause in shock at the sight of the cab waiting for her at the curb. She was opening the car door and getting in by the time his brain seemed to kick in and tell his legs to start moving again. It sounded like he was running.

7

"June, dammit, I mean Marybeth, please, stop and think about this. Talk to me!"

She pushed the suitcase onto the floor ahead of her, got in, and closed the door firmly. "Let's go, quickly please," she asked the driver. It took all of her resolve not to look to see what Ken was doing, but when the cab turned the corner, she had a brief glance and the tears she had held in came pouring out. He was a good man and he looked so forlorn. He wasn't even yelling. He just stood there on the sidewalk, watching her go. She hoped he would remember her promise. She was coming back for him, for their boys, for their life together. She just had to find something out first.

The cab was out of the neighborhood quickly and as they reached highway speed Marybeth forced herself to slow her breathing and lean back into her seat. She took her glasses off and set them on the seat beside her, then rummaged through her backpack for a tissue. Disappointed in herself for crying, she tucked the wet tissue into her pocket and actually smiled for a second, imagining how mad Ken would be. As the head launderer in the house, he had forbidden anyone from putting tissues into pockets. Oh well, if this was what the wild side looked like, it was time to embrace it. She cleaned her glasses with the hem of her shirt and settled them back on her nose under the newly feathered bangs.

Marybeth had dressed casually for the trip, black jeans and a light zippered jacket over her plain white top, her favorite black clogs ready for quick removal at the terminal. She fingered the zipper pull and hoped that the airport screening process would go quickly, since the argument had delayed her more than she'd expected. As the cab delivered her to the departures door she shouldered her backpack and pulled the small suitcase behind her. She made her way through the relatively short security line and headed to her gate.

* * *

ON THE PLANE, the dreaded moment arrived when she had to lift her suitcase up into the overhead bin. It looked so easy when Ken did it, but she was barely five feet, and it proved to be the challenge she had feared. Luckily, she'd decided to bring her tablet rather than the pile of library books that she normally traveled with, so she managed to maneuver it into place. Sliding into her seat, Marybeth hugged her backpack to her chest as she watched the people stream onto the plane. A young man in headphones and a hooded sweatshirt settled into the seat next to her. They nodded cordially but neither one seemed to feel the need to speak. Marybeth put her pack on the floor and stared out the window, wishing she could get Ken's bewildered face out of her mind. The Harrisburg airport was a small one and she could see the farmland spreading out away from it, the river flowing on either side of it. As they lifted into the air, she felt as though she was watching her life disappear. Would she ever get it back?

After her final meeting with Donald's mother, the last of her yearly parent meetings, she'd stood near the door to the conference room, trying to memorize how it looked—the three upholstered chairs next to the shorter, metal ones, the sweaty, smoky smell of the three teenagers waiting in the outer office, the clacking of the secretary on his computer. She wanted to remember it all. Marybeth liked Donald's mother and was glad that she'd seemed pleased with the meeting. If Marybeth was being honest, she liked Donald's mother a bit more than she liked Donald, but that wasn't usually the case. On most days, she loved her job. She liked the classroom with its big wall of windows. She loved hearing the kids talk before class started, imagining their lives, so different from her own. Special education students seemed like the bravest kids in the world to her. Every morning that they came to school, knowing they were different and worrying that their lack of skills would be noticed, seemed like an act of courage. She felt privileged to witness it. Of course, afternoons still managed to last an eternity, especially with a summer breeze blowing in the window, carrying the kids' attention with it, but it was a life she wanted to return to.

She opened her backpack and pulled out her tablet. She put it on airplane mode before pulling up the familiar file, a newspaper headline and photograph from the *Times*. Marybeth still remembered the moment just weeks ago, when she'd scanned the news and come across the article. The shock had been visceral.

Fifth period had just ended and she'd taken a minute of passing time to look at the news on her laptop. At once, Marybeth was frozen, her eyes fixed on the computer screen in front of her. There was a photograph of a mountain jungle with the tail fin of a plane barely visible above the foliage. A large headline screamed, *Plane Crash in South America Linked to Suspected Drug Kingpin Walter Warren and Son*. The article went on to detail the suspected passenger list, Walter Warren, his son Jay Warren and an unknown pilot. What did it mean? The screen had dimmed as it prepared to shut off, while her brain felt as though it was spinning out of control. Could he really be dead? Could the entire ordeal finally be over? She had wanted to run out of the school building and jump in her car to go home.

"Mrs. Rogers? Can you help me with this? I'm stuck on number twenty-three." A student in her sixth hour class had settled down into the seat beside her at the table, the fat, red algebra text falling open with a thud next to her elbow. The sound finally reached Marybeth's conscious level and she turned to the girl, closing the laptop. She blinked to push away the beginnings of tears and forced herself to smile at the student.

"Of course, let's take a look at it. Are you graphing these equations in order to solve them?" After more than twenty years of supporting high school students with learning issues, this was one topic she could have handled in her sleep. Given the state of mind she was in, she figured that was a good thing.

Now, settled into her seat on the plane, Marybeth brought the article up one more time. She'd saved it weeks ago, but it was one of many that she still pulled up regularly to read over. She supposed, if it had been an actual newspaper, it would have been worn and brittle by now, the edges starting to curl and tear, but on the tablet it still looked like today's news. The photograph showed the small section of tail fin rising above the densest-looking woods she'd ever seen. No amount of staring brought the plane into focus or made it clear who had been on board. The author of this first article, and many articles later, reported three fatalities—Walt Warren, his son Jay, and a pilot. Much of the wreckage had burned, along with a small section of the forest around it. It seemed there was little more anyone would learn from that site.

The letter from her friend Gregory had come to her school address just days later. She'd dropped by the mailroom between classes and was surprised to find what looked like an actual letter. At first, she couldn't imagine what it was, or who might be sending her something. Her box was usually filled with catalogs for special education materials and notes from building staff about various items. Real mail was almost unheard of. When she got up to her office, she settled her computer on the desk and then tore open the envelope. On the front of a single sheet of folded paper was a photocopy of a more detailed article about the crash. On the back, in neat black printing it said "Ding dong the witch is dead!" with the smallest letter G under the quote.

CHAPTER TWO

*T*he flight to Pittsburgh took less than an hour. Marybeth wasn't sure why she'd chosen to fly instead of just driving her car to Pittsburgh from Chambersburg, but it felt right. She'd needed that quick break, the immediate distance that flying had given her, much more than she needed the car. She took another taxi to her hotel. It wasn't fancy, but it was close to downtown and the restaurant where she was meeting Gregory for dinner. She hoped he could help her decide where to go from here.

It felt odd to be checking into a hotel on her own without Ken beside her or busy wrangling the kids in the car, and she felt a little sad as she wondered again about all of them and what would happen in her absence. She'd made a point of seeing both boys last week, but of course, hadn't let on that she was going to be gone. She and Jimmy had talked in the laundry room about his summer plans as they folded the mounds of clothes that he'd brought home. She had no idea how anyone went weeks without washing their clothes, but it seemed that owning dozens of T-shirts was one of the keys. He appeared to be happy with the roommate he'd secured as well as his summer job at the hardware store. It was a Mom and Pop business rather than a chain, with aisles and aisles overflowing with goods. She laughed at his description of trying to memorize the floor so that he could direct customers as needed. Marybeth didn't think she'd have been up to that challenge, but it was clear that he was proud of his accomplishment. She thought back to how quickly he had memorized piano pieces as a child and figured he must just have the right sort of mind for the task.

Marybeth's older son, Grant, had been harder to pin down and she'd gotten the first inkling that this young woman he was seeing might turn out to be more important than the others she'd met over the years. He'd finally agreed to coffee with her one afternoon on his way home from work, but his conversation had centered much more around Amy than it had about his work. He had few questions for Marybeth but talked at length about the summer plans that the two of them were making. She'd told him he was welcome to borrow the camping equipment they kept stored in the basement and he was off again, rhapsodizing about their plan to go white water rafting with friends. She loved seeing him look so happy.

As she settled her few things in the hotel room, she tucked her phone away with her suitcase and wished fervently that all of them would be fine.

It was just a short walk from the hotel to the restaurant. She'd made a reservation but when she saw the nearly empty dining room, she realized she needn't have bothered. Oh well, if she'd accidentally picked the worst place to eat in the city, it didn't really matter.

Marybeth settled into a booth near the middle of the dining area and waited for her old friend. She realized she had no idea what he looked like now and wondered about herself, how different she must look. She had been so young the last time she'd seen Gregory, young and scared and so confused. Now, her hair held nearly as much gray as it did brown, and her backside had expanded a little more than she was comfortable with.

She saw a man she thought was about her age walking toward her and realized that he really did look much the same. He had a slight build, a pitiful sort of beard that spoke of neglect rather than style, and an unattractive knit cap. Slung over his left shoulder was an old, beat up leather satchel that she recognized from his college days at Penn State. It had been new then, and the decades since had weathered the leather to a deep brown. For some reason, she was pleased, reassured somehow, to see that he was still carrying it around.

She stood up nervously as he drew close, then saw the big grin spreading across his face. He enveloped her in a hug and she held on for a long moment. He even smelled the way she remembered him, a combination of Dial soap and mints. Finally, she released him and they settled into their seats. "I can't believe we're here," she said. "After all these years, I feel like I've been holding my breath or something."

Once he sat down, he tossed the hat onto the seat beside him, ruffling his short, curly hair into its proper shape. He, too, had a fair amount of gray mixed in with his blonde.

"I know what you mean, but are you sure we should be here?" he leaned forward just as she was leaning back, the smile replaced with a look of concern. There was a deep crease between his eyebrows, as though some kind of worry had settled in years ago and stayed. "I sent you that note so that you could put it all to rest, Sarah, sorry, I mean Marybeth, not stir things back up. I thought you told me you had a great life now, grown sons, a husband that you care about, right? Isn't that enough?"

She shook her head. "I wish I could say it was, but I can't. You know why I'm doing this."

"But it's probably the same for her. I bet she has a great life too, maybe even a husband and kids of her own. Why do you want to risk messing all that up?"

"I don't want to mess anything up, I just want to see my daughter, to know that she's safe, that she has a good life, one that makes her happy."

"I don't buy it. That's not enough of a reason and you know it. What are you really after here?"

"Fine," she dropped her napkin beside her plate and took a deep breath. "I'd like to see if there's a place in her life for me, if that's possible. I'd like to get to know her, for her to get to know my husband and my sons, and for them to know her too." She shrugged and put the napkin back into her lap. "I know it sounds crazy. Especially since she might not even want to talk to me."

"You're right, it does sound a bit crazy. But if she's happy, then shouldn't you let her be? For God's sake, why risk her happiness, or yours?"

Marybeth was surprised at how calm she felt now that she was here, especially after the scene that morning. "Look, if you don't want to help me, I understand, I really do. I can take off now and we can just be old friends again."

"You know that's not what I meant. I do want to help." He rubbed at his beard nervously. "You got a raw deal, there's no two ways about it. If you want to find her, I'm in. The timing seems better now than it ever was before."

"Thank you, Greg, you have no way of knowing how much it means to me to have you here."

Marybeth smiled and squeezed his hand again briefly, just as the waitress arrived with coffee and took their orders.

"So, where do you think we should start?" he asked as he poured sugar into the thick white mug. She wasn't sure a cup of coffee could even dissolve that much sugar and she laughed at the thought.

He looked up quickly. "What, I hate coffee, I only seem to drink it when I'm planning something unthinkable. Give me a break."

"I'm sorry I make you drink coffee, Greg." She felt her back relax as she drew her shoulder blades together and leaned against the seat. "You know, this feels like the first time I've laughed since I heard about the crash. I feel taller, lighter than I have in a long time."

Gregory leaned back, the leather squeaking audibly. He let out a long breath. "I know what you mean about feeling lighter." He sighed, a small smile on his face.

The waitress set their plates down gently and returned to the kitchen.

Marybeth changed her tone to a more sober one. "Can you believe it? I can't even bear to think about that crash."

Gregory sipped at his drink, then set it down and stretched his arms along the back of the booth. "My friend in the FBI was joking that they're going to have layoffs now that the case is out the window."

The Warren family had been in the news a lot before the crash as the FBI was reportedly building a new case against the well-known crime family.

"There's no one else to try? Surely Jay and his dad weren't the only ones running the business."

"They're the only ones the FBI cared about. The others were all small potatoes in comparison, not really worth the expense, I suppose." He cut off a bite of pork chop, then picked up a forkful of corn on top of it. "So, where do we start?"

At least that's what she thought he said through the food in his mouth. Now that the meal was here, Marybeth wasn't sure she could eat any of it. She pushed her mashed potatoes against the meatloaf and poked at it before setting her fork down on the edge of her plate. "Okay, let me tell you what I've done so far and maybe you can help me figure out where to go next. Once I got over the shock of the crash I couldn't help but think about her. I mean, I've always thought about her, she was so tiny when I had to let her go. But the only resources I had were a photograph and a baggy from the hospital when she was born. Years ago, I had an age projection photograph made from the baby picture that I had, but she was so little, they weren't very confident in what they produced."

"A baggy?"

Marybeth took up her fork again. "I felt silly doing it at the time, but I wanted anything I could have of her. I cut a few pieces of her hair, even kept the little bandage that the nurse had put on her foot. Then two years ago, once I started hearing about all of those DNA services, I sent everything in, hoping it would lead me somewhere. Unfortunately, I got zip. The only relative it found was her Great Uncle Edward Clark, but I already knew about him. Then I got online and looked further to see if there were any resources for linking birth parents and their adopted children."

"Don't tell me, you found tons."

"Yep, and I scoured them to see if anyone had been looking for me, but I didn't find anyone. I located an adoption reunion registry but it's huge. Have you heard of it?"

"No."

"It's got thousands of names and it's all organized by date and by city, but there were too many variables for me to sort through. That's where I thought you could help. You're with the police, right? You'll have more access than I can get."

Gregory stiffened and set his silverware on the edge of the plate. He wiped his mouth slowly before looking up at her to answer. "Actually, I'm not with the police anymore. I've gone out on my own as a private investigator."

"Really? Do you like that more than the police?"

"No, I don't." He shrugged. "But it is what it is and I still have access to a few more resources than you would have." He sounded resigned in a way, and it made her wonder about his life in the years that she'd been gone. Then his tone changed to a lighter note. "Why don't we meet up in the morning at the library branch around the corner? They've got a good microfilm section that has a lot of old city records."

Marybeth brightened at the idea of a concrete starting point. "That sounds perfect." She smiled broadly at her old friend and they relaxed into the meal, sharing stories about their lives. Marybeth was sorry to hear that Greg wasn't married, and in fact sounded a little lonely as he told her about his life since college. She wondered about all that he wasn't saying, but she enjoyed talking with him about her sons and her experiences teaching and they finished their meal slowly, dawdling over a shared dessert and a last cup of coffee. Once they finished, the two of them made plans to meet in the morning.

As Marybeth walked toward her hotel room, she wished briefly that she'd gotten a rental car and driven past the old neighborhood, maybe looked for her old house. But something about that just seemed too sad. After more than twenty years, there would be nothing worth seeing now.

Marybeth returned to the hotel room, settled her backpack on the bed and wished like anything that she could call Ken. She looked at her phone briefly, saw the number of missed calls from him, and with some regret, tucked it away again. She would call in a day or two, she promised herself, once she was feeling a little more settled. The room was nearly empty. She'd hung her few clothes in the small closet and tucked the suitcase in as well. She'd have to talk to Gregory tomorrow about how long the search might take. She hoped he could help her find a room to rent or some other less expensive place to stay. She had been saving a little bit at a time for years without really knowing why, or rather, without admitting to herself why she was doing it. But there was no way her funds would last if she were paying hotel prices.

She made a cup of tea in the little machine on the counter, then put on her nightgown and stretched out on the bed. After some fiddling, she figured out the remote control and surfed the

TV channels for something to settle on. It made her wonder what Ken was doing, and before long she turned it off. She fished her tablet out and called up the book she was reading. It was a light romantic comedy that lifted her spirits a bit, but before long her eyes were closing. She crawled under the covers, turned off the light and tried to settle into the unfamiliar bed but the space felt enormous. She and Ken had a queen-sized bed at home but without him, the hotel's king bed felt like an entire continent sprawling away beside her, one that was piled with a mountain range of pillows, all of which were too soft. She tried to settle in and not watch the numbers on the small clock, but it proved to be impossible.

After an hour, Marybeth got out of bed and used the bathroom, then opened her backpack again before climbing under the covers. She retrieved the photograph that she'd brought with her, a three-by-five print that she remembered picking up from a drugstore after the baby was gone. She traced her fingernail around the small face and wondered again why she had made the decisions she had.

CHAPTER THREE

$\mathcal{W}$hen Marybeth left, Ken felt like collapsing on the sidewalk, in fact, his knees started to give way, but the walk was covered with puddles, pooling in the seam between the squares of concrete. He was in shock, he thought, actual shock. He could feel his systems shutting down, until a drop of cool water fell from the branch above him, directly down his collar. "What the hell." He jumped and pawed at the collar of his shirt. What the hell, he thought again as the cab took the last corner and moved out of sight. He grabbed at his pockets frantically. Where were the damn car keys?

He dashed inside, dug through two different sets of pants pockets before finding them, and then ran outside to start the car. Once in the seat, though, he paused. Where would she have gone? The airport in the city, a train station, the bus? Who knew what she was planning, how far she was going? He punched her number into his phone, over and over again, listening to it ring and ring. He sagged in defeat and pulled the keys from the ignition. All he could think to do was get on the phone to her friends and see what they knew about all of this.

Thirty minutes later he didn't know any more than he had

before. He couldn't find a single friend that knew anything about her leaving. That in itself seemed both frightening and amazing and it made him wonder again just how long she'd been planning to do this. He went to their bedroom first, searched through her drawers, the bedside table and the little-used space at the top of the closet. Bookcases, the kitchen junk drawer, even odd spaces in the basement held nothing. Her desk was an antique rolltop one, and he was staring at more than a dozen cubbyholes. Searching this was going to take some time. He returned to the basement and brought up an old card table, then set it up next to the desk. Dammit, he was going to do this thoroughly. He was convinced that something there would explain what was going on.

He sat down in the padded office chair. His large frame bumped up against the lower edge of the desk, and he reached to adjust the chair from her build's smaller setting. It occurred to him suddenly that he'd never sat down at her desk before. Why was that? He supposed he just wasn't curious by nature, or maybe, honestly, he was just lazy about the kinds of things that she took care of at this desk.

He found one cubby that held requests for donations from the charities that they typically gave to. Another one held an old fashioned three-ringed notebook that was labeled *bills*. He opened it to find a page for each month of the year, each one clearly marked with the bills paid, the dates and amounts next to each one. In front of these sheets were pages for each account, with copies of the bills tucked into sheet protector pockets behind each one. Old fashioned, he thought. "Does anyone still handle bills this way?" He pulled out the first one, a gas card, and then looked at the past bills. They only seemed to go through April. The same was true of the electric bills and the car payment. What had she said, "they were all being paid electronically?" So the old fashioned way had been fine until she'd settled on this scheme? He looked at the last bill. *Go paperless* was circled. Jesus, had she been planning this for a while or was it just a coincidence? He tried to remember if she had talked with him about switching to online bill paying. There was a vague recollection of a conversation over dinner one night, but nothing that he could put his finger on.

"Dammit, what is going on?" Ken shoved the chair back from the desk and stomped up the stairs to their bedroom. He felt the anger radiating off him in sheets, as though it might melt the paint around him. He wanted to destroy something and cry all at the same time. He threw himself across the bed and lay back looking up at the blades of the ceiling fan. Shit, they needed to be vacuumed.

CHAPTER FOUR

*M*arybeth had been Sarah Dawes back then, the name dissolving on her tongue like a small mint. A quiet girl, she had arrived at college with few of the social skills that she would need to cope. Sarah's father had taken off not long after she was born and by the time she left for college, her mother had remarried and started a new family. The relationship she'd had with her mother had grown strained, then weakened even further. She had earned a scholarship with her grades and a work-study job helped her cover the costs. She remembered how excited she had been to start college, but when she got there, everyone around her had seemed so sure of themselves, hustling from class to class, meeting up with friends to study. She had felt so out of place.

Even after nearly a year and a half, she was embarrassed to admit that although she had a large number of acquaintances, she still hadn't made any really solid friends. After two semesters of difficult roommates, she'd decided that she must be the problem and had found a small apartment on her own. She got along well with everyone in her classes, but it just never seemed to go any further than that. Her tight budget made it hard, as she found herself saying no to activities that cost more than she could afford. Making matters even worse, to keep her scholarship, not only did she have to maintain stellar grades, she also had to put in twenty hours a week at the library's circulation desk. She had hoped that it might be a good way to meet people, she'd even been looking forward to it, but the supervisor was partial to blondes, it seemed, and they were always given the best shifts. Shy, dark-haired Sarah got the five to nine evening shift, which meant everyone else was out to dinner, relaxing and hanging out with friends while she was stuck in the library.

She could remember now how vulnerable she'd been when Jay Warren first appeared on campus, the answer to her loneliness and disappointment. She'd always been so careful around him back at home. All of the warnings, the rumors about his father and their family had been ingrained in her. Drugs, gambling, and money laundering were all in the mix and she had kept her distance from him.

In spite of the press about his family, Jay had been popular in school although well out of her league, to be sure. Some of her friends had called him stuck up, but she'd only ever seen the sweet side of Jay. Daniel, Jay's brother, had been in the class in C hall. He'd had meningitis as a baby and went through school in special needs classes. She'd volunteered in his classroom during high school and that was how she'd met Jay. He was picking up Daniel after school one day and she was there helping put his winter coat on. Danny hated that coat she remembered, the zipper scared him, so she and Jay were trying to work around his wiggling. It seemed like Jay was pretty gentle with his brother and Daniel clearly doted on him. His face lit up the few times that Jay came to the door of the classroom. It was one reason why she had found it so hard to believe that his family could do the things they were accused of.

It was a Friday evening, the deadest of dead shifts and Sarah was checking the big clock over the doorway one more time. She didn't see the young man until he was right in front of her. "Sarah, is that you?"

She was mortified. In protest of the Friday evening shift, she was wearing her worst t-shirt and rattiest jeans. She couldn't even remember if she'd combed her hair before sticking it into a messy ponytail. And here was Jay, the baddest of the bad boys from her hometown. His dark hair had grown and spread out around his collar and his deep brown eyes captured her attention and held it.

"Jay, what are you doing here?" She tried to smooth the front of her shirt down while straightening her ponytail at the same time.

She'd forgotten how disarming his smile could be, how it moved into his eyes and seemed to light up his face. "I'm working on getting a business degree, but I'm so late starting that I feel like a bit of an idiot. I don't know anyone at all." Sarah knew exactly how that felt.

"How's Danny? You know I'm getting a teaching degree in special education here."

Jay's head dropped and his tone changed when he looked up. "He's gone, I'm afraid. His funeral was just last week."

"Oh Jay, I'm so sorry. He was so sweet. I know you must miss him."

Jay shifted his feet back and forth briefly before looking up. "You were always so great with him, I can see you getting that degree. I never had the patience for it."

"Oh, I remember you being terrific with him."

Jay brushed his hair back from his forehead. "I don't remember that, but I do remember you."

"I remember you," she thought. That was all it had taken for the warnings to fly out of her head and for Jay to enter her life.

It had felt like such a magical winter, the two of them holed up in her tiny apartment. She'd been by herself for so long that she loved having his company. The fact that they didn't see any other students or head home for the holidays hadn't seemed strange, although looking back now, she knew it was a warning sign that she'd ignored. When he'd asked her to keep their relationship a secret, she'd readily agreed. After all, there wasn't anyone close enough to really care.

CHAPTER FIVE

"*D*ammit all to hell!" Agent Ray Sanchez slammed the newspaper down on his desk, kicked the trashcan that sat beside it, and then threw himself back into the old desk chair. How many fucking years of his life had he poured into this case, how many nights had he sat in this goddamned office instead of at home relaxing or dating even, just working this single case? He slammed his fist on the desk and picked up the article again. Above the fold of the newspaper was a grainy photograph and an enormous headline. *Warren Case Down in Flames?* Down in flames was right. The FBI had been tracking the activities of the Warren family for decades. Almost thirty years ago, his department thought they'd had it all sewn up, witnesses, broken alibis, disgruntled ex-employees, a solid case of gambling and racketeering.

Of course the indictments hadn't included everything they'd known about the crime family, but they thought the angle they'd picked would work. Until it didn't. A dead witness or two here, a re-hired employee with a new office there. The old man, and possibly the son, had taken care of every single piece of the case. Ray had been working for the last ten years putting together a new, stronger case, one that included the more recent businesses they'd gotten into including drug dealing, numbers running and prostitution. And now it was gone, literally up in flames.

Ray shoved back from his desk, tossed his glasses down and rubbed his hands over his dark, unfashionable crew cut. He had to get out of here. The office even smelled like failure—old coffee, dirt, and sweat. He couldn't think over his own anger. Death was too easy, too pat an answer for this case. And someone in the press had started talking about an "honor suicide flight" as if there was any honor to be found in that clan. He needed to know more about the damn plane crash.

A smile started across his face as he leapt up, propping his glasses on top of his head. He took the steps two at a time and found Cindy O'Brien, one of their best analysts, working at her desk, news articles and data sheets covering her computer screen. He dropped into the chair beside her, impressed that she wasn't even startled by him. "Please tell me you have some damn information about this crash."

She leaned back in her chair and pulled off her earbuds. "Nice to see you too, Sanchez. Thanks for the coffee and power bar you brought me."

Ray shoved his hands into his pockets and stretched out his long legs. "Sorry, I'm an ass when it comes to those kinds of things. We've been working this case for so long I can't even think straight anymore. Do you know I've racked up over a hundred vacation days working to put a lid on this mess?" He bent over and pushed against his knees, trying to stretch out his back.

Cindy nodded, holding his gaze for a moment before nervousness seemed to take over. She leaned forward and resumed pressing keys on her computer. "We're all in that boat. I've got over fifty, and I took some days last fall when my aunt passed away down in Texas." She shook her head gently. "Not gonna happen this week either, I guess." She shrugged and turned back to her computer before continuing. "Okay, let's just say you owe me coffee and a power bar next time. Here's what I know so far. The plane crash had some bodies in it, not sure how many, but no evidence of anyone walking away from it."

"What do you mean, 'some?'"

"Let me tell this. First, the plane was sabotaged, rigged to go down in those mountains once it hit a certain altitude."

Ray looked up quickly. "That's not in the news I've seen."

"No, and it won't be, if we can keep a lid on it. Once the plane went down, it broke into two big sections. One burned quickly and completely and we got nothing from it. In the other section, we found some metal dog tags as well as two bodies."

"But everyone here says that there were three." He ticked them off on his fingers. "The pilot, Walt and Jay."

"Wait." She held up her hand and pointed back at the computer screen. "I'm getting to that. The authorities were able to recover two partial bodies. Some kind of accelerant was used and the fire was especially hot. One body is definitely Walt Warren. We've identified him three or four different ways. The second body we think is a pilot calling himself Skip Jones. We're checking to see if he was ex-military. Our hunch is that Skip Jones wasn't his real name."

"Yeah, 'cause why would it be. Okay, what else?"

"This is the interesting part. At the airfield, there were four guys scheduled to work. One was running what they call a tower. I'd call it a stepladder. Two others were cleaning out a hangar for a rich client who was arriving that night. A fourth was a mechanic. The tower guy told us that the mechanic took off before we got there, sometime close to when they heard the crash. They can't ID him at all. We were told he was new and no one knew anything about him. We've got some men looking for him. The guys in the hanger didn't see much at all. One of them was in the can when the Warren plane came in to re-fuel. Whatever he was doing in there, weed or something else, took him a long time. He couldn't tell us anything. The other cleaning guy was taking a break, listening to his music and having a beer. He saw a group get off the plane and then get back on within about ten minutes."

"Three men, right?"

"He's not sure."

"What do you mean, 'he's not sure?'"

"For God's sake, Ray, it's an airfield where the people in charge are drinking and smoking weed. Then they get shocked to hell and back when a plane crashes just over the mountain from them? Even now, they're still scared shitless. It's a wonder they didn't all take off running."

Ray sank back in his chair, pulled off his Buddy Holly glasses and rubbed his hands through his crew cut before kicking the leg of Cindy's desk. He looked up and straightened back into his seat. "Sorry, do we know anything about Jay Warren in all of this?"

"Well, not definitively. The plane stopped in Dallas and the airport there shows both Jay and Walt Warren in the premium lounge having dinner. They were using a private plane but it was following the typical schedule, leaving in the evening, arriving in the early morning. The last photo from Dallas shows them boarding around seven-thirty."

"Do we know why it landed at the small airstrip?"

"Not yet, we've got people on the ground but the entire place is a wreck. It's going to take time."

Ray stood and reached overhead trying to stretch out more of the aches that were beginning to plague him. "Okay, I'd appreciate it if you'd let me know when you hear anything more."

"You got it, bud." Cindy smiled and despite the discouraging news, Ray couldn't help but feel a little bit easier.

CHAPTER SIX

*M*arybeth remembered the winter of her sophomore year as a particularly cold and bitter one. She and Jay had huddled in the apartment for much of it and the only family that they had seen was his Uncle Edward. His mother's brother, Edward Clark, had been in town on business and offered to take them both to dinner. When they walked in, Sarah was taken aback by the beautiful restaurant. It was obviously very expensive and well off the beaten track typically followed by the college crowd. She tugged at the side of her dress, wishing she'd worn something nicer. "What is this? Who is your uncle again?"

Jay grinned and gave her a quick kiss on the temple. "Edward Clark is my uncle, the king of dry cleaning. Can you imagine a more boring business to be in?"

They were ushered to a table where a short, wide faced man stood to greet them. Jay smiled broadly, extending his hand. "Uncle Edward, I'd like you to meet Sarah Dawes. Sarah, this is my uncle, Mr. Edward Clark."

"Oh now." He reached a hand forward and shook hers gently. "Call me Eddie. Please, sit down." She noticed that he was quick to smile. "Now, tell me a little bit about yourself, what are you studying?"

Sarah sat on the edge of the plush green chair. She was nervous at first, but her leg resting against Jay's gave her a bit of needed confidence. "I'm studying special education. I want to be a teacher."

"Why, you know, a very good friend of mine works there at Penn State, in that department. His name is Dr. Charles Wright."

"Dr. Wright? He's my favorite." Sarah would love to have talked more about her classes but Jay stepped in and turned the conversation toward business and finance and Sarah had said very little more. The elegance of the meal and the restaurant might have kept Sarah's nerves jangled, but Eddie had made her feel comfortable in spite of the surroundings. Coming home in the car afterwards, Sarah was eager to hear more about Edward but Jay said little in reply.

"Oh, Uncle Ed's okay, stuck in the nineteen seventies if you ask me." Jay looked at Sarah and patted the wallet in his front pocket. "I'm surprised his business does as well as it does, given how little he knows."

Sarah was puzzled at the change in Jay's tone. He'd been so warm and friendly toward his uncle while they were out, but now Jay's voice held nothing but contempt. Sarah's head spun with the contradiction.

In the weeks after the visit, she remembered how sweet Jay was with her, asking about her classes and listening when she shared stories from the library. She loved it when they'd sit at the table studying together in the evening. Sarah would look up from her textbook and see Jay concentrating on his work, so happy to be where she was.

As the winter wore on, though, Jay started to grow short tempered. Sarah had the vague sense that he might be having money trouble. He didn't talk about it with her, but there were rumblings in the newspapers about an FBI investigation and a possible court case against his father. Jay began to disappear for a few days at a time but he always seemed to return with an explanation of where he'd been.

One day in January, she was enjoying a brief release from winter's grip, her step lightening as she crossed campus. She had arrived at their apartment late in the evening, excited to tell him about a test she'd done well on, but when she got there, she could see the bottles and knew that he was already on at least his third beer. He'd been drinking more and more often, and she worried that his business classes might have been forgotten. Their evenings together studying had grown few and far between.

She eased into the room, her good mood suddenly dimmed, the smell of the beer making her slightly nauseous. Instead of looking up or chatting, Jay sat silently in his chair at the kitchen table. When she couldn't take the suspense any longer she asked, "What is it?"

His backhand across her cheek came out of nowhere. She staggered to a chair, her hand against her face, blood seeping between her fingers. His ring had broken the skin under her eye. She grabbed a handful of paper napkins off the table and pressed them to her cheek, waiting to see what he would do next. She was silent, sensing that any kind of sound might somehow make things worse. Five minutes, then ten minutes passed with no more reaction from him. When he got up to get another beer she eyed him, then quickly ducked into the small bathroom and locked the door.

She hardly recognized herself in the mirror. She peeled away the napkins and washed her face gently. She didn't think the cut was deep enough to need stitches, but her eye was swelling and blackening quickly. She knew she wouldn't be able to go to class the next day and that triggered the tears. She loved Dr. Wright's class on language development, the stories that he spun to get his points across. What could she possibly say to explain this? She pressed a cold washcloth against her cheek, wishing she'd grabbed some ice from the freezer before slipping into the bathroom.

She was still sitting there, not knowing what to do when she heard the phone ring, one quick half a beat before it was answered and then the handset crashed back onto the base. The front door opened and slammed shut after that.

She sat on the side of the tub, crying silently, listening for what would come next. Finally, as the quiet grew, she ventured out. The apartment was empty. She hiccupped twice as she tried to stop the tears, then focused on getting some ice and taking care of her face. She locked the front door but knew it wouldn't make any difference since he carried the keys with him. She finally climbed into bed in her clothes and drifted off to sleep in the early morning.

Two days later, he returned, smiling and kissing her as if nothing had happened. For a week it felt as though she must have imagined the whole incident. After her shifts at the library, they'd have dinner together and then study on into the evening. Not long after that, though, the winter weather returned, and with it came a new tension in the apartment. Jay became unpredictable, and Sarah began having trouble focusing on her schoolwork. She never knew what to expect. He could be smiling and sweet in the morning, then drunk and angry by the evening. It felt as though she were tiptoeing through her days, always listening for a raised voice or an angry comment.

Looking back now, Marybeth knew that the only good thing that had happened to her that school year was Gregory's arrival. They hadn't been close friends in high school, more acquaintances really. Long ago, friends had persuaded them to go on an actual date, but there'd been no chemistry between them and they'd spent little time together after that. But when she'd seen him interviewing with her supervisor, she'd been thrilled to see a familiar face. She had given him a glowing recommendation and he'd been hired that day. She had no idea how she would have gotten through that spring without him. As Jay's behavior became more unpredictable, her shifts at the library started to feel like the best part of her day.

Gregory's shift often overlapped with hers since he had the late night hours, and she was happy to see him when their days coincided. She loved having someone she knew to talk to and sometimes dawdled at the end of her shift. Once he saw her eye, she had no choice but to tell him what had happened. He couldn't do anything about it, she knew that, but just sharing the horrible experience with someone else seemed to help. From the very beginning, he had urged her to stop seeing Jay, but it wasn't that easy. There were so many moments when she still saw the man she fell in love with, when she thought she must have made a mistake, must have misjudged the situation somehow. Because nothing made any sense to her, she ended up doing nothing.

The Thursday before her last midterm exam, she had gotten home later, about ten thirty. Before she even had a chance to say hello to him, Jay yanked her in the front door. "What are you hanging around the library so late for? I've been hungry for hours," he screamed, his face ugly and sweaty with anger, his breath reeking of alcohol. He flung her across the small living room. Her head snapped back as she hit the sofa, her arm smashing on the coffee table. "Fuck you," he yelled and stormed out, the door crashing open and then shut behind him.

Where had that come from? She couldn't make herself straighten the arm and knew that she'd have to go for treatment this time. But it was so hard to make herself get up, she wanted to just stay there, curled up in a ball on the floor beside the sofa, crying. She thought about calling her mother or Gregory, but either way she would have to admit how stupid she'd been. She'd been warned about the Warren family more than once, and now she couldn't bear to hear the "I told you so's" that they had every right to deliver. Tears ran down onto the collar of her shirt as she stood up slowly, cradling her arm against her chest. In a painful haze, she pulled a coat around her, found her keys and purse, opened the front door carefully and looked up and down the block, relieved to see that Jay's car was nowhere in sight. Slowly, her mind spinning with pain, the scene playing over and over again in her head, she managed to walk the endless blocks to the school clinic.

She remembered lying to the in-take clerk about what had happened, describing a fall down the apartment steps. The process of getting X-rays and having the break set felt as though it took hours. She didn't have the energy left to walk home and was tempted again to call Gregory, but instead she spent the little money she had with her on a cab. When they pulled into the lot, she looked up at the windows of her apartment and was relieved to see that they were dark. She prayed to God that he would stay away again. She managed just a few hours of sleep and the next day took her exam on painkillers and sheer determination.

CHAPTER SEVEN

*T*he clock radio seemed to come on louder than usual, and Carolyn had to resist the urge to smack the button down hard as though she was in some old cartoon. Stupid *Love Shack*. She wondered who in the world had ever liked that idiotic song? Instead, she stretched briefly, then checked the baby monitor to see if PJ was stirring yet. In the ghostly black and white screen, she could see him sitting up and playing with his stuffed bear, then laying back down as though he wasn't ready to get up yet either. She relaxed at the thought of the few extra minutes it would give her and headed in to take a quick shower.

By the time she emerged, dressed for work except for her shoes, he was calling out to her, and she went in to get him. The best part of her day was that first glimpse she got of him, when he spotted her and a wide grin spread across his face. "Hey there buddy, are you ready for the day?"

She leaned over the edge of the crib and stroked her finger along his warm cheek. He still had blonde, wispy baby hair although it was growing a little bit darker as more grew in. His gray-green eyes looked up at her as he raised his arms. She picked him up, and he allowed her one hug before starting to wriggle around, so she laid him on the changing table and got a new diaper on him quickly. There was a brief disagreement about the day's clothes, but then he happily settled on a soft blue T-shirt and a pair of lightweight cotton pants.

Once he was dressed, she set him down in front of her and tidied up his room. It was just an alcove really, but she had turned it into his own space with big truck and plane decals on the wall and periwinkle blue curtains by the small window. She was proud of how it looked and was happy to take a few seconds to keep it looking nice.

"What do you feel like having for breakfast, little man?" Carolyn held his hand as they walked around the corner to the kitchen. She opened the pantry cupboard and he pointed to his new favorite cereal. Once she'd settled him in his high chair, she put the cereal and some cut up banana in front of him along with his sippy cup of milk and then started the coffee maker for herself. She had to admit, some mornings were a lot easier than others. She smiled over at her son and turned on some music for them to eat by. At a year and a half, PJ already loved music, dancing and jumping to the beat whenever possible. She looked over at him and saw bits of cereal and banana in each hand, waving to the beat of the morning's tune. She waved her arms with him as she waited for the coffee to finish.

Once the bread was ready in the toaster, she took her breakfast to the table and sat down next to PJ. She scooped some of his food back into the bowl and then opened her laptop to glance at the morning paper. Uh oh, it looked as though squabbles about education funding were back in the news. Carolyn had worked at the Children's Center of Baltimore for three years and budget planning, or "making do" as it was more appropriately called, was an annual concern. She flipped through the screens to the comics and told herself she'd read the budget article this evening once PJ had gone to sleep. She took just a few more minutes to look at the lesson plans she had been working on, then closed the laptop and slid it into her bag. She took one last big sip of her coffee and stood.

"Ok, PJ, are you finished here? How about one more bite?" She scooped up the last bits of banana and offered him the spoon, then swapped that for his milk cup and went to the sink to wet a washcloth. Once he was cleaned up, she set him down to play while she finished getting ready for work.

It was such a relief to be finished with coat weather, and it took just minutes to get their teeth brushed, shoes on, and toys and work items gathered. She settled PJ in the stroller and fastened the harness, then slipped her workbag, diaper bag and purse over her shoulder. She sang a silly ABC song with him as they negotiated their way out of their apartment, then through the big front door and onto the sidewalk. It was a beautiful, late spring morning and Carolyn was happy that her best friend and sitter lived just down the street. She took her time covering the distance, enjoying seeing the faces of neighbors who'd been indoors since the snow had begun last fall.

CHAPTER EIGHT

*M*arybeth cringed at the thought of how vulnerable a young woman she had been back then. Thank heavens she'd been alone at the apartment resting her broken arm when the clinic called to tell her about the blood work they'd done. Now, in addition to being terrified, she could no longer ignore her suspicions. She was pregnant. She knew enough about basic psychology to recognize that she'd been in denial. She had attributed the absence of periods to the stress she'd been experiencing as Jay's moods had soared and fallen. Now it also explained why she'd felt sick, not just at the smell of beer, but at all sorts of unexpected times.

She hated to call off work since that would mean sitting in her apartment, worrying about Jay's return, so she went on in. That evening she had been sitting at the circulation desk, staring at her watch, her arm throbbing and her spirits the lowest they had ever been, when the FBI agent first approached her.

Sylvia Nowicki had not been what Sarah imagined when someone said "FBI agent." There was no black suit or dark sunglasses, just a woman in her forties with a loose jacket and blond hair pulled back in a bun. She'd greeted Sarah by name, frightening her at first, but as the woman talked, Sarah found herself comforted by her steady tone and quiet demeanor. They had met a few times after that as the FBI was building their case.

In hindsight, Marybeth believed it was a very small miracle that she was still alive at the end of May. She remembered so clearly the last time she'd seen Jay all those years ago. She'd been in the bedroom fumbling with getting ready for work, the arm in its cast itching like mad and making every movement more difficult. She heard the front door open and tried to rush.

"Hey listen, I just got off the phone with my dad. He needs me to come home for a while," Jay called out as he entered the apartment and moved toward the bedroom. She reached for a bulky sweater, trying to pull it over her head as quickly as she could.

"What's that?" He sucked in his breath, pointing at her stomach. "You're getting fat?"

She tried to pull the sweater down but he grabbed it back up and looked at her hard.

"Jay, I wanted to tell you. I was just looking for the right moment."

"Are you kidding me? You said you were using birth control. What the fuck happened?"

"I was, I did, they're just not one hundred percent…"

His harsh voice echoed in the small bedroom. "I told you, I am *never* having kids, ever. Do you understand me?" He grabbed her by the collar and pulled her up to his face. It was a deep red color that she had never seen before. "There will be no more fucking freaks like my brother, do you hear me?"

"But Jay, Daniel wasn't a—" She was lifted into the air and thrown onto the floor, her breath rushing out of her all at once. The corner of the dresser gouged her back in the fall and she was struggling to pull in air when his foot connected with her stomach.

"We'll take care of this one right now."

She screamed and tried to curl herself into a ball. He

continued kicking at her midsection before connecting with her right temple. Her world went black.

* * *

SHE AWOKE in the dark and sensed that the apartment was empty. She had no idea how long she'd laid there. Hours, she guessed. She tried to lift her head but it spun and her stomach lurched before she put her head back down. Her broken arm was twisted behind her awkwardly and she struggled to free it and bring it down in front of her. She sensed there was blood, she could smell it even, but in the dark room it was impossible to tell where it was coming from. She reached her good hand around her stomach and rubbed but an ache was starting deep down inside of her and she cried at the thought. She fell back into darkness.

When she came to again, it was to the sound of someone pounding on the door. "Sarah?" a male voice called out loudly. She tried to make a sound but seemed to have forgotten how.

"Sarah, the door's unlocked. I'm coming in."

Sarah sighed with relief. It was Gregory, everything would be okay, she thought as she drifted off again.

* * *

THE STEADY BEEP worked its way into her thoughts first, then she tried to open her eyes but the lights hurt too much to keep them open. She thought that she smelled some sort of antiseptic, but how could that be? Then it seemed that someone was calling her name. It was a woman's voice but not one she knew.

"Sarah, this is Doctor Phan. Can you hear me?" Sarah blinked and turned toward the voice but could only cough when she tried to speak. The doctor, a small, dark haired older woman brought a cup with a straw to her mouth and she sipped eagerly at the cool liquid.

"Thank you," she managed to get out. She reached for her stomach again as she looked toward the woman. "Doctor?"

"Sarah, the baby is fine. We need to thank your friend Gregory. He found you around ten o'clock and waited for the ambulance to come. Can you tell me what happened?"

Sarah hesitated, looked around the hospital room and paused again. She looked back at the doctor who gestured for someone to come in. It was the FBI agent, Sylvia Nowicki. She looked worried.

"I'm here, Sarah. You're safe." She took a seat beside the doctor.

Sarah looked at her and whispered, "He's gone, isn't he? Back to Pittsburgh? He said his dad, I mean before this happened, he said his dad was bringing him home."

The agent nodded.

"Can you tell us what happened, Sarah?" asked the doctor again as both women leaned forward slightly.

Sarah took a deep breath and then another sip of water before beginning. "He came in and said he had big news, he was going home. But I was trying to get dressed and my cast made it so hard to do everything..." She paused, tears forming and falling silently down her cheek. "I had planned to tell him I was pregnant, I had. I was just waiting for the right moment. You don't understand, he can be the nicest man, really." She paused again but saw the look on the women's faces. "Well, sometimes. He could be so charming and lovely, I was just waiting for one more of those interludes."

"But it didn't come?" the doctor asked.

Sarah lowered her head. "No, it had been a while actually. He'd gotten so busy, always in and out of the apartment. I'm not sure he was even going to class anymore."

"And yesterday?"

Sarah gave a small sigh. So it was only yesterday? "Like I said, I was trying to pull my sweatshirt down and he saw my stomach looking a little round. I started to explain, but he just went into a rage, said he was never going to have kids." Sarah swiped at the tears impatiently. "He had this really sweet brother named Daniel who caught meningitis as a baby. Jay said he wasn't going to have any more freaks like him around. I started to explain that Daniel's issues weren't birth defects, but I didn't get the chance. He grabbed me by my collar and threw me down on the floor. Then he started kicking me in the stomach and I just tried to roll up into a ball. I think he might have kicked my head because I passed out."

"What time of day was that, Sarah?" the doctor asked gently.

"Around four-thirty maybe? Doctor, can you tell me what's wrong? Is the baby really okay? He kicked me so hard and it hurt, way down inside."

The doctor stood and smoothed Sarah's hair off her forehead to reveal a wide bandage. And then she smiled. "You're going to be all right, but you've had a concussion and I believe your head is going to hurt for quite a while. How is your vision?"

Sarah turned her head slowly looking around the room and out the door at the hallway. "It seems fine."

"Good, that's a good sign. Such a long wait for treatment could have had a lot of negative consequences, especially since you were bleeding."

"From where?" she tried to sit up but felt a line of pain across her shoulder blades.

The doctor nodded. "From there, your back. I'm guessing you hit something fairly sharp on your way down. The good news, though, is that you landed on your back and that seems to have stopped or at least slowed the bleeding a good deal. The rest of you, your legs and arms, reflexes all seem fine." She paused and then put her hand gently on Sarah's stomach. "Luckily for us, your little one is still fairly small. The fetus got jostled for sure, but all of our tests indicate the baby's fine." The doctor rested her hands on the stethoscope that hung around her neck. "Overall,

I'm pleased with how you're doing. I'll be back to check in on you later before I leave for the day."

Sarah thanked the doctor and then Sylvia pulled her chair closer to the bed. Once the doctor had gone, she spoke quietly. "He's gone, really. Our agent that's watching the father's place in Pittsburgh has seen Jay going in and out. There doesn't seem to be any move to have him return here."

"The case? It's getting stronger?"

"We're hoping so. But Sarah," she paused. "We need to take photographs of this, you know that, right?"

"I understand." She lowered her gaze. "It's just so embarrassing. Do you think I can go back to my apartment, to school?"

"I think school is fine." She hesitated. "But I think the safest bet is to close the apartment and move you onto campus. As far as Jay Warren knows, he killed you and the baby. We'll concoct a story for the landlord in case anyone should come looking for you there. In the meantime, I'm going to back off until we're closer to moving forward with the case, then we can talk more." She stood. "You just take good care of yourself and that little one."

Sarah tried to smile at the agent as she left, pulling the door shut quietly behind her. Then she winced and her head swam a bit as she moved to sit up straighter in the bed. She noticed that the cast on her arm was new and a little shorter, which made it easier to move. She placed both hands on the small mound of her belly. "Okay little one," she whispered. "It's just you and me now."

A knock sounded at the door and Gregory walked in, carrying a small plant with tiny purple blossoms. "Hey there, champ. You look a lot better than the last time I saw you." He bent over to give her a careful hug.

"Oh, Gregory." Tears came to her eyes again. "You saved me. What made you come to the apartment?"

"Well you were late for work, silly, and you're never late. So I got one of the other students to wait while I went and checked on you. Are you going to be all right?"

Sarah dried her tears on the arm of the gown. "Yeah, I think I'll, I mean we, will be fine. He's gone, back to Pittsburgh."

Gregory's shoulders dropped in relief and his face lit up at the news. "Oh thank God."

Sarah watched his face. "Why do you say that?"

Gregory paused and took a seat on the edge of the bed before answering. "When I first started working at the library, I couldn't figure out why you liked him, but it didn't feel right saying anything." He set the plant on the bedside table. "I never told you this before, but I saw him one night in the parking lot after the football team lost the regional game. He and Jeff Stone had the other team's mascot up against the gym door and were beating the hell out of him. I think the kid was already unconscious when I saw him and they were still hitting him. If coach Dawkins hadn't opened up that door, I'm not sure the kid would have lived."

"I never heard anything about that. Everyone seemed to like Jay so much in high school, even with the suspicions about his father. He was always so friendly and funny." She paused and considered. "The coach never said anything?"

"Of course not. Jeff and Jay were his star players and he knew what Jay's dad was capable of. He got the poor kid to the hospital and covered up the rest. You may not have seen it, but I think there was something twisted in Jay even back then."

Sarah leaned her head back against the pillow. "You're right, I didn't see it." She closed her eyes and felt the fatigue wash over her.

Gregory rose and pulled the cover up a bit. "I'll be back later. You rest now." Sarah managed a smile but fell back to sleep quickly.

CHAPTER NINE

*D*ays later, Ken had no more idea about what was going on with Marybeth than he'd had the day she left. He'd tried calling, over and over, just to have it go straight to voicemail.

The only neat spot in the house was now Marybeth's desk and the card table next to it. They were covered in tidy stacks of papers, many related to her school, a few about the house, a stack for taxes and the smallest pile of all, a few sheets that didn't fit with any others. In the mail today was a bill from the water department. That didn't seem to follow her plan so Ken looked through the bill book until he found the account information, and then headed to their bank.

Once he got there, Ken realized how long it had been since he'd actually been inside. Aside from the ATM, he never did any kind of banking. Why was that? As he stood in line for the teller, he wondered again what pieces of his life he'd been ignoring. He knew he'd been crap at keeping a checkbook when he was in college, was that how it had started? With a sense of chagrin, he handed the bill to the teller. "It's my understanding that this account is being paid automatically, so I'm wondering why I received a bill?"

The clerk smiled. "Oh, we've had a few of these issues recently, the water department changed its billing address and didn't notify customers in time for this month's processing."

"So, do I need to do something to correct this?"

She typed in the information for the account. "No, my records indicate that it was taken care of yesterday."

"What do you mean?"

"Electronically, someone went in and corrected the address. You can ignore this bill."

"Someone from the bank did that?"

"No, someone who is on the account, Marybeth Rogers it says." She looked up at him. I'm guessing that's your wife?"

Ken stood there, dazed. Marybeth had been in their account yesterday? "Can you tell where the transaction took place?"

"Oh no, sir, we don't have access to that kind of information." The clerk looked baffled by his question and she adjusted her thick-framed glasses to bring him into clearer focus.

"Can you tell me if there's been activity in any of the other accounts, please?" Ken tried to make sure that his smile was genuine but he was struggling, clenching the keys in his pocket, feeling them dig little trenches into his knuckle.

"I'm just seeing activity in her other checking account sir."

"Other checking account? Not the one that we share?" Now the clerk looked flustered and he saw her eyes darting past him.

"I'm sorry, perhaps I shouldn't have said anything. You don't go online and look at these accounts sir?" The teller looked over his shoulder toward the manager's desk, seemingly relieved to see that it was empty now as he stood at a distance chatting with a client.

"No, I haven't. How would I do that?"

She smiled. "Well, your wife could share her password with

you or we can set you up with your own access. Would you like me to do that for you sir?"

"That would be great. And I can see all of the account activity?"

She paused as she answered apologetically. "Well, only the ones that have you listed on them. This would not include the accounts where she is co-signer with two other individuals, your sons?" She looked up questioningly and he nodded as she continued. "Also, the other checking account, you wouldn't be able to access that, unless, like I said, you had her password." The teller typed in a string of information, then copied it carefully onto a sticky note. "Here you go, these codes will get you in and then you can set your own password." She handed him the paper.

He didn't trust himself to say any more so he gestured thank you with the slip of paper and left. Once in the car, the first thing he did was text their boys. *Have either of you seen anything odd on your bank accounts recently?*

Jimmy, the youngest, answered quickly. *No, why, you thinking about giving me my allowance early?*

You're 20 and you still get an allowance?

Just kidding, Mom cut me off in January.

Ken felt like asking more but he let it sit. He could always give Jimmy a call that weekend, get together for a burger or something. He wondered if he and his brother had bought the story he'd told them, that Marybeth was helping care for a sick relative down in Virginia. It was all he could think of when Grant had asked him. Frankly, he was surprised that they weren't more curious, but he figured they were busy with their own lives now, not thinking much about Mom and Dad. He headed home, ready to log on and see what, if anything, he could discover about their accounts.

With Marybeth's laptop gone, he was forced to use the older desktop that was set up in the study. He got a beer from the refrigerator and waited for the unit to boot up. He was so used to his laptop at work that he rarely used this machine anymore, but the codes worked easily and within minutes he was looking at the opening screen. It showed just two accounts, savings and checking. It irritated him knowing that her screen would have shown so much more. Was this just one more price he was paying for having yielded all of the financial responsibility to her? Did he even know that the kids had accounts here with her? Should he have pushed to be more involved with all of that? He sipped at the beer and then leaned forward again. No, dammit, what did it matter? They were grown now and when they were younger it was Marybeth who'd been working in town with more opportunities to deal with that stuff.

He pulled off his baseball cap and dragged his fingers through his hair. It was getting shaggy he realized and slapped the hat back on before he could get sidetracked further. Forget it, there was no time to worry about any of that. He scanned the first screen for the checking account and found the water bill payment. It was weird, the amount had gone out, then returned, then gone out again. He quickly figured out how the pages of transactions loaded and then began going backwards through the history. He wasn't seeing anything that seemed out of the ordinary.

Finally, on the third page back, he spotted a transfer of thirty-six dollars out to another account. It seemed like an odd amount. On the next page there were two transfers out to the same account, one for forty-two dollars and another for fifty-five dollars. Again, they seemed like odd amounts. He went back and looked at the first one he'd seen, then noticed just above it, thirty-six dollars to Pine Lake Golf Course. On the next page, the forty-two had a charge above it in the same amount to the Oak Ridge course. Below that fifty-five dollars had been transferred out right below a charge for fifty-five to Ravenwood Golf Course. He remembered he'd gone with Randy and they'd had lunch afterward. He went back page by page through the account history until it made him pause and request more dates. There was no need, though. Once the pattern was there, Ken was able to trace back hundreds of dollars that had been taken out. Of course he was feeling a little embarrassed at how much he'd been spending on golf. It really did add up faster than he realized.

He sat back in his chair and flipped a ball point pen around his fingers and back again over and over, a habit from middle school that he'd never been able to break. Well, at least he knew how she was funding the damn sabbatical. He'd taken up golf almost ten years ago so it was possible she'd saved thousands of dollars, especially if he counted the handful of weekend trips he'd made with Randy and Stu. He wasn't sure why, but for some reason he felt a little relieved to know that she had some money to support her.

He was so angry, though, that she'd never said anything about it, about the cost of golf or his involvement with it. Had some sort of resentment been building this whole time? He'd have stopped playing, quit spending the money or even given her the money if she'd asked for it. Hell, he'd have gone with her on her research trip if she'd asked.

The whole thing just made him feel so damn pathetic, like he'd been duped just because he'd been busy with his ordinary life, their ordinary life. But then he dropped the pen on the desk and settled his feet flat on the floor, puzzled again at the whole series of events. No, he didn't believe that she was mad or resentful, that just wasn't like her. They joked about the golf a lot and it really hadn't seemed to bother her at all. He paused again. And the water bill, she had to be checking in to make sure that everything was all right with their accounts. It didn't seem like someone on a wild sex trip to Europe would be making sure that the water bill was paid. He felt a little foolish, but a tiny corner of his mind registered the smallest amount of something like hope.

CHAPTER TEN

*1*986 was such an amazing time to be in special education, Dr. Charles Wright thought, sitting at his office desk, worn running shoes propped on an open drawer, his gaze focused on the dried leaves of the oak tree outside his window. In the years since the passage of the new law, students and, even better, funding had been pouring in. Classes were full to overflowing and he had never felt so lucky or engaged before, as if he were in exactly the right spot at exactly the right time. His expression suddenly darkened though, as his eyes focused on the young woman walking beneath his oak tree. She had an ugly knitted hat crammed too far down her face, an ill-fitting brown coat that she held tightly closed at her neck, and an air of what could only be called defeat pulling her chin down as she pushed forward against the winter wind.

He remembered the first time Sarah had come to his Introduction to Child Development course in her freshman year. She'd been shy, but bright and eager and he knew as soon as he saw her that she would take a seat in the front, not hide away with the masses in the middle of the small lecture hall. Sure enough, second row, center, he'd been right. She looked to be a good note taker, a thoughtful student not panicked and trying to write everything down, but smart enough to watch and listen, absorbing the class experience rather than waiting for it to be over. After the first few weeks she had begun to ask questions and to stop by his office for discussions about her writing. She'd earned an A that first semester, a step ahead of her other classmates from the very beginning, and according to his colleagues, she had continued to do well. But now, he sighed and lifted his feet, planting them on the floor with a sigh of resignation, this semester's class on the development of language had been another story, and he knew who was to blame for that.

Charles had been friends with Edward Clark since they'd been a couple of junior high numbskulls together in Philadelphia. He'd also had a crush on Edward's sister Kathryn when they all entered their senior year of high school, but she'd never once looked his way with anything more than disinterest and boredom.

Eddie, though, had none of her haughtiness, despite having grown up in the same affluent family. The two of them had been running partners for years but now that they were in their late forties, Eddie's work commitments and spreading midsection had curtailed his interest in exercise. Their friendship, though, had lasted nearly two decades now, and Charles had come to value it above all others. In fact, Eddie had been the one to see him through his disappointment when Kathryn married that idiot Walter Warren.

Now, her son Jay was keeping company with Sarah and destroying her before Charles' very eyes. Although he had never mentioned it to Edward, Charles didn't entirely buy the persona that Jay presented. Something just niggled at the back of his mind, preventing it. What worried him now was that the reserve and hesitation that Sarah had entered college with seemed to be back tenfold, and in class he saw her struggling to focus. That Friday when she'd come for the weekly quiz, he'd seen her eye. It was puffy and dark despite the makeup she'd used, with a bright crescent line arcing underneath it. He'd had enough, and called Eddie to meet him for coffee to discuss what could be done.

The drugstore was old fashioned, with a counter that still served drinks and sandwiches to the college crowd. Charles resisted the urge to spin his stool the way he had as a youngster and instead watched the broad mirror for signs of his friend. Eddie had said he was downtown checking on one of his new dry cleaning stores, so it was an easy walk over to the drugstore. Charles spotted him outside, kicking his boots against the brick wall to knock the snow off before walking in. Then, with a big grin, he plopped down on the next stool. Eddie gave it a quick spin and Charles laughed to see him there. When he came around, Charles clapped his friend on the shoulder as the counter clerk looked at him askance. He wondered what the young woman would think if she knew how wealthy this goofball was.

"Charlie, how are you doing? How are the halls of academia these days, still bursting with eager young minds and hearts?"

"You know it buddy. How's the dry cleaning empire going?"

Eddie waved his hand dismissively. "Aw, it's good, you know it seems everyone has dirty clothes and no one has the time to wash them anymore."

"So what number is this latest one?"

They ordered their sandwiches when the young woman came by, and waited politely while she handed them napkins and silverware and filled their coffee cups. Once she'd headed back to the kitchen, Eddie's grin returned. "This one is the big five-oh, number fifty if you can believe that. I need to buy a new car in fact, I've about worn my old one out traveling back and forth between them all."

"Don't you have employees for that? Why is the boss traveling everywhere?"

Eddie spun his stool and managed to look a bit sheepish despite his age. Charles could still see the longhaired bohemian he'd once aspired to be, and thought again how incongruous it was that he'd ended up with so much money. As a young man Eddie had been embarrassed by the family fortunes and downplayed his connection to the Clark name whenever the opportunity arose. But somehow, he'd ended up with a head for business that no one had expected. "Oh, I just like to keep busy, keep my hand in and make sure things are being done right, you know? Or maybe it's just habit. I don't know. Either way I'm busy and..." He gestured awkwardly.

"And that's the way you like it. I know. Well, I think your success is terrific. It couldn't have happened to a nicer guy." Charles rested his hand on Eddie's back and then squeezed his shoulder for a second. The waitress set their plates in front of them and Charles began to eat, pausing with a potato chip in his hand. "I was so sorry to hear about Daniel, Eddie. He was such a sweet boy, or young man I should say."

"That's kind of you. You know, I can't thank you enough for helping me find that wonderful school for him. He just loved it up there. I'd go up and visit him once or twice a month and bring him down to the city for the big holidays. He was just as happy as could be."

"And how's Kathryn doing? I never really got over my crush on her, you know."

Eddie paused, his smile dimming. "I'm afraid she's not going to win this latest battle."

"I'm so sorry to hear that, Eddie. I know she never did fancy me much but I've always liked and admired her."

Eddie set his fork down and turned to Charles with a more serious expression on his face. "Thank you, I appreciate that. Cancer is such an ugly disease."

Charles nodded and ate a bit more before returning his silverware to the plate. "All right Eddie, here's the tough part of the conversation."

Edward wiped his mouth on the thin, paper napkin before

looking up. "Geez, what could be tougher than death and cancer?"

"Are you still in touch with Kathryn's son, Jay? He's here on campus, you know."

Eddie finished a bite of sandwich and took a sip of coffee. "Yeah, I'd heard that. Kathryn told me he's working on a business degree. Why, he hasn't been in your classes has he?"

Charles shook his head and waited long enough that Eddie turned and looked at him curiously. "I'm sorry, Eddie, I know he's family to you, but I think he might be hurting a young gal I've got in one of my classes. Have you spoken to him recently or met a student named Sarah?"

"Sure, we had dinner together last month. I thought she was a real sweetheart, said she knew Daniel back when he was in high school. She and Jay seemed like a great couple. What makes you think there's something wrong?"

"You know I loved your sister, Charlie, and I thought the world of Daniel, no matter what anyone said about him." There was a pause then, and Eddie watched as Charles struggled to find the right words. "I'm afraid I just don't like Jay. Never have, to be honest. He's always seemed like a bully to me, the worst kind of bully, the kind that's mean but seems to kind of enjoy it, you know? I heard him talking to his mother that way one day and I had to walk away. Walt was there and didn't say a damn thing, so I think that says even more about the boy's character."

"Oh I don't know, Charlie, that sounds a little harsh." He waved his hand in dismissal and took another bite of his sandwich before continuing. "I don't think he's like his old man. And besides, he and Sarah seemed pretty happy to me."

Charles wiped his mouth, then settled his napkin on top of the plate and pushed it aside. "I don't know, she's just one of those bright lights that teachers get from time to time. She was shy but engaged in the classes and now," he paused, "now, she looks like a shadow version of herself. I first saw them on campus together in mid-December and she looked pretty happy but this spring has been a different story. She missed class last Wednesday and when she arrived on Friday she had a cut under her eye and a shiner she was trying to hide with makeup. Frankly, I'm worried about her. Do you think there's anything you can do?"

The waitress cleared their plates and Eddie left two twenties under his coffee cup before they got up. They pulled their coats on and buttoned them against the cold before heading back out to the sidewalk and pausing beside Edward's car. "Let me see what I can do, Charlie. I'll try to get in touch with Jay, maybe invite the two of them down to my place in Pittsburgh and see what's going on. You know, last summer he became eligible for the first half of the trust I set up for him. Maybe the money's just gone to his head somehow. I'll let you know what I find out, okay?"

"Hey, never underestimate the powers of a dry cleaner, right my friend?" Charles slapped Edward on the back and opened the car door for him.

"You got that right, we've got all sorts of secret resources. I'm on the case, my friend, I'm on the case."

Charles laughed and saw his friend away before walking back toward his office. His step was just a shade easier as he thought about what those resources might be, and he was glad Sarah had someone with that kind of influence in her corner.

CHAPTER ELEVEN

*B*ack at his desk, Ray Sanchez felt like there was nothing to do except start over from the beginning. The original agent on the case had been Sylvia Nowicki, a fifteen-year veteran at the time. When he'd gotten the case originally, his first step had been to try to interview her, but Sylvia had been killed in a car accident years before. The circumstances of the crash had looked suspicious to Ray, and he'd investigated a bit, but no one at the time had seen any red flags so it'd gone no further. He pulled the old files out from under a stack and began thumbing through them for what felt like the millionth time. He knew there was something in here that was key, there just had to be.

Nowicki's first interviews had been with the family, Walt, Jay, and the mother Kathryn, just before she passed away. The family was well known in the city even back then. Their notoriety had had a philanthropic patina at that time which seemed to have dropped off somewhat once Kathryn passed away. Although Jay Warren remained a man about town with his face on the society page, often with a beautiful woman, philanthropy no longer seemed to be a family focus. The FBI had been investigating him right along with his father, but the agent had to admit that not much seemed to stick to Jay.

Ray continued to read Agent Nowicki's notes as she commented on the look of the home, a large, three-story brick house that occupied nearly a block of the downtown neighborhood. Crime, on the rise all over Pittsburgh at that time, had been conspicuously low in the area around the house and indeed, for a three block radius in every direction. Ray could picture Kathryn Warren walking to the little market, talking to the small shop owners. He wondered if she was aware of the fear that they reported when Nowicki interviewed them or if her oblivion protected her from those types of thoughts.

Ray had found a separate file just on Kathryn, detailing her birth and upbringing within a wealthy New York family. She had attended an exclusive women's college and had met Walter Warren at a college mixer. Apparently, he'd spun a tale of his so-called studies at the nearby school and she seemed to have bought it hook, line and sinker. Nowicki's notes in the margin questioned how she'd had the brains to attend the college even with her family's guarantee of admission. Ray snorted as he re-read that section.

Walter's charm and persistence had clearly won her over, though, and even seemed to have quelled her family's initial concerns. Once he began rising in the financial circles of Pittsburgh, he'd married her, and she had moved from the insular world of her wealthy family to the world that Walt had created for her there. She'd died of breast cancer at forty-one. There was a dark, scribbled note further down on the page. "Her estate?" At the bottom a hand scrawled note reminded Nowicki to investigate this further. Ray had followed up as well and found that while a chunk had gone to her husband Walt, the larger part of the estate remained in the hands of her brother Edward. Agent Nowicki's notes indicated that Jay had inherited a sizable chunk of the money once he turned twenty-one. He was due to collect the rest once Edward Clark died.

Ray sifted through the other original files and noted that the one on Jay was relatively small. The first paper in it was an article clipped from the Post about a school mascot who had been beaten into a coma. Nowicki had put question marks all over the brittle paper and circled Jay's name in the article, which mentioned a football game that his team had lost. An index card clipped to it indicated that the boy's medical bills had been paid until his death three years later, complications from pneumonia related to the coma. Nowicki had tried to find out who was paying the bills but hadn't been able to follow that trail. It had been another one of the first avenues that Ray had followed up on and Nowicki's suspicions had been correct. Ray had followed the money trail back to the Warrens and then interviewed a retired coach who had witnessed the beating. He remembered too, that he'd had to promise the coach protection if anything ever came out of that discovery.

Behind the article were three photographs apparently taken on the campus at Penn State. In the first, Jay looked fresh and eager, walking beside a young woman who was looking up at him with a smile on her face. The trees around them were bare and there was snow piled next to what looked like library steps. *December 1985, Jay Warren/Sarah Dawes* was written on the back. The second one showed the two of them walking into an apartment building carrying groceries and was dated late January 1986. But the third one was the most interesting as far as Ray was concerned, because it made no sense. It showed the young woman, her head down as she walked along a flowering walk. Jay wasn't in the picture at all, and he had always wondered why Nowicki had included it in the file.

Ray studied it for a long time. There was something about that photograph that still bugged him. The back of it said June 1986, Sarah Dawes. It wasn't digital so he couldn't zoom in on it, but he remembered a gag gift he'd been given years ago, a Sherlock Holmes style magnifying glass that he'd gotten at a party when he graduated from Quantico. He found it buried in his bottom drawer, pulled it out, and focused it on the woman. After a few minutes of study, it came to him. Damn, she looked pregnant. It had never occurred to him that Jay had a child. Holy shit, where was this woman?

Ray pawed through the rest of the pages but found no more entries about her. He got on the computer and began searching records, drivers' licenses, marriages, even death certificates, nothing. He broadened his search to include records of any sort including financials. Nothing again. Even when he located a social security number for her he still couldn't find any current data that attached to that number. What the hell, he wondered and turned back to Nowicki's file, taking each set of papers and index cards apart, searching for something he might have missed.

CHAPTER TWELVE

*I*t took a bit for Carolyn to bump the stroller up the three stone steps to Janine's place but she managed it. The home was old, one that had seen better days, frankly, but Janine loved it. It was a bit tattered around the edges but it was a full three stories. On the first floor was the sitting room, a powder room and the kitchen, the next held the two bedrooms and a small nursery but she knew that the third was Janine's favorite. It was a bright sunny loft where she got to spend time creating big, beautiful paintings.

When Carolyn knocked, Janine's daughter April came running to the door, her little eyes peering just over the wood-work at them.

"Hi there." Janine opened the old door and took April by the hand as she welcomed Carolyn and the stroller inside. She gave Carolyn a quick hug once she was disentangled from the door.

"Good morning. How are my favorite people?" Carolyn asked as she bent over to scoop April up in her arms and give her a loud, slobbery kiss.

"Auntie Caro, Peej!" April squealed and Carolyn put her down as she bent over to release PJ from the stroller. The two of them took off running for the kitchen.

"C'mon in Carolyn, got time for a cup of coffee?" Janine was wearing her favorite bathrobe, an ugly old striped terry robe that had belonged to her ex-girlfriend. Her wild, frizzy, shoulder length hair was pulled back in a reckless ponytail, making her morning look complete.

Carolyn set her messenger bag and purse down by the door. "A quick one I think. It's so much faster getting ready without all of the coats and scarves and hats."

"Oh my God, yes."

"Plus, we think the water's on at the park now."

Janine set a fat red mug on the small table by the window, then filled a second one for herself before the two of them sat down. "How long until you're sprung? Isn't it summer vacation time yet?"

"Just one more week after this. City schools may be done a day or so earlier. I'm not quite sure. But then, we're back at it after a two week break."

"Ah Caro, I hate that you have to work all summer too. Most teachers have the summer off."

"But the bills, the bills." She laughed. "You know I'm lucky to have summer work that's with the program. A lot of teachers have to go out looking for extra jobs to tide them over. Besides, if I wasn't working I wouldn't have an excuse to see you, now would I?"

At the sound of heavy footsteps on the stairs, PJ and April tore off down the hall. Carolyn stood and set her empty cup in the sink before she and Janine followed them. At the bottom of the stairs she was caught off guard by the scent of chocolate and man. Janine's brother Sean was standing at the base of the stairs. At well over six feet in his flip-flops, he towered over Carolyn's small frame and she had to look up to see the dark crumbs on his T-shirt. "Are you eating brownies for breakfast again Sean?"

"Busted. Janine made them yesterday for April to have a little tea party and I couldn't resist."

"I swear, only a runner could eat the way you do and not weigh four hundred pounds."

April came toward them, squealing. "Uncle Sean, brownie peeze?" she reached for him and he lifted her easily, tossing her into the air gently before he winked at Carolyn and headed off toward the kitchen.

Janine swiped at the hair trying to escape her scrunchy and then gave Carolyn a quick hug. "I give up, I guess everyone is having brownies for breakfast today." She opened the door and took a dramatic sniff. "Isn't it beautiful out? I am so happy that summer's here."

"I know, it's almost hot today already. I love it." She called toward the kitchen "Ok, PJ, I'm taking off, buddy." She bent down to meet him as he came running toward her and launched into her arms. She gave him a quick kiss and he was off again in a heartbeat. "Bye, Janine, I'll see you tonight. Thanks again."

"Sure thing, Caro, have a great day with the monsters."

"You too." Without the diaper bag, Carolyn's step was lighter, and the walk to school seemed to take no time at all.

CHAPTER THIRTEEN

*A*fter the attack, Sarah was in the hospital for two days before she was released. In the meantime, Gregory had seen to it that the things in her apartment were either stored or moved to the dorm room. Agent Nowicki had met with her twice and assured her that Jay was still home in Pittsburgh and that agents there were keeping a close eye on him.

It looked as though Sarah's information about Jay's whereabouts throughout the winter was going to be key in breaking some of his alibis. The FBI checked in with her off and on throughout the summer, but Agent Nowicki discreetly did not mention the pregnancy. Sarah kept working at the library as much as she could, sticking close to the route between there and her dorm room. Gregory was still her only confidant and she treasured the few minutes she had each day to chat with him.

But as the summer wore on, the agents began to have a grim look about them. Sarah had heard rumors of a witness in Pittsburgh found strangled in his home. By late August, she was starting to panic. The baby was due in just a few weeks and she had yet to make any real plans. She had talked to Gregory about it all summer, but she was so ashamed, she'd made excuses to her mother and never gone home for a visit.

She was finishing a Friday night shift when Agent Nowicki walked in looking exhausted. Sarah hadn't seen her for a week or more and she was shocked at how worn out the woman looked. "We need to have a serious talk," Agent Nowicki said as she led Sarah to her car. "Something has happened."

The agent held the passenger door for her, then walked around and climbed in behind the steering wheel. The windows were rolled up in spite of the heat, so she started the car and got the air-conditioning running before turning to face Sarah.

Sarah could tell by the agent's face that she was struggling to find the right words. "Just tell me, don't sugar coat it, please?" she asked.

"It's bad, so bad I regret ever making contact with you."

"The court case isn't going to happen, is it?"

"No. They just pulled another witness out of the Mononga-hela. They wouldn't have even found the body except for a freakish current generated by the rain last week. Sarah, it's just not safe for you anymore."

"Do you think that the Warren family knows that I've been talking to you? Do they know that I'm pregnant?" She took a deep, shaky breath. "Sylvia, you didn't see his face when he said he wasn't going to have kids. He tried to kill it."

"I'm not sure exactly what the family knows. But my agent, Chuck, happened to be outside your old apartment building today when he saw one of Walt Warren's thugs go inside. The man didn't stay, and we don't know for sure that it was your unit that he was checking out, but we do know he talked to the super. He gave him our story that you dropped out and moved away somewhere to find work, but it was a pretty flimsy tale and I don't want to risk one of them digging into it further. They've been gone all summer long, so the fact that one of the Warren people was here today tells me they're looking to tie up loose ends."

"What should I do? I can't go home to Pittsburgh, that would put me even closer to them. Besides, this baby is due soon." She was embarrassed by her tears but didn't know how to stop them.

"Actually, I think we need to have a talk about this baby. We need to hide you, for good."

"What does that mean?" She pushed her fist against the pain in her right side. The outline of a foot pushed back.

"It means witness protection, Sarah, getting you out of here and out of their grasp. Your information about Jay's whereabouts this winter was a key piece that connected him to his father's illicit businesses. With the case in shreds, you're one of the remaining threats to the family and to Jay in particular."

Sarah was horrified, the pain intensifying as she reached in her purse for a tissue. She was crying for real now, and had trouble getting out the words. "You think Jay or his dad would kill me? The baby too?" She blew her nose and tried to sit up straighter in the seat.

"I think I don't want to take that chance. We need a plan that takes care of both of you." Suddenly Sarah doubled over, the pain in her side having morphed into a stabbing pain that felt like it was going right through her. She felt the seat growing wet beneath her.

"Oh, God, I think we'd better make a plan quickly, I'm pretty sure this is labor," she shrieked as a second pain began to build. Agent Nowicki threw the car into drive and sped toward the campus clinic.

Sarah wasn't sure why the agent stayed, since it surely wasn't in any FBI manual she'd ever heard of, but Sylvia Nowicki, a mother herself, had settled into the hospital room with her and taken on the role of labor coach. Of course Sarah did all of the work, but the agent stayed the night and helped talk her through it. At dawn, Sarah had given birth to a little girl.

She held the baby against her chest and looked hard at the agent. "Sylvia, what does witness protection really mean?"

The agent's tone was somber. "It means letting go of everything, I'm afraid. Your family, your town."

"My college?"

The agent nodded yes.

"Could I go to another college? Would I have to start all over?"

"No, you wouldn't have to start over completely," Agent Nowicki shook her head. "We could arrange for your college credits to be transferred."

"But I couldn't keep my scholarship, could I?"

"I'm afraid not."

Sarah looked at her baby's face and imagined the cost of college without a scholarship. It would mean working even more hours and with a baby, how would she ever manage that? She looked up at the agent briefly. "And money?"

The agent's shoulders sagged. "I'm sorry, the FBI would move you, help you get settled with a little bit of money but it wouldn't last." She took a deep breath. "It might be easier for you without the baby."

Sarah's head whipped up. "Without her? What do you mean?"

"Being a single mom is tough, really tough, and you'll be cut off from every connection, every resource that you might have had. It might be hard to finish school."

Sarah looked up at the agent. "My mom was a single mom."

The agent spoke quietly. "So was mine."

Sarah sat silently, the baby sleeping in her arms. As far back as she could remember, her mother had worked at the diner on the edge of their neighborhood. In the winter she'd come home in the dark, her face chapped from the frigid weather. Summer hadn't been much better as the diner's air conditioner barely kept up with the eating area and was even less effective back in the kitchen. Sarah had lost count of how many nights she'd sat in a cracked red booth practicing her letters and numbers, dozing off as she waited to go home with her mother. At fourteen, she'd gotten a job there as well, hoping to ease the financial strain on her mom. It was only when her mother met and married Frank that anything had really begun to change and by then, Sarah was well into high school. Emotionally, there had never been the kind of closeness that Sarah had seen between her friends from school and their mothers. It was as if her mother had never really had the energy for it.

She pulled the blanket back from the baby's face and adjusted the tiny pink hat. She pictured herself working as a waitress, an endless string of minimum-wage jobs, coming home exhausted with little energy or joy left to share with her child. She wanted so much more for her daughter. Then she thought of something else. "Would it be more difficult to hide the two of us than it would be if I was on my own?"

"That's hard to say. We don't think they knew about the pregnancy but we're not sure. If they did, yes, it might be a little harder to hide the two of you. We'd definitely want to move you farther away, out of state most likely."

It was so hard to think about being alone. Adding hundreds of miles to it frightened Sarah even more. She felt as though she were tearing in half at the choice laid in front of her. She rubbed her finger along the baby's cheek and watched her eyes flicker in sleep. What kind of life was waiting for her little girl? For her? If they were ever discovered, would they be on the run again, starting over and over, a new town, another new name? Sarah sat, staring at her child and then struggled to sit up straighter. She kissed her daughter on the forehead, pulled the little blanket tight around her and handed the tiny infant to the agent. "I love her too much to put her through that. Hide us both, but separately."

Even now, Marybeth was shocked at how quickly it had all happened. She had gotten to hold her little girl for just a few hours more before the nurse spirited her away. Agent Nowicki had made arrangements for the adoption through one of the bigger hospitals in the area, deliberately not sharing the details with Sarah. Other agents packed up her room and gave her just one more opportunity to step on campus before they left.

She sat with Gregory for a few minutes on a worn, wooden bench outside the School of Education building. She tried not to notice the fact that her coffee cup was shaking slightly in her hand. Her arm had healed but she had developed a habit of holding it close to her, just over her stomach. "You're not going to see your mom first?" he asked.

"No, I wrote to her, told her that I got a different scholarship and was planning to change schools. We're not close. She's busy with Chrissy and her new husband now. It's fine. But I wanted to ask, if I write to her again, would you forward it on to her? I don't want her to worry." They both knew that technically they were violating the witness protection rules, but she just couldn't stand to disappear altogether. It had been so incredibly hard giving up her baby. To go to a new town now, all by herself without telling anyone, just felt too hard, too frightening. "I picked out a name, want to hear it?"

"Sure."

"It's Marybeth White."

"How'd you come up with that?"

"Well, Mary White was the most ordinary name I could think of but it sounded kind of dull." She managed a small smile. "When I was a little girl my favorite book was *Little Women.* Beth was the sister that everyone loved the most, so I thought I'd add that part in." Tears were forming in her eyes and she looked away, digging in her purse for a tissue. "I'm so scared."

He put his arm around her shoulder and held her close to him. "Sarah, I mean Marybeth. It'll be okay. You're going to get back into classes and make new friends. You're going to have a great life. No one's going to hurt you anymore."

CHAPTER FOURTEEN

*R*ay Sanchez had been searching the files for hours and he had a pain in his back to prove it. He'd found no other mention of the young woman in the file. Why had Nowicki stopped looking for her he wondered? Or had she? Within minutes Ray was back upstairs at Cindy's desk.

"What, again and still no power bars, I see?" Cindy swiveled her chair to face him as he thudded into the chair.

He waved his hand in the air. "I know, I know, I'll owe you a whole box of the damned things. Look, if someone had been in college in 1986 and you looked for them now but couldn't find any record of them, what would you think?"

"I'd think they were dead, that's years ago. Why?"

"But wouldn't there be something, anything, a death certificate at least?"

"Well, if they died in the US, yeah, I think there'd be something. It's all computerized now so it's usually pretty simple to search."

"I know. That's what I've been doing and I've found zip. I can't even find out if she graduated from the college. So it got me thinking, what if we put them under protection back then? I couldn't find that record, or at least I shouldn't be able to, right? Witness protection information is kept secret for a reason."

Cindy shook her head. Ray watched as the curls shifted and then settled around her face. For a second he was distracted, suddenly realizing how beautiful her blue eyes were against her dark hair.

"Witness protection, really? I think you've been watching too many cop shows. Hardly anyone gets put into witness protection, ever, and why would they do that to some college student?"

Ray leaned back in his chair and folded his hands together. "What if they were Jay Warren's girlfriend?"

"Seriously, someone dated that asshole?" Cindy turned and looked at Ray again. "I know he was good looking, but even back then people knew that the family was trouble at least."

"I think trouble is exactly the right word. I think this woman got pregnant and was put into witness protection when they did the investigation back in 1986."

Cindy laughed, then retreated at the look on his face. She picked up a chain of paperclips and began adding another one to the length. "Sanchez, do you know how crazy you sound? She was probably just some tourist who died on vacation and the death didn't get reported right. Witness protection is a huge leap."

"But can you find out for me? Can you trace her name?"

She coiled the paper clips into a pile and turned toward him once again. "You know I'm not supposed to do that. Those records are sealed for a reason, to stop loonies like you, for example." He stood then, pacing within the tiny cubicle before throwing himself back into the metal folding chair.

"Dammit Cindy, you're the only one I know with the skills to hack in and find that record. What harm is there in looking? I'm not planning to out the woman, for God's sake. I just want to know what happened to her."

Ray saw Cindy looking at him and wondered what she must

think. He set his glasses up on top of his head, resting them on the crew cut he kept because he was growing self-conscious about the amount of gray in it. He was realizing just how much he liked this young woman and hated to see her looking at him pityingly. Then he saw her face soften and change and he couldn't help but smile. "Okay, fine," she said. "This damn case is making everyone crazy. Give me her name, let's see what we can find."

Ray forced himself to sit back in the chair, to smooth his pants down over his knees and try at least to look patient. Inside he was jumping, though. He hadn't had any new information in this case for a very long time. Until that moment, he hadn't quite realized just how frustrating it had become, how defeated he'd been feeling. He debated running across to the market for a case of power bars just for a distraction, but Cindy looked up at him with a quick intake of breath.

"What?"

"I'll be damned, you were right. Take a look."

Ray got up and leaned over, resting his hand on Cindy's shoulder as they read the entry together. "Marybeth White, and there's an address with a photo, 316 College Lane, West Chester. Do you see anything about a baby?"

"Hold on, let me see."

She typed a bit more then leaned aside so that he could read the new screen. "The minor child, female, closed adoption 1986."

"So they were separated? That's surprising."

"Why?"

"I don't know, from the picture she looks like a nice person, I wonder why she would give her kid away."

Cindy looked up sharply. "Are you kidding me? Maybe because she was twenty years old and terrified of a crime family?" She shrugged. "Who knows, maybe the agency talked her into giving the baby up, told her they'd both be safer that way."

Ray wanted to run back to his desk and begin searching for

this new name, but he forced himself to sit back down and consider the situation. "So she's young, she has a baby with Jay Warren and then disappears. Will I be putting her in danger if I try to find out more? The Warrens are dead, right? They can't hurt her now."

"Need I remind you that we still haven't located the body of one Jay Warren?"

"There haven't been any sightings, though. I thought the consensus was that he died in the crash and the body was just too far gone to be identified."

"Is that what you think?" Cindy turned and looked at him as he fell back into the chair.

"No, I don't, to be honest. I'm just grasping at straws."

"Why would you want to find her, anyway? What information could she possibly have if she's been away from them for so long?"

"Well, don't you think the baby is a big deal?"

"But she won't know where the baby, actually the adult woman, is."

"Damn, you're right." Ray slumped into his chair and tapped his fingers on the edge of Cindy's desk, down, back, an even tempo that was designed to make anyone scream.

After several minutes she slapped her hand down over his to stop it. "What're you thinking?"

"I'm not sure. I keep thinking about all of the money involved and where it goes now. Walt Warren was rich, maybe not as rich as he once was, but he had some. His wife's family has even more."

"Remind me who they are?"

"Kathryn Clark Warren was the daughter of Frank Clark. He started a chain of dry cleaners in New York that spread all over the country. You've heard of Clark Cleaning, right? Her brother Edward took it over after the father died, made an even bigger success of it."

74

Ray saw Cindy look down at her worn corduroys and wondered for a moment if he'd insulted her by asking. "Sure, I've seen their signs." She leaned back over her screen to try to hide what he thought might be a blush creeping into her cheeks. "What are you thinking?"

"Before the crash happened, we were starting to see some connections between the supposedly squeaky clean Jay and his father. When they tried to make the case initially, this woman was one of their links to him."

"But she wouldn't know anything about him now, she's been in hiding for years and years."

"Dammit, you're right. I'm not making any sense."

"Hey, look at this. There's a way to track whenever someone accesses this file. Here's a list. There's us but there was someone else about three weeks after the adoption and then another search just after the crash. There's also a note here that says anyone accessing the account needs to contact Sylvia Nowicki immediately."

"Oh no, she's dead, that's why no one noticed the access. She probably had a system to warn her, but her personal records, whatever wasn't in our files, are gone. Can you tell who it was? Three weeks after the crash makes me nervous."

Cindy typed, frowned, and then typed some more before slapping her hand on the desk, dislodging the paperclips with her. "I'll be damned."

"What? Do you know who it was?"

She nodded. "I have no idea why, but it was the assistant director, Ronald Perkins."

Ray stood up suddenly and stretched his long body out as far as it would go, nearly touching the ceiling squares above him, then tucked in his shirt and straightened out his tie. "Hold that thought. I'm going to go see if I can talk with him."

Cindy looked up surprised. "What? Really? Are you kidding me? You can't do that. He's probably not even in the building."

"Guess I'll find out. Wish me luck." He loped toward the front stairs but thought he noticed Cindy shaking her head at him as he took off.

Forty-five minutes later he was back, grinning. "You are not going to believe this."

"They told you to make an appointment and come back in three months?"

Ray plopped down onto the seat. "No, he was walking into his office and I just followed him in."

Cindy laughed. "Unbelievable."

"No, here's what's unbelievable. Turns out the guy is friends with Edward Clark. He talked to him not long after the plane crash."

"Are you kidding me?"

"No, and get this. Clark wants to find the baby, the niece."

"It's about the money, isn't it?"

"Yep, you got it. When Jay was born, Clark set up a trust arrangement so that he inherited a big part of the estate when he turned twenty-one. He gets the rest of it as well as control of the dry cleaning business when Clark passes."

"And now, with the crash?"

"Perkins said that Clark told him he met the mother back when she was dating Jay in college. Now that the Warrens are dead, he wants to find his niece and settle the estate on her."

"So what now?" Cindy looked up as Ray stood next to her.

"I'm going to find this witness and talk to her, see if she knows any more than we do."

Ray felt taller for a second, as though this new lead had lifted something from him and caused him to stand up straighter. He smiled broadly at her, and he thought he saw the blush starting again.

"All right, get the hell out of here Sanchez, and don't come back again without the power bars."

Ray leaned over and gave her cheek a loud, smacking kiss. "I'll buy you shares in the damn company if this amounts to anything." He stood quickly and practically sprinted for the stairs, then stopped and came back around to stand by her desk. "If anything comes of this, you and I need to take some time off. Are you the photographer?" He gestured toward the pictures tacked to her cubicle.

She looked up. "Yeah, it's what I do when I'm not working seventy hours a week trying to close a case."

"I think they're terrific, and I'd like to see more if you have some. When this is done..." he smiled and turned away, charging toward the stairs once again.

Ray found himself grinning all the way to his desk but once he got there, he wasn't sure if it was because of the lead in the case or Cindy herself. Come to think of it, she sure had smelled nice when he leaned over her shoulder to look at the screen. Either way, he felt stoked, for the first time in several years. He settled down at his desk to find out all he could about Sarah Dawes/Marybeth White.

CHAPTER FIFTEEN

$\mathcal{A}$fter the sprawling campus of Penn State, the small campus outside of Philadelphia had reminded Marybeth of a nostalgic little town from an old movie. The buildings were located in a small section of streets and reflected such a mishmash of architectural styles and materials that it was hard to know exactly what the founders might have had in mind at the time it was built. In a way, though, the effect was of an unfashionable living room where the furniture didn't match but the room was still filled with comfort and ease. From her first days on campus she had felt surprisingly at home.

In order to maximize the funds that the FBI had settled her with, Marybeth chose a shared dorm room on campus and a simple meal plan. She could still remember the trepidation she'd felt on meeting her new roommate, but Niko Kim, a whirlwind in rainbow colored clothes, had been something else. Her straight black hair was cut short in a fluff of bangs that rarely settled evenly on her face, especially as she was prone to raking her fingers through it as she talked. She'd been on the phone with her mother talking in a mix of what sounded like Japanese and English when Marybeth walked in. A big grin crossed her face as she rolled her eyes and gestured to indicate that she was trying to wrap up the conversation. Finally free, she dropped the receiver into the cradle and laughed. "Hi, I'm Niko and I'll tell you right now, my mother calls more than once a day so please don't kill me. She's a worrier and I can't seem to do much about it."

Marybeth tried hard to hide the nerves and sadness that threatened to overtake her. "Well, I'm Marybeth and my mother will never call so we should balance out just fine."

Niko threw herself onto the dark green bean bag chair that occupied the one free corner of the room. "Wow, so you're coming from Penn State, right? Why would you want to move to this little burg?"

Confronted so quickly with all that was new and false in her life, Marybeth dropped her bag on the unmade bed and sat down uneasily beside it. She took a deep breath and with a newfound resolve, forced herself to move toward something, not away from it. "I just wanted something a little smaller, I guess. I'm studying special education and this program is ranked really highly."

"Hey, me too, how cool is that?"

"Really?"

"Yeah, there's only about twenty of us so we're a pretty tight group."

Marybeth worried immediately that she'd be the outsider once again, but Niko wasn't having any of that. "Come on, drop your stuff and come meet Ruby and Aisha. They're just down the hall." She laughed, pulling Marybeth gently by the arm. "This is awesome, our study group definitely needs some new blood."

And just like that, she'd become part of the gang. Classes were held in one of the oldest buildings on campus, a leftover from its days as one of the state's Normal Schools. Although beautiful and imposing on the outside, the worn desks and outdated labs reflected the status of teaching in so many places. "Put your heart into it but don't expect there to be any money" seemed to be the motto here just as it had been at Penn State.

Programs differed around the state and the new one she'd entered varied just enough that Marybeth was surprised at how quickly she was expected to choose a specific area to focus on. Feeling a little embarrassed and ashamed of herself, she had to admit that she really wasn't interested in working with the developmentally disabled. Repetition was the key for those children and she couldn't imagine herself lasting in that kind of a classroom. What really interested her were the students with emotional issues. After all, she felt like she'd barely escaped a truly damaging situation and she was an adult. How much harder would it be for children caught up in their own desperate situations?

The second week she was there, the students in her cohort group had all scattered to do observations in a range of placements, including hospitals, pre-schools, elementary and high schools. They gathered in the classroom on Friday afternoon to share their experiences. One young woman talked with gushing enthusiasm about working with brain damaged adults on pre-attending skills. Marybeth couldn't even imagine what it would take to work with such individuals, people rendered less capable than a dog or cat. The woman, Rebecca was her name, would clearly be in line for sainthood.

When Marybeth's time came to talk, she found herself describing a therapeutic hold that a teacher had used with a young boy who'd been trying to hurt himself. He had kicked and flailed but the woman had held him firmly while maintaining a steady, soothing tone. Marybeth had watched a calm descend on his features and the tension flow out of his limbs. It seemed remarkable.

She saw Rebecca shake her head, unable to understand working with the type of children that Marybeth liked so much. Suddenly, it really did feel as if each of them was meant for something just a little bit different and that was okay. She found she was happy knowing that, as well as feeling a little less guilty.

The social scene at the small college was also a lot different from that at the big university. Here the intramural programming took the place of big time athletics and nearly everyone seemed to participate. Niko had talked her into partnering with her in ping-pong and Marybeth found herself enjoying it with a freedom that she realized she hadn't felt since elementary school. Once everyone finished playing, Marybeth had tried to beg off the party, preferring to head back to the dorm on her own. She still didn't feel very comfortable in many of the student groups, as though all that she had gone through had somehow rendered her twenty years older on the inside if not the outside. But again, Niko had been insistent. In fact, Marybeth had met her husband Ken at the house party following that final tournament.

"Come on, you can't bail out now. Besides, I don't think it'll be a huge party. It's just over at the house the Brehm boys are renting." Once they stored their paddles and helped to break down the tables, Niko hooked her arm in Marybeth's and smiled so persuasively there really wasn't any way to say no without being rude.

At the front door, the smell of beer wafted out over the porch and Marybeth balked, immediately associating the smell with the nausea that had accompanied her recent pregnancy. But Niko forged ahead, making quick introductions, so Marybeth forced herself to follow along in her wake.

Soon though, Niko was swept into a deep philosophical discussion about death and Japanese art and Marybeth was left on her own. She grabbed a cup off the table and filled it with water from the tap. The kitchen door opened onto a small porch and she stepped outside where the music was slightly less deafening. There were iron steps leading down to the small lot below and she was considering walking home, when Ken walked out behind her and leaned on the railing.

"A little loud," he commented, pressing his ears shut for a moment. "I'm Ken. You're Niko's roommate, aren't you?"

Marybeth put out her hand. "Yes, Marybeth White." She hoped that the fraction of hesitation she still felt with the new name wasn't noticeable. "Are you in education too?"

"No, I'm in the business school. Niko and I went to high school together." He pointed off to their left. "Just over there in fact."

"Another townie, huh?"

"Yep, the guys that rent the house too. We've known each other for a ridiculously long time."

"It must be nice to have a history with people. I've always been the outsider myself." She shrugged and finished the water in her cup.

"Can I get you another beer?" He gestured with his own cup but she shook her head.

"No thanks, I'm not a beer drinker."

He reached in his shirt pocket, pulled out a pack of cigarettes and offered her one of those instead. "Cigarette then?"

"No." She laughed. "I don't smoke either."

"Well Marybeth, you don't drink, you don't smoke, what do you like?"

She was ashamed that the first thoughts that popped into her head were, *what should I say? What does he want me to say?* But just then she spotted a young mother walking along the sidewalk with her son, a comfortable grip on his hand as she balanced a bulging sack of groceries in the other. In an instant, Marybeth realized she was done trying to figure out what everyone else wanted her to say. She gestured toward the bag. "Cantaloupe. I like cantaloupe a lot."

Ken tilted his head and beamed. "Well, all right then. So do I."

Afterwards, she and Niko had talked into the wee hours of the morning about the party. Marybeth figured she had scared Ken away with her prudish behavior but Niko seemed to think otherwise.

"I dunno, MB, he looked pretty interested to me. I've seen

some of the girls he goes out with and to be honest, he never looked at them the way he did at you tonight." She could hear sleep overtaking her friend's speech as the night deepened and Marybeth found herself wondering again at the new life she had fallen into.

CHAPTER SIXTEEN

*J*ay felt at home in hotels and the resort he'd chosen in Caracas was an especially nice one. The room smelled of flowers that were cut and placed there each morning and his view of the beach and nearby mountain was stunning. He didn't expect to stay there long, just until he was confident that the FBI investigation was firmly focused on his father and not him. His lawyers in Pittsburgh and Philadelphia were discreetly keeping him posted on what was going on.

Jay had been surprised at first that the media seemed to think he was dead as well. He'd thought that a private plane wouldn't have attracted so much notice. But who cared, he could work it into the plan. It was irritating that his bank accounts had been frozen but the offshore account he'd set up in the fall would serve his needs for the present. He figured that it would probably take the crash investigation team a few weeks to determine that his body was not in the wreckage. That would give him enough time to finish his preparations and plan for his grand re-entry. He thought he'd have a nice black suit tailored for him here and then make sure that the cameras caught him in his stylish mourning attire. He would claim to have sustained a head injury and only recently learned of his father's death. In the bathroom mirror, he practiced what he called his funeral gaze.

Downstairs, the hotel bar wasn't bad. Its expanse had been crafted from local hardwoods and polished until it shone as brightly as the mirror above it. The waitresses were stunning, he thought, long-legged beauties in tropical skirts that opened on one side from floor to hip. He smiled politely at the young woman who sidled up next to him to take his order. "I'd like a top-shelf Long Island iced tea, please sweetheart, and some real peanuts, if you've got them."

"Of course, anything else I can get for you?"

He gestured toward the wide-screen TV in the corner. "Do you get anything besides soccer on the sports channels down here?"

She shook her head. "Sorry, not around here, I'm afraid. I'll be right back with your drink."

He watched as she swished her way around the end of the bar, then turned back to the screen. Goddamned place, fucking tortilla chips and soccer everywhere you looked.

He moved from the bar stool to a small table closer to the pool. He would love to have worked on his tan while he was here but that didn't quite fit with the image that he was creating, so he chose a table with a broad white umbrella that would shield him from the sun. There were a few decent bodies that held his attention. One blonde in particular was bent over, making quite a show of gathering her beach things and putting them into her bag. He caught her eye and saw her wink as she moved away from the pool deck toward the bar.

Jay thought there were a lot tougher places to sit out a couple of weeks.

CHAPTER SEVENTEEN

*M*arybeth tucked the photograph away but managed to get very little sleep. Her first morning in Pittsburgh, she was awash in nervous energy, panicked at the steps she'd already taken. The nervousness shifted into sadness as she turned her phone on and saw the number of missed calls. The texts from Ken had been lengthy at first, then they'd grown increasingly terse and angry. Tears filled her eyes as she sat cradling the phone in her hand long enough for the wallpaper to reappear. It was a favorite photo of Ken and her boys taken last Christmas, all of them armed with Nerf guns, a split second out of the epic battle. She turned off the Wi-Fi setting and put it back into airplane mode so that the calls and messages couldn't come through. Then she tucked it away in her suitcase, put that back into the closet and closed the door firmly. She would call him back this evening, she decided, or tomorrow at the latest. Gregory would be waiting for her.

The library was a short walk away and she found Gregory easily. He was just ahead of her, walking in to the second-floor reference area where they commandeered a table. He set his laptop on the table between them and plugged in a small USB drive.

"What's that?" Marybeth asked.

He looked sheepish. "It's a kind of lock for my computer, makes it safer than just a password."

"Oh, that's neat."

Marybeth got her laptop out as well and sent him the information that she'd learned so far.

He pulled an old-fashioned steno pad out of his satchel and flipped through several pages before landing on a blank one. He turned to the computer to begin typing and within twenty minutes had their first bit of information. "Okay, so I checked over what you had and then looked a little further. It looks like the year we're talking about there were over three hundred kids adopted from the western Pennsylvania area."

She slumped against the back of her chair. "Oh my God, so many,"

"Yeah, well, you've already started narrowing that total down." He resumed typing. "We have to start somewhere."

By the end of the day Marybeth was convinced that she'd made an enormous mistake. She had risked losing everything she had with Ken for a search that looked even more impossible than she had imagined. She picked up a sandwich on her way back to the hotel and sat eating it, staring at the black face of her phone, and then looking around at the rest of the room. There was something unnerving about the light in here, as though a bulb was close to burning out. She got up and turned on all of the lamps in the room, but the feeling persisted. It probably wasn't the room at all, she told herself, just her own melancholy surrounding her. She turned her phone back on for a minute, watched as the number of missed calls and messages doubled, and jumped as a call came through. She knew by the ringtone that it was Ken. She watched the phone register the call then go blank and decided it was better not to look at it at all. She just wasn't ready yet.

After a second fruitless day, Marybeth and Gregory took the time to explore some Airbnbs in the area. She'd gotten the idea to start her own checking account when she'd opened accounts for their boys when they were young. She would put in small amounts over the years if she earned an extra fee for tutoring or testing a student, but she hadn't really thought much about it until she'd seen how Ken's golf expenditures had started to add up. He wasn't extravagant by any means. He'd been given the set of clubs that he used, but weekly outings, even to local public courses, had started to add up. Marybeth wasn't a shopper or a spender by nature, probably because she'd had such a tough go as a young woman, but she had wanted something that was just hers, a reserve in case she ever did decide she wanted to spend money on something. So, she'd begun matching his golf outlays with deposits to her checking account. The small amounts over the years had added up so that there were several thousand dollars in the account by the time she saw the news clipping and began to formulate her plan. But plane fare and hotel rooms would eat into that account quickly.

They finally decided that a room in a house owned by an older, Italian grandmother named Mrs. Finelli, seemed like the best choice. For a small additional fee, she could have dinner there as well. Marybeth checked out of the hotel and settled in within just a few hours. Since the library hadn't offered them any more assistance with the search, they settled on Gregory's usual coffee house as their meeting spot. It wasn't one of the chains, but locally owned, with a good Wi-Fi system that made it a comfortable place to work.

At the end of the third day, she made her way back to her room, dropped her pack on the narrow bed and washed her face in front of the old, speckled mirror. Physically, she felt better than she had before she left home, since she walked everywhere she went in the city. Mentally, though, it was a different story. It was becoming harder and harder to ignore the phone that lay tucked away in her backpack. She set up her laptop and took a minute to look at her bank records to see that everything was all right. There was something funny going on with the water bill but she discovered it was easy enough to fix. Then she went down to dinner.

The first evening in the house she discovered that the owner, Mrs. Finelli, was a true delight. At eighty-two, Rosemary, as she insisted on being called, was more fit and agile than many of Marybeth's younger friends back home. Her blonde hair, though she said it was thinner than it had been as a young woman, was still carefully washed and styled each week. She had half a closet full of pastel colored pantsuits that she liked to accent with a variety of scarves and pins as well as matching tennis shoes.

There were no other guests so early in the summer so it was just the two of them at dinner, but Marybeth loved hearing tales from Rosemary's day. She wondered if, given the chance, her mother might have aged into someone a little bit like Rosemary. So many of her expressions seemed to be taken straight out of Marybeth's childhood. When she'd first gone into hiding, Marybeth had planned to write her mother regularly, but during the first winter, a truck driver had lost control on the ice and her mother had been killed instantly.

After dinner that night, Marybeth returned to her room and thought about how much she missed shopping for her favorite ingredients, planning and cooking meals that she and Ken would enjoy. They'd have been eating on their back deck by now, she thought, if she hadn't taken off. God only knew what he'd been eating. She didn't know if he'd go the frozen route or if he'd become the grocery store deli counter's favorite customer. Both choices just made her sad. She pulled her phone out and sat with it in her lap before finally dialing the familiar number. Ken answered before the first ring.

"Marybeth, thank God! I've been going nuts. Where are you?"

Marybeth tucked her free hand under her leg to keep it from shaking. "Ken, I'm fine. How are you?"

"What do you mean how am I? What the hell's going on?"

"Ken, it's okay. I'm in Pittsburgh." She dragged her shoe across the fringe of the old rug.

"Pittsburgh, where? I'm coming, I can drive there right now."

"No, Ken, don't say that. I'll hang up if you do."

She could hear a quick intake of breath. "No, for God's sake, don't hang up. Please, just talk to me. I deserve to know what's going on."

"I know you do and I know I'm not being fair."

"Fair? You're right, there's nothing fair about this situation. Talk to me."

"I can't Ken, there's just no way to explain everything over the phone. I'm looking for someone and it's taking me a little longer than I had hoped."

"Looking for who? I don't understand." He paused and Marybeth could hear him take in a long breath before continuing. When he did there was a flat quality to the tone. "Who is he, Marybeth?"

She rushed to answer. "Ken, I swear to God, it is not a man that I'm looking for. I'm in love with you, no one else. I know this is hard, but please, I just need a little more time. I promise I won't be much longer."

"Time, what do you need time for? I don't understand. Jesus Marybeth, we worked so hard to get past all of this nonsense. I thought you trusted me."

The anger in his voice had been replaced by hurt and tears formed in Marybeth's eyes. Her finger reached for the button to disconnect, then hesitated. "Soon, Ken, I'll be home soon and I promise I'll explain then. No more secrets. I love you Ken, believe me. Once I know a little more, I'll tell you everything. I promise. I just need a little more time."

She knew it was cruel, but she pushed the button and then turned off the phone. She tucked it back into her bag and then fell onto the bed. She pulled the pillow tight to her chest and let the tears fall.

CHAPTER EIGHTEEN

*P*rofessor Charles Wright, Retired, pulled off his Kangol hat and tossed it to the butler as he walked through the foyer of Edward's ridiculous house. He had no idea why his friend still chose to live in this mausoleum. The butler, he'd forgotten the man's name, nodded briefly and then disappeared down the hallway with the hat. Charles knew that it would be returned to him silently, almost mysteriously, at the end of his visit like a scene from some old Hollywood movie. The whole setup still seemed crazy to him. Years ago, Charles had chosen Pittsburgh for his retirement and he enjoyed his little apartment that looked out over the river and the lights of the city. He had simple hooks by the door for his hat.

Years earlier, when Eddie's wife had died, Charles had tried so hard to get him to sell this place and move in with him or near him, but nothing could persuade him. Charles had to admit to himself that he'd begun worrying about Eddie lately, they weren't getting any younger, that was for sure. He wished he knew if the staff here was as tuned in to Eddie as he was. Would they notice if something was wrong?

Charles walked through the echoing house and found his old

friend planted in his usual spot at the kitchen counter. The house had a library, a study, a solarium even and where did the man choose to work? The kitchen island, on a leather stool. It made Charles's back ache to think about it but as he watched Eddie swivel slowly side-to-side, he had to smile. Some things never changed. In his late sixties now, Edward Clark had grown wide around the middle and somewhat shorter, but he still sported a full head of hair. The money, the house, the luxuries that he could call up, none of that tweaked at Charles the way that head of hair did. He rubbed his hand over his spotted dome and smiled at his friend. "What's new with the billionaires' club?" Charles slapped Edward on his shoulder and took the next stool over.

Edward grinned. "Not much, not much. How are you? Still getting in some running I see?"

Charles looked down at the pitiful old sneakers he wore. "No running for this old dog, just walking along the river when the weather's nice. You should join me some time, get out of this place and see how the little people live. What's up?"

Edward swiveled to face his old friend. "How would you like to go on an adventure?" Edward got up and went to the enormous refrigerator. He pulled out two beers and what looked like a platter for a dinner party, heaped with cut-up fruits and vegetables, even some sort of crackers and dip were included.

"What's all this?" Charles leaned over to inspect the platter as Edward laid it on the counter in front of him and removed the cover.

Edward gestured toward the tray, opened the two beer bottles and settled himself back on his stool. "Oh, my cook, oops, I should say my chef Helen, doesn't think I'm looking after myself well enough. She keeps hiding the potato chips and making up these platters of healthy foods for me to pick at. I know she means well, but I have to say, I miss my damn potato chips, Charlie." They both laughed and reached past the vegetables for the crackers and dip.

"So what are you talking about, an adventure? You planning on taking us on a safari or something?"

"No, nothing like that." He paused. "Although, if you'd like to go on a safari, I could arrange it."

Charles popped a cherry tomato into his mouth. "No thanks. I think our safari days might be behind us anyway."

"Well, if you're sure. The adventure I'm thinking about is a little closer to home, but to start with, I have to tell you a secret. It's one I've kept for over twenty-five years if you can believe that."

"I thought I knew all of your secrets, Eddie. Are there skeletons and closets I'm not aware of?" He reached around to rub at his spine. "God, what have you done with all of the comfortable chairs?"

Edward stood up and pushed the stool back under the counter. "Of course, let's take this in to the dining room and sit like civilized people." Charles carried the platter along with his beer, while Edward closed his laptop and led the way into the next room. The chandelier over the beautiful, polished walnut table, seemed a bit much when he turned it on, so Charlie was relieved when Edward flipped it off and they settled instead on chairs near the floor-to-ceiling windows. "This secret actually starts with a conversation that you and I had back at Penn State one day. Do you remember telling me about a young woman you thought my nephew might be hurting?"

Charles leaned back in his seat and was surprised at how easily Sarah's face popped into his mind. He had been so sorry to see her drop out of school and had wondered for years just what had happened to her. "You remember that after all this time?"

There was almost a twinkle in Edward's eyes as he leaned conspiratorially toward his friend. "Indeed, I do."

"After she dropped out I kept hoping she'd return but when I got back from my trip that summer, I never saw her again. Do you mean you know what happened to her?"

"Well, I can tell you this much, she wasn't a dropout." He paused and studied his hands for a moment. "I admit, for a long time I just didn't think that what you were saying about my nephew could be true. I even called Jay and talked with him, tried to get him to bring Sarah down for a visit, but no such luck. It was then that I started seeing more and more in the paper about a court case regarding his dad, Walt Warren. I had a few connections, so I poked my nose in. I discovered that something much bigger *was* going on. The FBI was building a case against Walt but they were also looking at his son Jay, and your Miss Dawes had stumbled into it."

Charles set his beer on the table. He hesitated to ask his next question, but he just couldn't avoid it. "Was he the one who hurt her? I seem to remember something else after the black eye that we talked about, another incident, right?"

Edward leaned back as he settled into his story. "A few weeks later her arm was broken." He rubbed his hand over his face. "I wish so much that I'd listened to you back then."

Charles slapped his hand on the table. "Yes, I remember that now." He caught his breath and nearly whispered his next question. "Did he kill her?"

Edward poked at the remainder of the dip with his cracker before putting the whole thing in his mouth at once. He shook his head as he chewed. "No, no, no, nothing like that. What he did, was get her pregnant."

Charles tried to think back to that spring but too many others crowded it out. He knew that he'd been caught up in preparing for his big trip to France that summer, but he just couldn't remember any more than that. "So, what happened then? Did Walt flip out?"

"He never knew. As far as I know, neither he nor Jay knew anything about it. Walt called Jay home to Pittsburgh that spring because of the FBI investigation." He paused and pulled at his watch, rubbing his finger across the wide dial. "My sister

Kathryn had just passed, and I felt absolutely no loyalty to that son-of-a-bitch, Walt Warren."

Charles nearly jumped out of his seat. "You worked with the FBI?"

Edward spread his hands wide. "Oh, not really. An agent named Sylvia Nowicki was in charge of the work they were doing up in State College and I..."

"You met with her? Were you undercover?"

Edward laughed. "No, nothing quite that exciting, I'm afraid. No, her supervisor was a man that I knew from my college days at Pitt. He came to my dry cleaning office to interview me about the family, and when I told him your story about Jay, he introduced me to the detective who was in charge up there. Once their case started falling apart, Agent Nowicki asked if I'd meet with her. That's how I found out Sarah was pregnant." With the crackers and dip finished, Edward picked up a carrot spear and crunched on it as Charles waited impatiently for him to go on.

"So, what happened then?"

He washed the carrot down with a sip of beer and reached for another. He waved it in the air in front of him as he continued the story. "Sylvia Nowicki called me at the start of August to say that the case was collapsing and she was worried about this young woman. The agent hoped that the Warrens had bought the story that she'd dropped out and moved away, but she wasn't certain. We were trying to figure something out when Sarah went into labor. Agent Nowicki called me that night and asked for my help. The FBI wanted to put Sarah into protection and she had decided that the baby would be safer on her own. I helped arrange the adoption through St. Vincent's here in the city."

"I can't believe it, and you kept the secret all these years. So why tell me now?"

Edward stood and walked toward the window, pausing as he looked out at the thick green leaves now covering the adjacent oak. He waved the thin, white curtain as he thought, then let it go and turned back to the table. He planted his hands on the back of his chair and leaned in. "I always hated Walt Warren, even before Kathryn passed. I'm getting up in years now and I want to settle my financial affairs. I'll give whatever I can to charities that work for children like Daniel, but they don't need all of my money."

He paused and sat back down in his chair, a thoughtful expression on his face. He spoke slowly. "I tried, but I could never really decide what I thought of Jay. Honestly, I didn't deal with him often, but when I did he was always polite enough. We usually met up once a year or so and talked business or politics. I know that Walt was dirtier than hell but I never saw Jay having any involvement in it." He rubbed his thumb along the edge of the table as he spoke. "But with the two of them gone now in that awful crash, I need to adjust my will. What I'd like to do is find my great niece and settle the rest of the estate on her."

Charles leaned his chair back, balancing on the back two legs while he studied his old friend. "Is something wrong Eddie? Are you ill?"

Edward waved his hand dismissively at his friend. "No, no, I'm fine. I'm just getting older. We all are." He looked at the beautiful room with its enormous, gleaming table. "You've been after me to sell this place and downsize a bit and I'm starting to think you're right." He settled back into his seat and picked up another carrot spear. "So, are you in?"

"In what?"

"The hunt for my great niece. Are you in?"

"What do you mean? I thought you'd just hire a private detective or something."

"Well, I made sure it was a very carefully closed adoption so that's really not an option at this point."

"What do you mean?"

Edward waggled his head. "There might have been a bit of forgery involved and I don't want any of that to come to light."

Charles landed the feet of his chair down hard. "Are you kidding me? What did you do?"

"Well, my secretary knew Walt's secretary through their bridge club, and I might have had my secretary borrow a signature stamp with Jay's name on it." He let the statement hover in the air above them as he watched his friend's face for any sign of disapproval. He was relieved to see that laughter was what spread across his face instead.

"Son of a bitch, never underestimate the powers of a dry cleaner, huh?" Charles slapped his old friend on the shoulder and reached to finish his beer. "Well Mr. Crime Master, what's your plan, then? How are we going to find this young woman?"

"I think we need to follow her mother."

Charles stopped just short of spitting out the last swallow of beer. "My old student? The one in witness protection? That's your plan? You think the trail of someone hidden by the FBI is going to be easier to follow than a closed adoption? Are you crazy?"

"Now hang on, here's the thing. Not long after the plane crash, I was at an alumni gathering and saw my old friend from the FBI. He's an assistant director now, so I told him what I wanted to do about my estate." Edward stood up and walked into the kitchen to bring out two more beers. He clinked the bottom of his bottle with Charles' and resumed his story. "Cheers. Where was I?"

"FBI guy?"

"Right, so of course he won't tell me anything directly but he does say that he'll look into it and get back to me. So I wait and I start to figure he's not going to tell me squat, but then I got a call yesterday. He tells me that an agent of his was looking into the case and discovered that she's just flown in to Pittsburgh herself and hired her own private detective, a guy that she knew back in State College."

"Sarah's here? Why?"

"My hunch is that she's looking for the baby. Think about it. She's had to hide out all this time, knowing her baby is growing up without her. She hears about the plane crash and suddenly she's safe. She can look for the young woman without having to worry about the Warrens finding out. I think that's why she's here in Pittsburgh."

Charles smoothed a bead of water down the side of the bottle with his thumb.. "Wow, that's a lot to take in. But I don't get where we come in. Are you going to contact her, ask her if that's what she's doing?"

"No, I don't feel comfortable doing that, at least not yet." He shrugged. "Actually, if I'm being honest here, I'm not sure whether I'm ready to come clean yet about helping with the adoption." He paused and looked up. "What I did do was look into the guy she's working with, and I found out that the private eye she hired doesn't really have an office, he's usually at a coffee shop down by the river."

"And we'll hang around the coffee shop and listen in? Are you crazy? For one thing, people in this city know what you look like. Your face was just in the Pittsburgh Magazine's business section. People recognize you." He paused and studied his friend's face as he took another sip of beer. "Wait, that's where I come in, isn't it?"

"That's why I called it an adventure. Hasn't a part of you always wanted to play at being a spy?"

"Don't you think she'll recognize me?"

"A professor she had three decades and a full head of hair ago?" He shook his head. "You keep a low profile and no one will know. People these days hang out in coffee shops all day long. It'll be a breeze."

Charles looked at the eager grin on his friend's face. "You are a crazy old coot, do you know that? Of course I'll do this. It's not like my appointment calendar is booked or anything."

"You have an appointment calendar?" Edward paused then reached out to shake his friend's hand. "Thank you."

"Don't thank me yet, let's see if this cockamamie scheme of yours is going to work first."

Their conversation turned to the logistics of the hunt as they cleared up the platter and beer bottles and took everything in to the kitchen. Sure enough, as Charles was walking out fifteen minutes later, the butler appeared with his hat and a quiet nod.

"Keep an eye on my friend," he said as he took the hat in hand.

"Of course, sir," the man intoned.

CHAPTER NINETEEN

*I*n the morning, Marybeth and Gregory met at the nearby coffee shop again. Summer had arrived for good and the streets were radiating heat. The cars in the tiny parking lot were steaming and a compact car with a dent in its front bumper caught her eye. She was trying to remember if she'd seen it before. Perhaps it had been there the day before.

Oh well, it felt great to step inside. The air-conditioner was making a grinding noise as they settled into their seats and she hoped it wouldn't give out. Gregory had his laptop out as he sipped on a glass of iced tea. "So here's where we are so far. We've narrowed it down to the four hospitals here in the city. They seem to have facilitated most of the infant adoptions and a lot of those were pre-arranged. I think I can get computer records from three of them, but the fourth one may be tougher, St. Vincent's. They had far and away the most adoptions and they're currently under investigation."

"Figures, the Catholics have been spiriting babies away for centuries."

"Right, so this is where you come in. I think our best bet is for you to physically go in and get access to St. Vincent's records. You'll probably have the best chance if you pose as a nun."

She looked at him incredulously. "Are you serious, impersonate a nun? In that white outfit thing they wear?"

He waved his hand dismissively. "Nuns don't wear that stuff anymore, most of them dress like everyone else now. You just have to go in like you mean business and convince them that you belong there. Some outside groups are questioning St. Vincent's methods already and I think that someone coming to set the record straight for them would have a good shot at getting in. Are you up for it? Do you think you can do it? You're not a very good liar as I recall."

Marybeth leaned back in her seat and eyed Gregory for a moment. "Are you kidding me? I've been lying forever."

He dropped his face into his hands before sitting up straight. "Oh right, sorry about that. Well, let's work on getting the computer records from the other three, and then we'll see whether or not we have to take that on."

The computer records held no matches, so later that afternoon, Marybeth straightened the unattractive glasses on her nose and reached into her purse one more time, touching the letter of introduction that Gregory had written and the plastic ID card that he'd made for her. They had gotten her outfit from the thrift store, an unflattering maroon suit that itched around the waistband and some cats-eye glasses that looked like they'd come from an old sitcom.

Marybeth was thinking about scratching again when the door to the records office opened and a stooped, older man in a wrinkled white shirt walked out. She stepped aside as he exited, then set her shoulders and entered. The clerk looked up briefly from her desk then returned her eyes to the computer. A young woman with five rings in her left ear alone, her posture made it clear that she was not on her chosen career path. "Yes?"

"Hello, I'm Sister Marybeth King. I was told to see you about the adoption records review?" She handed the prepared letter across to the young woman.

"Today? You're here today? I wasn't expecting you until tomorrow." Irritated, she closed the screen on the computer, what looked to Marybeth more like a Facebook page than work. The young woman glanced casually at the papers and then handed them back to Marybeth. "It's this way. We haven't quite gotten everything entered into the computer system yet, but we're close."

"That's fine, our agency is only going back as far as 1985 at this point."

"Well, that should be okay." One of those purple, stretchy wristbands held the key to a small office, a closet really, with a square table and an ancient looking desktop computer. Marybeth was glad that she'd brought her own laptop to download and save the records. There would never be time to look them over properly here.

The clerk flipped on a feeble looking light and shrugged by way of apology. "Sorry it's so dark. Like I said, we were told you were coming tomorrow. My supervisor should be back soon so I'll have her come and check on you once you're settled in."

Marybeth tried to smile accommodatingly at her, as if she handled this sort of thing often. "I'm sure I'll be fine. I'll come find you if I need anything."

The clerk backed out of the room quickly, no doubt eager to return to her Facebook posts.

Marybeth booted up the old desk unit and then set her laptop beside it. With the cord she'd brought, she hooked the two units together and began her search on the older unit. She was trying to hurry, knowing that a supervisor would see through her scam too easily. The search was starting, but the old unit was clearly taking its time. Her watch said ten minutes had passed. She didn't think she'd have ten more. "Come on, come on you piece of shit." Marybeth's knee was jumping just like her son Jimmy's did as she sat waiting for the years of adoptions to appear. "Finally," she breathed, then instructed the machine to copy all of the records for 1985 and 1986 for good measure. She watched the progress bar on her machine, a quarter, half, there was a noisy door opening and shutting nearby and she thought she heard the clerk's voice. "Come on, dammit," she whispered. Three quarters, a trickle of sweat was dripping down the back of her shirt.

"Miss King?" she heard a new voice call out. As the door opened she saw the bar finish, closed the lid to her computer and whisked the cord into her pocket. She stood and greeted the large woman who entered.

"Oh good, a supervisor. I'm so glad to see you. This is all a mistake. These aren't the records I'm supposed to be reviewing. I don't know what was going on in that clerk's mind." She quickly put the items into her bag and began moving to the door.

"What exactly are you supposed to do? Do you have any papers for me?"

"Well, I gave them to that clerk, of course. This sort of incompetence really can't be tolerated. I'll have to be sure to share this information with the lawyers."

The woman began sputtering in distress as Marybeth shouldered her way out the door as quickly as she could. She still had to go up two floors and get past the information desk and security guard before anyone realized she didn't belong there. The old-fashioned briefcase she'd brought banged against her leg as she took the stairs quickly.

She pushed open the wide front door and her breath exploded with relief as she spotted Gregory and his car idling at the curb. She jumped in and tugged her seatbelt on as he sped away. "Oh my God, that was close." She thought about tossing the glasses out her window but felt a little bit silly, like she thought she was a character in a movie or something. Now that it was over, though, she had to admit that it had been exciting, exhilarating even, to act out the part.

CHAPTER TWENTY

*B*y the end of the week, Ken had given up on trying to find Marybeth. He'd lied to the kids about where she was and told any friends who asked the same story—that she'd gone to her cousin's in Virginia to help with a sick relative. He was relieved that none of them questioned him deeply, as the lies had been flimsy to start with, and he really hadn't done a good job keeping them straight. He was just angry, all of the time angry. Every time he came home to an empty house, whenever he stopped at the market and bought prepared foods rather than the ingredients she used to ask for, he couldn't stop missing her. It had been days since that one phone call but there'd been nothing else since. Time after time, his calls went straight to voicemail. It was making him crazy.

He had gotten together with each of the boys but they didn't have any more information than he had. Marybeth had not called either of them. It looked as though Grant and Amy were getting pretty serious, and he wondered if Marybeth knew any of those details. Jimmy was busy with his friends and rarely stopped by the house. When their college town had emptied for the summer, he'd found a cheap sublet and was happy not to be living at home.

Unless Ken caught him on laundry day, a rarity, he saw little of him.

He had thought about telling both boys the truth, especially since he knew that their computer skills outstripped his and he could have used their expertise. But she'd asked him not to, and whether or not it made sense, he had chosen to honor that promise.

The only other thing that was weird, apart from the whole Marybeth leaving thing, was the sense that he had of someone watching him. The day before, he'd started to notice it, A black Ford, one he hadn't seen in their small neighborhood before, had been parked on the street. It was possible that someone had a relative or friend visiting, but with the great weather, everyone was out and about and no one had mentioned anything. It was starting to grate on his nerves. In their development, most people kept their cars in the driveway, so an odd one parked on the street seemed out of place.

Then, Ken started to notice it in other places. He thought that he'd seen it near Marybeth's school when he was feeling wretched and drove by there like an idiot. It also looked like the same car was leaving the grocery store when he was going in. He thought about getting the license plate number but didn't know what he would do with it. There'd been a few unidentified phone hang-ups as well, but they had stopped about the time he was starting to get suspicious. He worried that living alone was turning him into some sort of paranoid idiot.

That evening Ken pulled into the driveway and parked, ready to peel off his hot, sticky work clothes. He was trying to loosen his tie and unlock the front door all at the same time, his bag of food getting ready to fall on the porch when a voice startled him from behind. "Can I help you with that?"

Ken whipped his head around at the sound, dropping the bag of takeout in the process. A tall man with a crew cut, an old Steelers jacket and khakis was coming up the walk.

"Jesus, you scared me. Who are you? What do you want?"

"Mr. Rogers?"

"Who are you? How do you know my name?"

The stranger bowed his head and then began unfolding some sort of ID badge as he spoke. Ken looked at it carefully.

"Sorry to interrupt your evening, Mr. Rogers. My name is Ray Sanchez and I'm with the FBI. May I come in?" Ken looked at the ID and held the door in his hand, reluctant to let any stranger into the house given how odd he felt already. He didn't intend to be rude, but his tone wasn't welcoming. It was then that he noticed the black car parked in front of his neighbor's yard.

"I really don't see any need for me to talk to the FBI. I haven't done anything wrong. What do you want?"

"Mr. Rogers, I'd prefer to talk inside. Actually, I'd really like to talk to your wife. I was hoping I could catch her in."

Ken felt his shoulders sag and the bravado disappear. He picked up his food, pushed the door open, and then stepped back to allow the man into the living room.

"What do you know about my wife? Have you been watching me?"

"Watching you, no, well, not exactly. I was just hoping to find an opportunity to talk with your wife."

Ken dropped into the big chair near the door and motioned for the agent to sit. He dropped his takeout on the coffee table, put his head in his hands briefly, and then made himself look carefully at the stranger. "What do you know about my wife? Why do you want to talk to her?"

"Well, it's really more of a private conversation, if you don't mind."

Ken could feel the anger building as he stood up quickly, the chair rocking back from the force. "Why the hell would my wife be having a private conversation with the goddamn FBI? I want to know what's going on, and I want to know now. I've been worrying about her for days, and look where it's gotten me."

"What do you mean?"

"She's gone. She's been gone since last weekend." He strode back and forth in front of the fireplace. "I've been going out of my mind trying to figure out what's going on."

"Wait, you mean she's gone, gone, not just at the store or something? Have you reported it?"

Ken collapsed back into the chair. "This is going to sound ridiculous. It *is* ridiculous, actually. Get this. She asked me for a sabbatical. She said she wanted to go and do research. Who the hell takes a sabbatical from a marriage?"

"Did she say where she was going? When she was coming back?"

"No, well not where she was going, but she did say she'd be back before our vacation starts in July. Then she called me, real quick one evening, said she was in Pittsburgh, that she was looking for someone. I tried to ask her more but she hung up. She's a special ed teacher, for God's sake, just an average person. I have absolutely no clue what's going on."

The agent stood awkwardly and then followed Ken's route, pacing for a moment in front of the fireplace. Ken watched him moving back and forth. Clearly he was trying to come to some sort of decision.

Finally, Sanchez picked up his jacket off the end of the couch and fished in the pocket for one of his cards. "Mr. Rogers, I'm sorry I can't help with your questions. I wanted to talk with her about an old case that I'm working on. I'm not at liberty to say anything more than that, but can I give you my card? If you'd have her call me when she returns, I'd appreciate it."

"Wait, you're not going to help me? Can't you do anything?"

The agent handed the card over as he opened the screened door. "You could file a missing persons report but I'm not sure it would be helpful in this case. Please call me if you see or hear from her. I appreciate your time."

CHAPTER TWENTY-ONE

*M*arybeth and Gregory were back in their coffee shop now, seated side by side on an old sofa waiting for the Wi-Fi to engage. She had insisted that they go by her room first so that she could dispose of the glasses and change into her regular clothes.

There was the usual group of patrons scattered around the room but nearly all were on their own laptops. Only the older gentleman sitting in the corner read an actual newspaper. She recognized his bald head and the odd constellation of age spots that covered the top of it, half hidden now by the paper. He seemed to be there just as often as they were, she thought, but a more careful look around the shop found a number of faces that seemed familiar to her.

Marybeth held her breath, clicked on the download and waited impatiently for it to open. Gregory put his hand on her arm. "Calm down. You're starting to look like a crazy person. Go get us some tea and coffee and a couple of pastries. It's going to be fine." He reached for his wallet but Marybeth waved it away and went to the counter to order.

A few minutes later she set the drinks down, nearly bobbling the cup as Gregory reached for the pastry. "I'm a nervous wreck, spilling drinks, seeing things. I could swear that old guy in the corner has been in here every time we've been in." Gregory turned toward him just as the man raised his paper up in front of his face. "Please tell me I got the information we need." She plopped down on the sofa beside him, took off the plastic lid and blew on the hot drink.

Gregory turned his attention back to the laptop. "Actually, I think we got really lucky. Maybe it's a good thing that they're being investigated. It looks like they've scanned in all of the records, whole files, not just the vital statistics. That means we have photos and letters as well as the certificates." He raised his hand in the air and she met it for a resounding high five. "You did an awesome job, Marybeth. Maybe you should be the detective in this partnership."

She looked at him. "So, whatever prompted you to become a private detective? I've been wondering that. Weren't you a political science major?" Gregory looked up from the computer,.

"Not sure really, when I started out in law enforcement, I thought I might try for the FBI but it didn't end up working out."

"Do you miss being a policeman?"

"I was a detective actually, and yeah, I miss it. A private eye wasn't what I wanted, but sometimes it seems like our lives are going down a particular path whether we steer them there or not." He turned back to the computer, apparently uncomfortable with the conversation track they were on. She could see his shoulders tense and Marybeth wondered what was behind such an odd summary.

"Let's start through these," he said, drawing her attention back to the computer. He clicked on one file after another as they read and then dismissed each one. After thirty minutes, Marybeth was ready to tear her hair out. She'd already used the bathroom and ordered a second cup of coffee when Gregory signaled to her. "Look at this one."

"The length and weight on the new birth certificate are perfect. Was that typical, to issue a new birth certificate?"

"No, not from what I've seen. But look, everything else on it, even the dates, times and attending's name are the same." Then he paused. "Oh, my God," he whispered, he's listed as the father." Gregory clicked on the accompanying documents and was surprised to see that two more papers had been connected to this child. The first was clearly a legal document with AFFI-DAVIT stamped across the top of it. The two of them leaned close to read it. It was a sworn statement saying that the presumed father gave his permission for the adoption. Marybeth felt as though a tremendous bandage had just been ripped off her skin, leaving her raw and vulnerable. She grabbed Gregory's arm.

"What the hell," she whispered urgently at Gregory. "The Clerk of the Court knew who the father was? They put it on record before the adoption went through? Greg, I never wrote his name on the birth certificate." Marybeth let go of his arm and turned to face him. "Do you think Jay or his family ever saw this? It has to be a forgery of some kind, right? Who could have written this?"

"I don't know. Look at this second page." The back of the sheet had been scanned as well and someone had scrawled Marybeth White, 316 College Lane, West Chester. It was the address of the first apartment she had in hiding. He looked at Marybeth, her face two shades paler than it had been. "Breathe, just breathe, we don't know what this means, except that we found the right baby. And look, we have her name. It's a good place to start."

"Greg, are you kidding? It means someone else is looking for her. Or for me."

"Or they were, a long time ago."

"What do you mean?"

He shrugged. "That information is old, isn't it? I don't think there's anything we can do about it now. Let's just focus on the baby, we have her name now, Carolyn Jacobs. It's a terrific place to start."

Marybeth leaned back and studied Gregory's face, trying to reconcile what he was saying with the look of concern that seemed to have settled on his features. "This matters, Greg. I don't know how or why but it matters. I know it does."

* * *

IT WAS GETTING LATE. They were still in the coffee shop, the table covered now with empty takeout containers, feeling discouraged again. They had found dozens of Carolyn Jacobs, the most likely one the daughter of a man who had been on active military duty for over two decades. This Carolyn, if it was her, had been in ten different schools by the time she was in the eighth grade, two of them overseas.

"Well, she's had an interesting life, it looks like, if not a quiet one." Marybeth tucked her hair behind her ear nervously.

"Could be, or maybe she just grew up to be outgoing and confident, like me."

Marybeth kicked him in the foot. She liked this man that she was getting to know. They'd never had more than a friendship at Penn State, and she'd wondered at the time about the lack of chemistry between them. Having spent so much more time with him now, though, she understood easily that he was gay. She thought back to the high school they'd gone to and wondered if it had been difficult for him. He'd said so little about his life now, she really would like to hear more of his story. She hoped that after the search there would be time. Finally she turned away and focused back on her laptop.

"Oh no, look at this, Greg."

"What?"

"It's a headline from the Pittsburgh paper. I was searching for the family name and found this. *Lieutenant with Ties to Pittsburgh*

Killed in Afghanistan. They're reporting it because it says that the widow returned to the area. There's no mention of a daughter, though. Do you think we could find her and talk to her?"

"Probably. Let's see if we can find an address."

* * *

THE NEXT MORNING, their drive out to the suburb of Butler took longer than Marybeth expected it to, but it still wasn't long enough to calm her nervous stomach. Nor had she figured out yet what she planned to say. How would she even get a foot in the door? As they got closer, though, the street began to fill with parked cars and Gregory was forced to circle around the block to find a space. "It looks like some kind of party."

"Or a wake maybe? Do you think we should come back later?"

She thought for a moment and then shook her head. "No, maybe it'll be easier with a crowd, we might raise fewer eyebrows than if we were alone. At least we put on good clothes."

They parked a block away and followed a middle-aged couple through the front door. Marybeth worried that there might be some sort of receiving line inside, but they stepped into the foyer easily and followed the couple toward the back of the house. A formal living room was on the left but it didn't appear to be in use. As they moved on into the open kitchen and den area, they found groupings of two and three scattered around the large room while a caterer in a sunny yellow uniform worked behind the kitchen counter loading a tray with hors d'oeuvres. Near the back wall was a tall, red leather armchair that looked almost like a throne, except that the small woman sitting slumped and dazed didn't appear regal at all. She looked ill, frankly, and Marybeth's heart sank. They crossed and spoke to her briefly, but all she managed to do was nod in return. Clearly this was the widow, and whether it was drugs or a deep depression, there was no way that anyone was going to be able to talk to her.

113

They served themselves small plates of food and leaned against one of the walls as they watched the small crowd. As she studied the widow, Marybeth looked more closely at her skin, the lines on her face, the sag to her shoulders. "Greg, I don't think that woman has been well for a while." Next to them was the couple that they had followed in, now speaking in quiet tones with a young man in uniform.

"Curt, we're so sorry for your loss. How are you doing? How's your mother?" The young man barely raised his eyes toward his mother before answering them. He rubbed his finger around the rim of his empty glass as he spoke.

"She's about the same, I'd say, she never really recovered from losing Tim and now to have Dad gone too, I don't know."

"Is there anyone here at the house helping her? You know we live just the other side of the city."

He stood and started moving toward the catering set-up. "She actually has some live-in help now. Carolyn gets up here once a month or so and I try to do the same. If you'll excuse me?"

"Certainly," the couple returned to their food, talking quietly to each other. The woman leaned toward her husband "Do you remember what happened to Tim exactly?"

"He was an MP at a base down in Georgia and some idiot, drunk off his gourd, rammed him at the check-in gate. I think he was killed instantly."

"Oh my, such a waste." They stood and moved to join a small group at the back of the room.

Marybeth set her empty plate on the counter and turned to Gregory. "Let's go, we're not going to learn anything more here."

"Yeah, I guess you're right."

They nodded respectfully to the small groups around them and then walked toward the front of the house. Marybeth looked down the empty hall behind them before ducking into the living room that they had passed. "I think I saw some photographs," she whispered.

A few photos sat on the mantle above the fireplace. One showed a young family on what must have been a vacation, four striking blondes and one small dark-haired girl. They wore matching T-shirts and lined the deck of what looked like a small beach house. Beside the group photo there were three single portraits, two young men in uniform and one young woman. Marybeth and Gregory spotted it at the same moment. "Oh, my God."

"It's you," Gregory said. "That's exactly what you looked like in high school."

Without a word, Marybeth took the photograph down, tucked it into her bag and led the way out. Gregory started to protest but Marybeth held up her hand.

"There's no way that woman's going to miss it."

The car was stuffy when they got inside. Gregory turned on the air-conditioning and opened the windows all at once. He looked in the rearview mirror as they exited the subdivision, and Marybeth saw his eyes widen as an SUV pulled up to the house and a man in a dark suit get out. He turned the next corner sharply, but the rest of the drive was smooth. In fact, she was largely oblivious to the trip back into the city as she sat staring at the photograph.

CHAPTER TWENTY-TWO

*O*nce he realized that the husband had no idea about Marybeth's background, Ray couldn't get out of there fast enough. On the highway out of Chambersburg, he called Cindy to fill her in. He hoped she was still at her desk.

"O'Brien here, what's up?"

"Hey Cindy, it's Ray. How's it going?"

"No complaints, how'd it go with the witness?"

Hearing her voice change from the distant, professional tone to a friendlier one made his breath catch. He was surprised at how good it made him feel. "It didn't. She's gone missing. The husband is going nuts. Says she took off to go and do some kind of research. She told him she was looking for someone. He had no idea what's going on."

"Do we?"

"Well, no, he said she'd never done anything like this before. But get this, she called and told him she's there in Pittsburgh."

"What do you think is going on?"

"I just keep thinking about that woman giving up her baby all those years ago. Now, there's a plane crash, and the asshole is dead, so maybe she got to thinking about the kid she gave up."

"You think she's breaking her cover here?"

"I don't know what to think. You have any ideas? Can you see if you can find a plane or train ticket for her? A hotel maybe?" He could hear her typing as he continued. "Have we heard anything yet on the mechanic?"

"You were right, they found a body not two miles from the airstrip, tools still on him, single gunshot wound to the back of the head. Face was totally messed up."

"Anything on the weapon?"

"No, too common, especially down there. No local interest in pursuing it either, since they know he's just some lowlife American that no one seems to be looking for. They're focusing everything on the crash site."

"Is there anything new at all?" Ray asked.

"Well, I was talking to one of the guys about the airport pictures, he's an older guy and he remembered working on the earlier case. Turns out he knew Sylvia Nowicki, said he helped her with some photographs way back then."

"Really, did he take the picture of the girl?"

"No, he didn't remember anything up at Penn State, he was on the family here in the city. But he suggested I look up Sam Duffy, see if he remembered anything."

"Who's that?"

"Turns out Sylvia Nowicki sometimes worked with a partner named Sam Duffy. I looked him up, and he retired right after Agent Nowicki's death."

"And the coincidences just keep coming. Wow. Were you able to find him?"

"You bought me any of those power bars yet?"

He spotted a convenience store just off the exit and flipped on his turn signal. "I'm going to buy them right now."

"Promises, promises." She laughed. "Okay buddy, this is your lucky day. Sam Duffy retired from the Pittsburgh office of the FBI at the age of thirty-five and went to work for the police force down in Fort Lauderdale. He retired from there twenty years later."

"So, any idea where he is now?"

"Believe it or not, the dude left Florida and retired back here in Pennsylvania. Who leaves Florida to retire? Anyway, he's in Camp Hill, not too far from where you are now."

Ray pulled into the parking lot of the convenience store and threw the car into park. "Text me the address, will you? I'll head there right now."

"Coming your way now."

"You are the best, absolutely. I'm heading in to buy the power bars this very minute."

"Sure you are. Anyway, drive safe, see you back here tomorrow?"

"You bet. Take care, Cindy."

"Will do. Later."

Ray pushed open the door of the convenience store, the aroma a mixture of stale coffee, singed hot dogs, and a bathroom that hadn't been cleaned recently. He headed over to the food aisle and picked out three each of all the available flavors of power bar.

* * *

By the time he found Sam Duffy's house, the sun was heading down and Ray was sick of being in the car. He was getting hungry, too, although not enough to eat one of those bars. How could she stand to eat them he wondered. As he pulled up, there were two cars in the open garage and a pickup truck in the driveway. A pair of legs in oily coveralls was poking out from under the side of it. Ray walked up and knocked on the side of the truck bed. A gruff voice barked out, "yeah, what is it?"

"Sam Duffy?"

An older man, his hair flattened by a backwards painter's hat, slid out from under the truck and stood up, wiping his hands on an already blackened towel. "Who wants to know?"

Ray pulled his badge from his pocket, but Sam waved him off. "Figured you for an agent. What are you looking for?"

"I'm Ray Sanchez, I've been working on the Warren case. Do you have a minute?"

The man's face turned stiff and he began stowing various tools in a massive tool cabinet. Ray followed him up the driveway as he closed the cabinet and wheeled it into the garage. Once they were inside, Sam hit the door control. Darkness fell along with the door, and when the mechanism stopped, the silence seemed oppressive.

"Why are you asking me about that case?"

Ray tucked his hands in his pockets and tried to focus on Sam through the gloom. "You retired because of that case, didn't you, right after Sylvia Nowicki died."

"After she was murdered, you mean." Sam's stance softened, and he gestured for Ray to follow him on into the house. "Come on in, let me get these coveralls off, and I'll grab us each a beer."

Ray settled down at the kitchen table and looked around him. It was a small but tidy house, everything put away in the kitchen or displayed attractively on the counter beside it. Either Sam had a flare for design or he was married to someone who cared more about kitchens than Ray ever had. "Nice place," he offered as Sam returned wearing a clean t-shirt and neatly ironed jeans.

"Yeah, it's small, but my wife and I like it fine. She's off with her sister today." He got two beers out of the fridge and set them on the table before settling into the seat across from Ray. "I know you didn't see my name in those files so how did you find me?"

"That was deliberate?"

"You're damn right. Took every piece of paper I could find with my name on it right out the door with me. Destroyed the hard drive on my desk computer too."

"One of our analysts ran into a photo expert who remembered working with you back on the original case. So, you didn't believe her death was an accident?"

He shook his head. "There's no such thing as accidents when you're talking about the Warren family. Sylvia Nowicki was a loose end that had to be taken care of. She was murdered, plain and simple. There was just no way to prove it." He paused and took a drink. "You know, it wasn't easy for her, being a female agent in the FBI back then. She was solid, though, tough but kind if you know what I mean. Tore me up, I'll admit it. After that," he shrugged, "the case against the Warren family collapsed, and the FBI felt like it had to move on. I know about the plane crash, so why are you still poking around all of this?"

"Do you remember a young woman, someone Jay had been seeing?"

Sam peeled the label down with his thumb, the nail black from the work he'd been doing. "Sarah, yeah, she was so young back then. No idea what to do about him or about the baby. I felt for her."

"Was it Agent Nowicki's idea for her to give the baby up before she went into hiding?"

"Well, yes and no. Girl was all alone, no parents around or anyone for her to talk to. We could have hidden the two of them, but I think Sylvia thought that it would be easier if they were apart. For one thing, Sarah was worried what Jay would do if he found out there was a baby. The man was a control freak, an abuser. He beat the hell out of her and tried to kill the kid when he found out she was pregnant. Even more than that, though, I think Sylvia was worried about the girl, about what kind of life she'd have as a single mother. Sarah was studying to be a teacher, and I always thought that the mother in Agent Nowicki wanted her to get that degree. Don't get me wrong, Nowicki may have nudged her a bit, but Miss Dawes made the decision in the end." He paused and looked up at Ray. "You're not going after her now are you, after all these years?"

"No, my concern is that she's left home on some sort of trip, and I'm beginning to think it's connected to her past. That worries me."

"Why? What's the real scoop on that plane crash? You wouldn't be here if something wasn't up."

"You're right, I'm grasping at straws, because I just don't think the crash reports add up."

"The father or the son? Which one aren't you sure about?"

Ray set his beer on the table. "The son, actually. We identified the father and the pilot but there wasn't enough left after the fire to tell more."

"You think the son got away?"

"Hard to say. It was a hell of a fire. But yeah, I have my doubts."

Sam stood and Ray took it as his cue to go, but the older man paused and rested his hand on Ray's shoulder. "Listen, I left that department clean, no hint of trouble in all the years I've been gone."

Ray nodded. "I get it. I was never here."

"That's right, but listen. You'd better hope that bastard *is* dead. Sylvia and I went to see Sarah when she was in the hospital the last time. He nearly killed her back then, nearly killed the baby she was carrying, too. And that was when there was a lot less riding on the outcome than there is now."

Ray tilted his head. "What do you mean?"

"Edward Clark is Jay's uncle."

"Yeah."

"Well he's worth millions and he's getting older, right? The will says Jay ends up with that pile of money once the guy passes, and my guess is, he's getting pretty tired of waiting."

"How would Jay get it if he's hiding out?"

"No idea, but I wouldn't put it past him to find a way. I bet that family's got cops, lawyers, even judges in their pockets. Jay Warren would crawl back from the dead for that money, kill or pay someone to kill whoever got in his way." He laughed but the sound was not a happy one.

"Shit." He paused. "More likely, he'll just waltz back into town and expect to collect. His lawyer will probably schedule a press conference. That's the Warren way, believe me. I've seen it up close." He rubbed the whiskers on the side of his face and his tone became more serious. "I've loved my wife more than fifty years now, hope for fifty more, but Sylvia Nowicki, she was special. Never met anyone in the agency who could hold a candle to her. Do what you can, but you keep that in mind."

Ray offered his hand. "Will do, and thank you, for everything."

"You be careful now." He gave Ray a serious look before opening the door. Ray walked out, his head buzzing with a combination of fatigue and anxiety as he climbed in to head back home. He spotted a text from Cindy as he started the car. *MB Rogers landed Pittsburgh 4 days ago flight 5201. Checked out of hotel two days later. Phone records indicate local contact with Gregory Hanes, private detective.*

He tried calling Cindy back but it went straight to voicemail, and he realized how late it had gotten. As requested, he texted the information he learned to Assistant Director Perkins before starting the car and heading back onto the highway. He tossed his phone on the seat beside him and thought he would prefer to tell Cindy in person anyway. He wondered if there was one of those warehouse stores open on his way back into Pittsburgh. He might need a lot more power bars.

CHAPTER TWENTY-THREE

*T*he ride back into the city from Butler passed in a daze and Marybeth was surprised when they pulled up to the curb outside of Mrs. Finelli's house. She hadn't known what to say to Gregory once they found the photo. When they got in the car, she noticed that he was looking in the rear view mirror a lot and cornering a little quickly, but it hadn't really registered with her.

As for the photo itself, she couldn't take her eyes off it. Gregory was right. This young woman looked a lot like her, the wavy brown hair, dark eyes and eyebrows. She appeared to be smiling but Marybeth kept thinking that the expression looked the tiniest bit off, as though it were forced. Did this woman hate being photographed as much as Marybeth did? Detective Nowicki had warned her about photographs when she'd first told her about witness protection. She'd hated being photographed anyway, so it'd been an easy enough guideline to follow. She'd always been their family photographer so there were albums filled with the boys at various ages, solo or in pictures with Ken, but there were precious few that included her.

She pulled out the two photographs she'd been carrying with

her, the baby picture of the infant she'd given up and the age-enhanced projection. She was surprised at how much the projection resembled the photograph that she'd taken from the Jacobs' home. Marybeth closed her eyes and imagined this young woman in the house they'd just left. Why hadn't Carolyn been at that wake? But, more importantly, what had life been like growing up in that family? The picture of them at the cottage had looked happy, but it had been taken when the children were all fairly young. What had happened to Carolyn when their mother started to decline?

The photograph she'd stolen looked like a graduation picture from Penn State judging by the colors. The year stamped into the corner of the frame was an added bonus. She knew with this much information they would find her quickly. That would probably turn out to be the easy part. The harder part, much harder when she was honest with herself, would come when she met Carolyn Jacobs and tried to explain.

When Marybeth and Gregory got back to their coffee shop later that day, she expected him to be relaxed, smiling even, given the breakthrough they'd had, but he wasn't. She couldn't quite decide what his expression was, but she noted the big cup of coffee in his hand. He smiled when he caught sight of her but she saw it drop quickly as she turned toward the counter to order a pastry. She scanned the room and thought that the small crowd looked a lot like it had the other days they'd been in, lots of singletons with their laptops open and the same older man with his newspaper over by the fake fireplace in the center. Must be his daily routine, she thought as she balanced her computer bag and purse in one hand, the Danish on top of the coffee in the other. When she got closer to Gregory, she could see his expression morph again. He brought the smile back up quickly as she sat down across from him at the narrow table by the window. "Greg, is something wrong? You're drinking actual coffee again."

He cleared space on the table and moved his backpack to the floor beside his chair. "No, I'm good, just a little tired, what about you? Did you get any sleep last night?"

Marybeth took a bite of the Danish before leaning back in her chair. She made her shoulders relax as she sipped at her coffee. "Some, but I was pretty excited about what we found. What about you?"

"Oh, I slept fine, I'm used to this kind of work." Marybeth heard what he said but she didn't really believe it. His shoulders were hunched and he kept stirring his coffee with the tiny plastic straw. She couldn't tell what was causing his odd manner this morning so she put the worry aside and leaned in to talk.

"Have you found her?" She held her breath waiting for his answer, jumping when the wind pulled the door out of a customer's hand and sent it flying against the wall. Everyone in the coffee shop seemed to jump, she noticed, except for the older guy with the paper. Hard of hearing she thought, noticing the flesh-colored earbuds he was wearing.

"Baltimore, she lives and works in Baltimore." He set the stirring stick aside and leaned back in his chair, brushing crumbs off his lap onto his wrinkled napkin. Marybeth was speechless. Her baby really was a grown woman now with a life of her own. She couldn't help but wonder why she had started on this quest in the first place. Why had she risked losing Ken for this wild goose chase? Carolyn Jacobs probably wouldn't even give her the time of day, much less be willing to sit down and talk. She set her Danish aside and tucked her hands under her legs to keep them from shaking.

"What kind of work does she do?"

"She's a teacher, believe it or not. She works with special needs kids in a center run by the city."

Suddenly Marybeth was picturing her first teaching job,

working with emotionally impaired students in a residential facility. The idea that her daughter had chosen a similar path was somehow both startling and reassuring. At least they would have some common ground. Out of the corner of her eye, she saw the older gentleman fold the newspaper and get up. Then he dropped it on the table by Gregory before heading out. Gregory startled and for a second Marybeth thought that there was something familiar about the man, but then she and Gregory quickly returned to their conversation.

Gregory leaned forward in his seat and looked carefully at Marybeth. He ran his fingers through his hair, then rested his elbows back on the table. "To be honest, I think I'm sad that we're done here, we accomplished our mission. I've enjoyed being a real detective again, and I think I'm just disappointed to see that coming to an end." He smiled more broadly at her. "You did it Marybeth, you found your daughter. We should be having champagne, not coffee shop lattes."

Marybeth grinned back at him. "We did it, didn't we? Of course, now comes the actual hard part, facing her. How in the world do you start a conversation like that? *Hi, my name's Marybeth and I'm your biological mother. Oh, and by the way, your father was a criminal.*"

Greg shivered in his seat. "You're right, tough conversation for sure. Do you want me to go with you, offer moral support? I could get away for a few days."

Marybeth leaned over the table and squeezed him in a quick hug. "Ah, Greg, that is so sweet of you to offer, and after I've monopolized your schedule so much already." She sat back, straightening her spine with a sudden resolve as she did. "I think I have to tackle this myself, though, before I lose my nerve. Do you have a phone number for the center? She's probably at work right now."

"Let me look, okay, here it is."

She looked over his shoulder and dialed the number. It rang

twice and she managed to take a quick breath before it connected. "Hello, my name is Marybeth Rogers and I'm calling to make an appointment with Ms. Carolyn Jacobs." She held her breath again as a young man's voice responded.

"She's in class right now, is this an emergency?"

"No," she thought quickly. "I'm a special education teacher and I'm going to be in the Baltimore area this week and I was hoping to talk with her and have a quick tour of the center."

"Oh cool, well we love visitors but I have to tell you, this week is a little crazy. Tonight we have a staff meeting until after five and tomorrow Carolyn's in parent/teacher conferences until six. Would Thursday after school work for you? Her class is over at two-thirty and she could meet with you right after that."

Marybeth looked at Gregory over the phone. "Thursday at two forty five would be just fine."

"All right, we'll see you then."

She tucked the phone back into her pocket and did a little dance in her chair. "I'm going to meet her on Thursday. Can you believe it?"

Gregory smiled back at her. "Good, that means we have time to celebrate a little. Would you like to have dinner together tomorrow night? You can rehearse what you're planning to say."

Marybeth laughed, "I don't think there's any way to rehearse for that, but I'd love to have dinner. Is six o'clock all right? I can spend tomorrow getting ready and then get on the road Thursday morning."

"Sounds like a plan." They stowed their laptops and headed out of the shop.

CHAPTER TWENTY-FOUR

*B*ack in her room, Marybeth tossed her computer bag onto the pillow and threw herself crosswise on the bed. She waved her feet in the air, unable to contain her excitement any more. She had done it. She had found her daughter. It was unbelievable.

She could imagine the young woman from the photograph standing in front of her own classroom and the fact that her daughter had become a teacher just felt remarkable. When Marybeth looked back at her time in West Chester she thought that learning to become a teacher had played a key role in helping her become the person that she was. She wondered if it had been the same for her daughter, Carolyn.

On Tuesdays and Thursdays the group studying learning disabilities and emotional impairment met together in the small conference room on the main floor. There was a wide oak table, gouged and worn that easily seated the eleven students and the professor. The intimacy of it contrasted with the crowded lecture hall at the bigger campus and as the semester wore on, Marybeth found herself speaking up and offering her opinions much more readily than she had over the last year. She slowly came to realize that Jay's looming presence in their apartment as well as his frequent criticisms of her had been eroding her self-esteem in other areas as well.

By studying emotional development and the ways in which children's environments could shape dysfunction, Marybeth had also learned more about the ways in which abuse could manifest itself. Now when she remembered incidents going back to her first meeting with Jay, she was able to see with much clearer eyes how his control had grown and how she had acquiesced to it.

Really, she saw it in Niko's interactions with her mother as well. Mrs. Kim was a small powerhouse, kind and friendly but with a formidable resolve. She had very clear ideas about what Niko should and shouldn't be doing with her life and Marybeth saw how much Niko struggled to hold her own in those confrontations. It was frightening what a powerful tool love could be in controlling another human being.

Marybeth had found that working with the kinds of children that she saw was also eye opening. Consistency was everything. The professor kept returning to the fact that kids like this needed to be able to count on their teacher. Their lives were filled with uncertainty and unpredictability and they needed a steady, reliable adult, an individual to test and push against who would remain even and constant in the face of that pressure. Marybeth found that she liked that idea of holding steady, of being someone who could be counted on.

Becoming that sort of person, though, had been harder than she had expected. Living with her mother and later with Jay, Marybeth had grown accustomed to an off-kilter sort of existence. Yelling and raised voices, even if it was for sporting events, would cause her to pull back and withdraw from the situation. It took time for her to learn the difference between an argument and an attack, to discover that a discussion could be heated but at the same time fair and useful. She was embarrassed now remembering how she'd had to actually learn to argue, to make a point and maintain it as disagreements emerged. At first she had found Ken's father, an ex-army officer, so loud and frightening that she was reluctant to visit with them. But with time she learned to recognize the bluster and good humor that accompanied the noise.

Now, in her room at Mrs. Finelli's, Marybeth put her feet back on the floor and thought about Ken. She had tried to stick with those ideas in her social life as well as her teaching one, but that didn't mean that she had found it any easier getting to know and trust Ken. In fact, from the beginning she had often been hesitant and cautious. She remembered the look he'd had on his face as her taxi pulled away, and her eyes filled, knowing the hard earned trust that she'd broken in that moment. She looked down at her hands and imagined him holding on to them. He deserved so much better.

She opened her phone and punched in his number.

"Marybeth, thank God. Don't hang up."

"I won't. Hi Ken, how are you?"

He paused, taking in a deep breath. "I'm fine Marybeth but how are you? Are you still in Pittsburgh? Do you need me? Should I drive there?"

"No Ken, I'm not quite ready and I'm not staying in Pittsburgh. I wanted to let you know that I have to go to Baltimore for a little bit."

"Baltimore, where? why? Can't you come home first? It's on the way. I'll drive you to Baltimore, whatever you need."

It was Marybeth's turn to take a deep breath. "I'm not done yet, Ken, I just need a little more time."

"For what?" His voice was louder now, his irritation and anger growing. "Dammit Marybeth, I just want to understand. When we first met, this is just what you were like. You never really answered questions. You'd veer off and change the subject like this, but I thought we were past all of that. Now it's starting all over again. Did you know that an FBI agent was here trying to talk to you?"

"What?" she gasped, her body instantly rigid with fear. "What did you say?"

"I told him I was worried about you. I wanted him to help me find you but he wouldn't say anything. We've been married forever, why can't you be honest with me, tell me what's going on?"

Marybeth wanted to hang up immediately, to think about why an FBI agent would be looking for her. Did they know somehow that she'd broken cover? Was she in trouble or in danger somehow? She had to think. "Ken, I don't know why an FBI agent was there. I wish I could tell you more, but I can't. Not yet. I promise, I'll be home soon and I'll tell you everything, everything you want to know. But now, I have to go."

She hung up quickly. My God, why was an FBI agent at her house? For decades, she had kept Agent Nowicki's card in the box she hid away with the baby things and the photographs. She tried calling her now but there was a recording that the number was disconnected. She turned her phone off, slumped back on the bed and considered her options. Giving up, going home when she was this close to finding her daughter? Nope, scratch that. She couldn't do it. The only answer was to go forward, to drive to Baltimore and find out what she could.

CHAPTER TWENTY-FIVE

*C*arolyn couldn't get enough of the late spring weather. She had just dropped PJ off with Janine, and was feeling only slightly disappointed that Sean hadn't been there this morning. Oh well, school was nearly out and she would have two whole weeks to spend with PJ. They could sleep in and take their time in the morning. They could pick up April and go to the park. Her step felt that much lighter as she neared the school.

She was nearly at the front steps when her cell phone chirped for a call. She almost pocketed it without answering when she saw her brother's name, but she knew it wouldn't do any good to ignore it. "Curt, hello. What's up?"

"Hey Caro, I just wanted to check on when you're going to be up to see Mom next."

Carolyn leaned against the stone stairs of the school, the day suddenly not quite as bright and beautiful as it had been a moment ago.

"I was just up there two weeks ago, why? Is something wrong?"

"The wake seems to have put her into an even deeper funk, if you can imagine that. Plus, I'm not sure she's taking her meds. I was just hoping you could come and spend some time with her."

"Curt, the school year isn't over yet and I already used up the few days I'm allowed. I told you that when you planned the wake. What about the home health care nurse? She's supposed to be there every day. Isn't she supervising the medicines?"

"She gave me some bullshit story about Mom dropping them all over the floor and not knowing what she'd taken and what she hadn't. She's nearly worthless, I'm afraid."

Or you've totally pissed her off by leaving messages on Mom's phone instead of going to see her, she thought. "I'm sorry, Curt, PJ and I won't be able to get back up there until school is out. Besides, you know she doesn't do any better with me."

"Sure she does, what do you mean? She looks at me, and all she sees is Tim and Dad."

"And I don't look like either of them. I get it."

"Carolyn, you know that's not what I meant. It's just that you're a woman. You're more understanding and patient than I am, and I think she relates better to women."

Carolyn pulled the phone away from her ear. She wanted to pitch it into the trashcan at the curb. It never changes, she thought. I'm the afterthought, the odd man out until someone wants something done. Then I'm the dear, adopted daughter. Her shoulders sagged as she brought the phone back up to her ear.

"... different healthcare service."

He'd been talking about changing the service since they'd hired them in the spring. "Curt, I already told you. The only other service people are crap. We're already paying for the best one there is. You just need to get over there and visit a little more. You work right in the city. Can't you go by after work one afternoon a week or something?"

"Work is crazy now. I'll never get over there that often."

She stiffened her shoulders and stood up straight. Enough. "Curt, I've already done what I can. PJ and I will be up after school is out and we'll stay with her for a little while. If I don't think the service is doing a good job then I'll look into making a change. In the meantime, you're what she's got. You have to—"

He cut her off. "Fine, I'll see what I can do." The call ended without even a goodbye, and Carolyn was furious at having her beautiful morning spoiled by Curt. Did everyone have these issues with their families, she wondered?

She wanted to blame her dad, a career military man, it had felt like he was gone for more of her childhood than not. A part of her, though, always wondered whether he stayed away more once her mom's depression had worsened. It seemed as though some people rose to deal with issues, and others chose to back away. Tim had been the one they counted on to step up, and Carolyn missed him so much. He was the one who could always crack a joke and get their mother to smile. With him gone, and now Dad, she and Curt were all that remained, and although it was heartbreaking to admit, neither of them had ever found a way to make their mother smile.

So much for her summer break.

CHAPTER TWENTY-SIX

*M*arybeth felt she'd made the right decision, insisting on making the trip to Baltimore alone and choosing a rental car over another plane trip. At dinner, Greg had offered again to drive them both. He'd been such a friend, such a rock, through all of this, but she felt strongly that it was time to do the rest of it, the tough part, on her own. She'd found a Baltimore hotel and he'd helped her choose a good route into the city so she was set. She had spent yesterday washing clothes and packing, as well as arranging to pick up the rental car. She hoped that her timing today would help her avoid most of the rush hour traffic.

Marybeth knew that years ago she would never have turned down the offer of help or acted so independently. How had she gotten to this point, she wondered? When had she really become the person she was today? It had been a gradual process, that was for sure. As she turned up the radio, for the moment at least, she chose to focus on the fact that she was happy. Scared and nervous, too, but there was an undercurrent beneath all of the jitters that just felt wonderful. The rental car smelled new, the GPS was helping her with the route, and she found herself relaxing into the drive. This highway had been so familiar to her at one time, the first highway she'd ever been on as a student driver in fact. She could still picture the look on the instructor's face the first time he'd taken them up the ramp, her friend Kitty trying to merge at twenty miles an hour.

Marybeth dialed the radio tuner until she found another familiar song as images from her life and marriage to Ken floated in and out of her mind. She thought of her son Jimmy and his "safe for Mom" playlist that they listened to on their trips back and forth to his college. She missed him and Grant so much. They'd been busy with their own lives recently and she hadn't expected it to be so hard to be away. Really, she wanted so much to call Ken back and chat, ask about the boys and their summer. Just to hear his voice again would have meant a lot to her but for now, she had to put it aside.

As she drove, Marybeth found herself remembering Grant's birth and how different that experience had been from her first. She pictured herself once again, a terrified young woman with a newborn, talking through the night with an FBI agent. It almost seemed like a scene from a movie. Except it wasn't. Even now she could still see her daughter's face, hear the nurses calling to one another in the hall, feel the weave of the little hat as it rubbed against her cheek. She knew that even overwhelmed with love for her baby, she had never felt so alone in her life.

Grant's birth had been so different. She remembered how excited and nervous Ken had been when her contractions started. This time, it was nearly an hour after they started that her water broke. He had ushered her gently into their car and alternated between driving really fast and really slowly as they made their way to the hospital. At the time, Chambersburg's small hospital was undergoing an expansion and the section for women's services was far from ready. Plastic curtains hung between the patient area and the hallway and the night before, water had leaked through a gap and flooded the ward. Ken wanted to turn around and drive to Harrisburg, but there hadn't been time. As a crew of construction workers and hospital staff worked to clean up the mess, she and Ken had been in their own little world, laboring hard and waiting to meet Grant, their first son.

When she first suspected that she might be pregnant, Carolyn had gone to see her OB-GYN doctor by herself. She'd met Dr. Elizabeth McCallister years before when she and Ken had first moved to Chambersburg from West Chester. Ten years older than her, over six feet tall with dark, close-cropped hair, Elizabeth made an intimidating first impression. But once she started talking with her, Marybeth realized she had found a friend. For the first time ever, she told someone about giving birth and having to give up her child. She remembered how Elizabeth had listened without judgment and somehow recognized what it had taken out of Marybeth to make that decision. Meeting Elizabeth and telling her story had managed to ease something in Marybeth, a tension she didn't even know she'd been holding onto. In some ways, that conversation had helped to mark the beginning of a whole new life.

When the new pregnancy came years later, the doctor had beamed. "Marybeth, yes, it's true, believe it."

Marybeth sat on the edge of the examination table, stunned and nervous and excited all at once. "Elizabeth, what am I going to tell Ken?"

Her face grew more serious. "What do you mean? Doesn't he want a baby?"

"Oh yes, yes, I think he'll be thrilled. But will he be able to tell?"

"What do you mean?"

Marybeth dropped her head and tucked her hands under her knees. "I never told him, Elizabeth. It was so hard when Ken and I first met. I was so scared, all of the time. For months I would jump if there was a strange sound and news on the TV about the Warren family practically made me faint. I certainly never thought I'd get involved with someone again." She thought back again to that time in her life, when her new life had really gotten started.

Getting to know Ken had frightened her. Conditioned to worry that she might say the wrong thing or make a wrong move, Marybeth would feel herself moving toward him and then backing off at the slightest provocation. After all of the fear and intimidation that had come with dating Jay, it took a long time for her to feel comfortable around Ken, nearly a year to finally realize that she didn't have to rethink or rephrase what she wanted to say. Unlike Jay, Ken never commented on her clothes or activities. He judged nothing. He'd made fun of her shoes, of course, called them baked potatoes, which they kind of looked like when she thought about it, but it didn't mean she had to quit wearing them. Even more telling, rather than separating them-selves from the group, Ken was always reaching out to his family, to Niko and other friends, happy to share their adventures with the people that they enjoyed.

She smiled at the memory. In contrast to the nervousness that she often felt, actually loving Ken, that part had felt almost effort-less. He was kind and funny, always slipping in and out of silly accents and he told her often how much he loved her, showing it in a million subtle ways. When they walked around the campus together he'd hold her hand and pull her close. If he needed his hand to open a door or pull out keys, he would transfer her hand to his other one, not wanting to break the contact. It was the gentlest, most caring gesture she thought she'd ever experienced. Even now, all these years later, he still did that, sought out her hand to hold and then took good care of it.

Once she came to know his parents and saw the same kind of generosity and caring in them, she knew she had found someone real, someone true who would mean what he said. She found that her confidence as a friend and lover had grown right along with her confidence as a student and a teacher.

Marybeth looked up at Dr. McCallister. "I never told him the truth, Elizabeth. Never." The doctor's eyes widened but she didn't say anything. "He knows I dated, that I was serious with someone. He asked me about the stretch marks on my stomach one time and I told him that I had a miscarriage. He was so sympathetic and kind about it, I didn't say any more." She paused and drew in a deep breath. "Will he be able to tell?"

Elizabeth waited, even took a minute to sit down in the chair across from the table. "Marybeth, that's an awfully big secret to be carrying around all this time. I don't envy you the weight of it. But medically, no, he shouldn't be able to tell. For you, though, perhaps it will be a different experience altogether, having a partner with you this time?"

"I think he'll be a pretty enthusiastic one, actually."

Elizabeth sat quietly for a moment, then touched Marybeth on the knee. "It's not healthy, you know, holding onto a secret like that. The weight of something like that, it unbalances a relationship."

Just then a car swerved into Marybeth's lane with what felt like inches to spare. She tapped the brake, giving herself some distance from the idiot before putting it back on cruise control and settling back into her thoughts. She remembered at the time she'd been angry with Elizabeth for saying that. But their friendship had grown in spite of it and eventually Marybeth had come to see the wisdom of her friend's words.

She pictured herself as a young wife, she and Ken settling into their first apartment together. The younger version of herself was aware even then, that she'd been spending too much time giving in, taking a step back in order to avoid arguments of any kind. The move had just brought it to light.

For some reason, Ken had taken it upon himself to unpack and put away the kitchenware. He'd been stuffing the cutlery into a drawer that was all wrong for it and for a moment she had hesitated, reluctant to say what she thought. But dammit, it was her kitchen. Ken could barely boil water and she knew that she'd be the one working in there. She couldn't take it any longer. "That's not where those should go." She'd stepped forward, not quite elbowing him out of the way. "They need to be here, closer to the plates." It was a tiny victory she knew, but it had been a start. She knew now, that move was also one of many opportunities when she could have, should have, told him everything.

Raising their children together had brought the importance of speaking her mind even more to the forefront because any time she and Ken weren't on the same page, the kids knew it. One thing every teacher knew for sure was that if a kid saw a crack in the foundation, he'd go for it. Grant and Jimmy had challenged their foundation more than once through the years and Marybeth had gotten better at holding her ground. But it hadn't always been easy.

The same had turned out to be true with her work. Learning to stand up for what she believed had made a difference in her classroom, but it had proven to be even more important with her administrators. When policies came along that were not in the students' best interest, she learned to speak up. All too often, what was good for most kids was not good for her students and they needed her voice in their corner.

The music changed to a familiar old song and Marybeth focused back on her driving even as she continued sorting through old memories. She had loved every stage of her sons' lives, the sweet smell of their hair as babies, watching them scoot around on the floor, the way they felt on her hip when they got too tired to walk.

She remembered one day when Grant was little and she and her neighbor had taken their children down to the playground. Her friend's son was a year and a half older than Grant and Marybeth had often modeled the way in which she dealt with Grant after what she'd seen with her friend. But that day, Grant had launched into an ear-curdling tantrum that had gone on for what felt like hours. When she turned to her friend to ask for her advice in handling the situation, her friend had looked on in horror and whispered that she'd never seen anything like it. Marybeth could laugh now, but she remembered at the time feeling completely unmoored, suddenly finding herself the outer planet on the ring of the solar system, no longer a guide in front of her to follow.

She and Ken had made a good team, though, she thought. Especially as each stage of the boys' lives had held a special quality all its own, the books they'd fallen in love with, learning to drive, when they first started to date, all of it was so amazing when she thought about it. But of course the challenges hadn't ended with toddlerhood. In many ways the boys' teen years had been even more confounding. And the volume, she laughed again remembering the yelling and screaming that had gone on during that period. That had been something else again. She'd spoken her mind, of course, loudly when she needed to, but she'd also learned the value of a quiet word. That seemed to work in the classroom as well as at home.

Taken altogether, her life now was so full, she was well aware of how much she had to be grateful for. Their sons were doing well and she and Ken both enjoyed the work that they did. Over the years, they had developed a strong set of friends and they enjoyed hanging out and spending time with the group. At the end of the evening, though, it was always Ken that she looked forward to going home with. She smiled, knowing that he felt the same way about her. So why hadn't she ever told him about her past? The question hung heavy in the air around her but she had no good answer to it.

Marybeth had thought of her daughter so often over the years. It didn't hit her quite as hard anymore, but every once in a while she couldn't help dawdling near the little girls' clothes in the store. Or she would watch her friend Stan braiding his daughter's hair and wonder just what she had missed. She knew she'd been a good mother to her boys, but she couldn't help but wonder what might have been. Of course, she wouldn't have the life she did now if she'd held on to her daughter. Marybeth shuddered at the idea of trying to hide with a baby, never finishing her teaching degree, probably working in restaurants the way she had during high school, never meeting Ken or her boys. It was impossible, she knew, but she wanted both lives.

The impression she had of Carolyn's life was part of what bothered her, she decided. The family photo with the matching T-shirts was so positive, but the strained graduation photo and the shrunken woman in the big red chair both spoke to something dark having come into her life. She hoped that she could find a way to talk to her daughter but what in the world could she possibly say?

* * *

AFTER CHECKING INTO THE HOTEL, Marybeth took her time getting dressed for the meeting. She wasn't sure why she felt so picky about what she was wearing, but she did, especially since she didn't have much of a selection to choose from. Whether she hoped it would give her courage or make her feel more comfortable, she wasn't sure. It was going to be a hot day, so that made the selection process even more difficult. How to look nice enough for a school building without sweltering on the way over there?

By one o'clock, the jitters were about to overtake her completely. She'd seen a coffee shop in the next block, so she headed out. The hotel lobby was bright and open, if a little bit dated, and she exited out onto a busy sidewalk. Everyone seemed to be on their way to or from lunch. She moved with the crowd, feeling like a typical tourist as she leaned her head back to get a look at the tall buildings at the city's center. She liked how it seemed to be a mixture of old and new, as though the city planners appreciated the history as well as the new business.

It was easy enough to find the nearby coffee shop and settle down with her laptop and a sandwich. She chose a high counter seat that looked out over the sidewalk so that she was able to watch the parade of people as she ate her lunch. She studied the clothes of the people passing by and tried to guess what their stories were. The tourists were fairly easy to spot in cool, casual summer outfits, the business people often had open collars and sleeveless shirts, but the skirts were longer and more tailored, the shoes striking a more serious note as well. Marybeth smoothed her hand over her summer skirt and wondered again if she'd chosen the right outfit to wear.

She was draining the last bit of coffee from her cup when her eye caught the traffic stopping for the nearby light. A small car with a familiar dented front bumper was waiting just to her right. It had to be a coincidence, but at the same time, she fought the urge to go dashing into the ladies' room. She turned her head away from the line of traffic, and then brought the large drink cup up to provide a bit more cover. This allowed her a veiled view of the car. The glare from the store window made it difficult to see the driver's face, but she could tell it was a bald, older gentleman with spots on his head, a thick gray mustache and the largest pair of sunglasses she'd ever seen. She could have sworn he looked just like the old guy she had seen at the coffee shop back in Pittsburgh. The traffic moved slowly on, and the car didn't stop or linger, but she'd gotten a brief glance of the passenger. It was another older man who was looking intently at the coffee shop, and a shiver went down her back in spite of the hot day. As soon as the car passed, she tossed her trash in the nearby bussing station and piled everything back into her backpack. She didn't feel safe sitting still any more.

CHAPTER TWENTY-SEVEN

he lawyers' offices in downtown Pittsburgh were luxurious, but both Edward and Charles were anxious to be done. Edward had been so eager to take care of everything, that he'd dragged them all in at the crack of dawn on Wednesday morning. They'd been there the better part of the day, rewriting the will, reviewing the accounts, and drawing up all of the paperwork involved in reworking the plans for the estate.

The business and the enormous home would go to the niece, Carolyn Jacobs. In addition, Edward had requested that they set up a separate foundation to manage the philanthropic use of the funds he'd designated for educational purposes. Charles had agreed to run it, at least for now. They both hoped that once they got to know Marybeth and her daughter, one or both of them might be interested in getting involved.

Since he knew nothing about the legal process, Charles settled on the job of keeping a close eye on his friend. He made sure that they brought water and juice, not just coffee, and that Edward had the opportunity to get up and move around every so often. He couldn't quite put his finger on what it was that was worrying him, but he had a sense that something wasn't quite right with his old friend's health. He was relieved to see that it looked as though they were finally wrapping things up. Edward motioned Charles to come over to the long table where they were sitting.

"Charlie, I'd like you to be one of the witnesses here. We're going to video tape this part of the proceedings, so that there won't be any questions about the propriety or anything."

"You want me to attest to the fact that you're of sound mind and body, is that it?" He put his arm around his friend's shoulder for a quick hug before settling into the chair beside him. "Get those cameras rolling, boys, I've known this old guy for a lifetime, and he's still as sharp as the day I met him."

They finished with the signatures and the taping and then headed across the street to a bar and grill owned by one of Edward's old friends. The two of them settled into a deep booth and ordered a pint each of the local IPA. With a basket of chips and a fresh dish of guacamole, they let themselves relax a bit. Edward dug into the bowl of dip. "I have to say, Charlie, that is a huge weight off my mind."

"Eddie, it sounds odd, I know, but I'm proud of you. The fund you've set up is going to help an awful lot of kids like Daniel." He looked at his old friend, a loaded chip half way to his mouth. It was so easy to forget the amount of money that this unassuming old man held sway over. Charles touched his friend's forearm before picking up another chip himself. "I appreciate your setting money aside for research as well as programming. That's what made the difference way back when I was getting started in special education, and it's going to make the difference again, I can feel it."

Edward ate the chip whole and clinked his glass against his friend's. "My God, yes, the science happening these days is amazing," he said, grinning over his glass.

Charles nodded but took a more serious tone. "You know I'm happy to run this shindig for now but I do hope one or both of these women will turn out to be interested in it. I think their backgrounds would be a really good fit."

Edward waved his hand. "I trust you'll know what's best, my friend. If they're not interested I know you'll find someone excellent who is." They finished off their beers, then decided to stay and order dinner.

* * *

THE NEXT MORNING the two of them took off for Baltimore to meet Carolyn Jacobs and share their news. Once he had Eddie settled in with his belt on, Charlie slid into the driver's seat, a look of satisfaction on his face. He didn't know whether he was Sherlock Holmes or Dr. Watson but either way he'd been having a ball. No AARP couch poker for them. The two of them had been doing some real sleuthing and he was loving it. He'd been their eyes and ears in Pittsburgh as Sarah—somehow he was still struggling to think of her with another name—and her friend had begun their search for Eddie's great niece.

It had been easier than he expected. Who knew that people really did buy a cup of coffee and then sit all day long in a coffee shop? How could they afford to stay in business he wondered? After his first day, he'd asked Edward to look into the shop and make sure it was economically viable. Eddie had laughed at him, but he'd done it anyway and assured Charlie that it was likely to stay open at least as long as they needed it to. So Charlie had settled into a routine—pick up the paper at the newsstand, set up the small microphone and pop in the special hearing aids that Eddie had given him, buy a cup of coffee and a blueberry muffin and settle in to listen and wait.

Charlie had heard the excitement in her voice, known the minute they'd figured it out. He heard the name, Carolyn Jacobs, and then the conversation about the death of her father. He'd left the coffee shop feeling cocky, even dropped his paper on the table near them on his way out. He had hurried out to Eddie's house to tell him the news.

Once the door was opened at the mansion, he blew past the sour butler and made a beeline for Eddie's kitchen. "We've got it. We've got the name. It's Carolyn Jacobs. She lives in Baltimore but her family is here in Pittsburgh." He changed his tone of voice then, realizing that his glee wasn't entirely appropriate. "Actually, there was a headline about her father passing away recently." Together, they found the article online and located the address of the home. They spotted an additional announcement about a wake being held the next day. Charles was ready for a rest so Edward had the butler drive him out to the home in the suburbs.

That evening Charlie was back, eager to hear the latest news from Edward's trip out to the home. "So, was she there? Was Carolyn there? Did you get to meet her?"

Edward shook his head. "No, the brother said she was still in the city teaching. The mother looked bad, though, I'm sorry to say. Apparently Carolyn had two older brothers, both of them in the service. One was killed just a year or so ago."

"And now her dad?" He sat down abruptly. "Oh that poor girl. That's an awful lot to go through. Are you sure we should be going after her this way? Maybe we should wait, give her some time."

But Edward sounded quite confident. "Nope, not going to wait any longer. I want to meet this young woman, this great-niece of mine. Maybe since she's just lost part of her family, she'll like finding out that she has more." It was hard for Charles to argue with that.

While Edward was at the wake, Charles had returned to the coffee shop one more time, feeling a bit sad that his spying days were over. He sat, reading over the newspaper and enjoying a small pot of tea as he watched the young crowd move in and out of the shop. The clientele had been a little different from that on the weekend, a few more babies and toddlers he noticed, and he'd liked the change from the regular student crowd. At least he assumed most of the coffee shop goers were students since they were usually there on what he considered to be workdays.

He had his paper folded on the table in front of him when he spotted Sarah and her friend Gregory come in the shop. He quickly fumbled to get the paper up before they could see him, nearly spilling the pot of tea in the process. He forced himself to calm down and tucked his special earbuds back into place. Once they'd gotten their drinks he'd been able to hear them planning her trip to Baltimore.

So here they were. He and Edward had put on their proverbial deerstalker caps and headed to Baltimore as well. Edward had wanted his butler to drive them but Charlie vetoed that notion right away. He couldn't imagine driving across town with the man, much less all the way to Baltimore. No, he insisted, it was his car or nothing. Besides, a small car would be perfect for city driving, even if it did have a dent in the front bumper.

CHAPTER TWENTY-EIGHT

*G*regory was afraid he was going to throw up. Seconds ago, he'd been having a pleasant morning, sitting in the coffee shop reading. Now he looked at his phone as though it were dripping with poison. In a way, it was. He hadn't recognized the number that was calling, but the second he answered, he recognized the voice. He was dead. How in the hell was Jay Warren calling him?

"Surprised to hear from me?" Jay's phony laugh made Gregory feel even sicker.

"What the hell? Where are you?" And for God's sake why are you calling me, he wondered. He rested his head on the small table by his computer, one hand holding the phone to his ear, the other fist clenching and unclenching in his hair as the voice continued. Greg was as sickened by the call as he was at the thought of what this might mean for Marybeth. She had asked him a couple of times about his past but he'd kept silent, too embarrassed to tell her the ugly truth about what he'd been doing.

"Where's Clark?"

Over the years one of Greg's functions for the Warren family had been keeping an eye on Jay's uncle, Edward Clark. As Jay rose within his dad's company, Gregory was expected to keep him updated on Clark's health and whereabouts. This past January, he'd had to spend a frigid morning installing a tracker on Clark's latest car, an SUV to replace his Lexus. God only knew why a man of that age needed an SUV.

Still in shock, Gregory pulled up the program on his computer and saw the indicator blinking at Clark's home address. "He's at home. Why, what are you playing at?"

"What's the matter, did you think I was done with you?"

The phone clicked off and Gregory put his head between his knees, wondering what it felt like to faint. He could remember exactly when he heard about the plane crash, how he'd felt like dancing. He'd been at Lulu's having dinner alone and he remembered how the feeling of relief had washed over him.

"You good, man?" Lulu's bartender, had jutted his chin in the vague direction of Gregory's plate, now smeared with cheese and littered with a small pile of chicken bones on a wilting piece of lettuce.

"Yeah, sure." Gregory pushed his plate toward the back edge of the bar, then tapped the side of his beer mug. "Let me have another one of these, though." The bartender lifted the plate away with one hand and wiped the counter with a white rag. The whiff of bleach was almost enough to make Gregory head for the door, but it started to dissipate just as the sportscaster yelled and the small crowd behind him fastened their eyes back on the game. He kicked at the legs of the stool and thought if he'd still been a betting man, he'd have lost his shirt on this one, that was for sure. He'd been a sucker for the Penguins since they'd started the franchise when he was a kid. But the Red Wings had just scored again as the set headed into a commercial and he was relieved that his betting days were behind him now.

He reached up under his knitted hat to scratch, the wool growing more and more uncomfortable in the heat of the bar. He would love to take it off, but his hair was too long and too filthy to uncover it now. He knew his friend Arnie would have looked at the sorry hat and teased him into getting a haircut. An accountant who'd also been forced to work for the Warren family, Arnie had been killed in a hit and run accident just a week before. Gregory was still mourning the loss.

He rubbed at his short beard and tried to resettle himself on the stool in an effort to ignore the damn hat. He focused in on his beer and closed his eyes for a few minutes, picturing the shitty day he'd had. He didn't know what club these high-income women were meeting in to share his business card. He'd spent the day in his cramped, compact car following yet another idiot husband and his twenty-something piece into a sleazy, suburban hotel. They didn't even have the sense to meet in the city where anonymity was almost a given. Was it marrying these rich women that made the men so stupid, or was it the other way around, he wondered? Either way he felt like scum making money this way. God, he detested being a private investigator. He swirled the beer in its oversized glass. The days of Philip Marlowe were definitely over.

He had loved being a real detective, badge on his waist, a cop with one of the best police departments in the state, solving real cases that actually mattered to people. He had made his way up from beat cop to detective in just over four years. But the Warrens, dammit, they'd ruined it. His last real case had involved numbers running and he'd gone undercover into one of the older neighborhoods to try to track down the leaders.

The numbers game and gambling in general had beaten him first. Before he knew it, he was $35,000 in debt and yanked from the case. The Warren family had been the ones running numbers and to stay alive with all of his body parts intact, Gregory had made a deal with the devil. Jay Warren would cover his gambling debt in exchange for his off-the-books assistance.

Gregory had left the force before they could find out the true extent of what he had done and he'd been trying to make a go of it on his own ever since, running a business out of his apartment and various coffee shops, renting a friend's office when he had to have a sit-down with a client.

Twice he'd nearly paid off the debt, but first his car had been totaled in a godforsaken parking lot downriver, and later on, his apartment had burned, his laptop and client lists inside. When he was feeling particularly paranoid, Gregory wondered if Jay had been behind the mishaps, somehow arranging for him to remain in his debt, but there was no way to know for sure. He sipped at his beer, turning the glass in circles as he stewed. Suddenly, the crowd around him started talking but it wasn't about the game.

"Oh my, God, can you believe it?" He heard someone behind him say. Gregory's eyes darted back to the TV where an Eyewitness News banner was flashing underneath the anchorman. The image of the newsroom was replaced by grainy looking footage of a jungle, with the tail fin of a plane visible above the foliage. The sound was turned off, but a ticker ran along the bottom of the screen: *Suspected Crime Kingpin Walter Warren and Son Killed in South America.* The photograph of the tail fin alternated with a grainy video from an airport showing the two of them getting on the small plane. Gregory's hands were gripped around the beer mug, the knuckles growing white with the intensity. He leaned toward the bartender.

"Hey, could you turn up the sound?"

The bartender shook his head. "Sorry, man, remote's lost and the sound button broke off last week." Gregory watched a little longer, paid his tab and then headed for the door. It was dark with a cold nasty rain falling, but he didn't feel any of it. He pulled his coat around him and tilted his head back to catch a few drops of rain on his face. It was over. His goddamn time in the Warren family version of hell was over. With steps that felt easier than they had in a decade, he walked toward his apartment, smiling at the rain-soaked pedestrians that he passed. Maybe life could finally be good again.

Now, in the coffee shop, Gregory began grabbing up the empty coffee cup and napkins. How could he have been such an idiot? Even worse, why had he not told Marybeth about his lies to the Warren family? He'd been so excited when he first saw the report of the plane crash that he couldn't get enough of the news stories. He'd tapped his one last connection in the FBI to get a preliminary report from the crash, and it wasn't until he had that in hand that he had dared to send a quick note to the address he found for Marybeth's school. Then, he had thought about celebrating. The Warrens had been ruining his life for nearly twenty years, and at last, he was free.

Seeing Marybeth again, Greg felt like he'd been given a fresh start, a second chance. He had liked coming here with her, working on their search together. For a little while he'd felt like a real detective again instead of some sleazy guy looking into phony insurance claims. It had made him remember what he'd once had, the life he had hoped to lead.

Gregory knew he'd been so distracted working with her that he had quit paying attention to anything else. Still trying to right his brain, he risked making a call to Clark's office. Answer the phone you damn, old fool, he thought. But it rang and rang. Just as he was about to hang up, a breathless voice picked up. "Edward Clark's office, how may I help you?" He scrambled to think of an excuse for the call.

"Good morning," he paused, rubbing his palm against the seam of his jeans. "I'd like to see Mr. Clark about some paperwork this afternoon?"

"I'm sorry, Mr. Clark is out of the office until late next week. May I take a message?"

"Next week? Where is he?"

"Sir, if I can get your name."

He cut her off, turned his voice a shade deeper, trying to

transform the terror he was feeling into a tone she might respond to. "Oh no, I wanted to meet with him. It's just that there's some family business that he asked me to take care of for him." He waited, holding his breath to see if it would work.

"Oh, is it urgent? Mr. Clark didn't leave me any instructions about family issues. Listen, if you have to reach him, he's in Baltimore at the Klimpton on the harbor. If you ring their main number they should be able to connect you."

Baltimore, oh God, he wasn't at home. What if Jay found out? Gregory felt nauseous all over again, barely managing to end the call without raising any more alarm. Dammit, he'd been nervous ever since they'd gone to that stupid wake. He knew there was something he was missing. That car, the back of the man's head as he walked into the house, some part of his brain had known it was Clark, but he had talked himself out of believing it, even forgot to check the tracker on his computer afterwards. It felt as though he was missing some key piece of the story, and without it, he had no way of assessing the real danger.

Gregory sat for a moment trying to control the fear and dread that was washing over him as he tried to figure out what Jay's reappearance might mean to Marybeth. Maybe it meant nothing. He felt hopeful for a moment. After all, they'd been living their lives without any contact, why would it matter now? Then Greg remembered a conversation he'd overheard years ago between Jay and his dad when the old man had been hounding him about getting married and having kids. His father had seemed taken aback at Jay's loud declaration that he would never be tied down by a wife and kids. Would the existence of a kid matter now? He just didn't know but it felt important to at least warn Marybeth of what was going on.

More importantly though, it was time to come clean to Marybeth, to tell her the truth about his connection to Jay Warren. After all, if she was through hiding, he should be, too. He would understand if she decided not to have any more to do with him, but at least he would try.

Gregory pulled the battery out of the phone and threw it in the trash, shoved his computer into his bag and threw everything else into a bin on the street. He ran into the phone store next-door, grabbed up a cheap replacement, and then hurried home. He surveyed his apartment quickly, packed a bag with the only clean shirt and pants that he had, and took off for Baltimore. He wanted to call Marybeth, but that didn't feel right. This was too much information to cover over the phone.

CHAPTER TWENTY-NINE

he confines of the hotel were starting to grate on Jay's nerves. It was one of several high rises located near the center of Caracas, but without his preferred penthouse view, life on the fifteenth floor was growing stale. Granted, he was pleased that the food was decent as was the free Wi-Fi, but sitting in one place, any one place, was hard to do. He was used to a busy life, running the backroom meetings, partying in the heart of Pittsburgh's elite social scene. The arrangements he'd made had been costly, but he was confident now that with his misdirection, the FBI case would die along with his father. He had just gotten word that the last ties linking him to the Warren family enterprises had been cleanly severed. Within the month, he'd have things back up and running the way he liked, quick and dirty but discreet. There'd be no more of that penny ante bullshit like numbers running that his dad had loved. What was it those surfers said, go big or go home?

Now for the fun part. Jay checked the app on his computer. Once he located Gregory Hanes's phone, he dialed the number. He was looking forward to the effect this call was going to have.

"Did you think I was done with you?" He hung up and had to laugh. What a joke. Time to start living again.

* * *

THE NEXT DAY, Jay sent a quick text for his car and driver. He'd be packed by the time they got downstairs. It was time to head back home, to his life among the movers and shakers of Pittsburgh. He would take over the family home and bring an entirely new level of glamour to the old building. He'd get his businesses going again.

Later, once he had his uncle's dry cleaning network in hand, he would use it as a front to expand some of the more lucrative international businesses that he'd been contemplating. After all, the man had to die sometime, didn't he? For God's sake, how old was he? Shouldn't something have gotten to him by now? He thought about taking steps to help the situation along, as they say. But coming so closely on the heels of his father's death, he didn't think it would be wise to risk it.

Near midnight, Jay was wading his way through the endless customs process in Miami. There was a line behind every kiosk, people looking rumpled and smelling even worse. He fiddled with his phone, waiting until it finally found a signal. It beeped once, and then loaded in a message. What the hell? He punched in the numbers quickly but a security agent stepped forward. "Sorry sir, no telephones in this area." Jay looked hard at the agent, then noticed the travelers around him. It wouldn't serve his purposes to be noticed yet so he pocketed it.

The line inched forward as he fumed, until finally "Your turn sir," the TSA agent gestured toward the open kiosk. Jay moved over and smashed at the buttons, jamming the screen until he had to exit the program and start all over again. Once through the process he stormed up the long corridor until it opened into the larger terminal. This late at night, few of the gates had any activity in them so he stepped into a quiet area and dialed the phone. He didn't bother with hello.

"What do you mean he's not in Pittsburgh?"

"We checked in on the uncle like you asked. His car's in Pittsburgh, he's not. He got a ride with some old buddy of his and they took off. By the time I had the license plate number and a trace on the car, they were in Baltimore."

"Baltimore, seriously? You idiots need to find that lying son of a bitch Greg Hanes. Then let me know what's going on with the old man."

He waited in the deserted gate area, time dragging by. The shops weren't even open yet to get a Goddamned cup of coffee. Around two, his phone rang again.

"Boss, you're not gonna like this. I've been calling around trying to find out what's going on. A lawyer we've got here in Pittsburgh says that two days ago, Clark was at their firm. Our guy said they brought someone in to video the whole thing, said Clark was changing his will and they needed witnesses."

"Fuck!" Jay slammed his hand on the flimsy table. "Changing the will, how? Get that lawyer on the phone now. I want to talk to him."

After another long wait, the call connected. He grilled the sleepy-sounding lawyer but learned little else. Rather than working to his advantage, it seemed that his imagined death had actually made things worse. He would have to talk to his uncle immediately. He knew he could change his mind, use his charm on the man the way he'd done all his life. It was tiresome but effective. He figured he might as well get on with it.

Jay was fizzing by the time he finished the call and headed upstairs to the single airline desk that was open. Changing the ticket from Pittsburgh to Baltimore involved a tedious conversation with the stupidest airline employee he'd ever met. He was ready to tear someone's hair out by the roots and the next flight to Baltimore wasn't going to leave until morning. He charged back down the concourse to the quiet area and stepped over to an empty gate just as his phone rang. "Talk to me." There was a pause. "Well if they're both in Baltimore then that should make it even easier. Get there, immediately. Book me a room at The Four Seasons. I should get in by ten." He sent more texts and emails, receiving confirmation just as daylight was breaking over the far runway. The press conference they had been quietly arranging would be moved from Pittsburgh to Baltimore.

After a long and bumpy flight, the plane took forever to taxi to the gate. Jay was stiff and brimming with anger as he shoved his way out of the plane door and up the hallway. "Sir." At the top of the concourse, Vince, the larger of the two Morelli brothers, stepped forward and reached for Jay's bag.

"Everything set?" The two walked rapidly toward the exit. "Where's the press?"

"They'll be at The Four Seasons this afternoon. We've got a back way in set up for you now."

They ducked quickly into a black SUV and were at the back door of the hotel in less than an hour. Jay handed the clerk his new, clean, card, then waited to see if there would be any issues when they ran it. There was a pause and he felt a tightness along his spine, but soon the printer was humming and the clerk brandished the sheet for him to sign.

"Thank you, sir, the elevator is just behind you there. Please let me know if we can be of any further service." The clerk handed over the key card folder with a bit of flourish and a broad smile but Jay ignored it as he turned without bothering to acknowledge him. He was punching more numbers into his cell phone before the elevator doors had opened. As he waited for the phone to connect, he gestured to Vince with his watch. The man knew what he meant.

"Press will be here at five."

Jay nodded and turned his attention to the phone. "Where are we with Hanes?"

CHAPTER THIRTY

*A*fter her scare in the coffee shop, Marybeth stepped cautiously onto the crowded sidewalk and continued with the flow as people moved about the city. With one eye on the street, she followed a group into a small art museum and spent a half hour admiring the paintings and enjoying the air conditioning before she ventured back out onto the sidewalk. The pedestrian traffic was reduced in the hot afternoon, so she tried hard not to find herself on the sidewalk alone. Luckily, there were plenty of small shops and touristy spots that she could check out so that she was able to keep moving. By the time her appointment with Carolyn came, she found herself farther away than she had intended, so she opted for a quick cab ride to get her back to the area of the school. Inside the cab, she took a moment to brush her hair and freshen her lipstick before they arrived in front of the center.

The center was housed in what looked to have been an old town house. The front stoop was broad, the stone worn smooth across the middle where it met the cracking steps. The building was old but seemed to be clean and well cared for. She rang the buzzer and announced her appointment to the intercom before the door clicked and she was admitted. An amazing blast of color coated the walls of the entryway, and she laughed at the contrast with the dark exterior. It reminded her of the building on campus years ago that had been shared by ROTC and the art department, where intrepid art students used to sneak over at night to splash bits of color where they weren't wanted. For some reason that memory made her relax a bit as she headed toward the office on her right.

A young man was at the office desk poring over a textbook as she came up. She reached her hand over the counter as she introduced herself. He tucked a slip of paper in his book and then stood to shake her hand.

"Hello, how are you? I'm Seth, just holding down the front desk for a bit while everyone finishes up in their classrooms. My older ESL students don't start until closer to five, so I try to cram in a bit of study time. But you don't need to know all of that."

Marybeth liked his easy manner as he fumbled with the old desk chair and came around the small counter. "It's nice to meet you, and I know all about cramming in some study time. This looks like a great place to work."

He smiled more broadly and extended his hand, directing her ahead of him down the hall. "It's terrific. We've got all kinds of special needs kids here in the daytime and then community-based classes that fill up the evenings." They paused by a large window. "If you look out here, you can see the ramp and main access point that we use out back."

Marybeth leaned on the wide windowsill and peered down at the long ramp and narrow lot before following Seth around the next corner to a classroom. She caught her breath as she looked inside and saw a slim, dark-haired woman on her knees, piling an enormous stack of blocks into a wide plastic tub.

He turned to Marybeth. "I'll leave you in Carolyn's capable hands."

Marybeth righted her shoulders, tried to force some calm

breaths, and moved toward her daughter. She knelt on the floor across from the big tub and began to pick up blocks.

"Oh, you don't have to do that." Carolyn said as she continued to drop in handfuls of blocks.

"I'm a teacher too, so it seems like a pretty normal thing to do." They finished the pile quickly and Carolyn pointed to two chairs at a nearby table.

"Welcome to the City Center. I have to say, we don't normally put our visitors to work right away, we usually like to ease them into volunteering." She dragged the tub into the corner and sat down across from Marybeth at the low table. "Luckily you and I can both fit under this table. Not all of my visitors can."

Marybeth studied her daughter's face, the eyes so familiar to her that she worried for a second that she might start crying right then and there. Carolyn's dark hair was pulled back into a thick braid with lots of loose strands softening the look of her face. She wore a simple blue top over lightweight pants with low sandals. When she looked again at Carolyn's face the young woman had a puzzled expression and Marybeth was afraid she'd been staring.

"I'm sorry, I lost my train of thought there for a second."

Carolyn smoothed a piece of masking tape with a child's name on it. "You said you're a teacher. Are you thinking of working here at the center? Because I don't think we have any openings. I don't want to get your hopes up."

"Oh, no, I'm not looking for work. I teach special needs high school students back at home." She paused. "Actually, I came to see you."

A guarded look came across the young woman's face as she shifted her chair back slightly. "Me, why me? You look a little bit familiar, but I'm pretty sure I don't know you."

Marybeth leaned back in the small chair and settled her hands in her lap. She didn't want anything in her appearance to seem frightening. "I think this is probably the most important conversation of my life and also, the hardest. I keep trying to think of some easy way to start, but I just can't."

She took a deep breath. "Twenty-eight years ago I was a student at Penn State. I was working on my teaching degree and discovered I was pregnant."

Carolyn gripped the edges of the seat, her eyes wide.

"When the baby was born, we were in incredible danger. The FBI needed to put us both into protection. It was an incredibly difficult decision to make but in the end I decided that the baby would actually be safer without me." She looked steadily into Carolyn's eyes. "That baby was you, and I've waited twenty-eight years for it to be safe enough to find you, to tell you how sorry…"

Abruptly Carolyn stood, the chair falling on its side as she moved to put more distance between them. The air echoed with the sound it made falling.

"Carolyn I…"

"Stop talking, just, stop talking." She shook her head and pulled on the edge of her shirt before striding over to her desk. She sat down in the wide chair and leaned her face into her hands.

Marybeth stayed just where she was, not wanting to frighten the young woman any more than she already had. She gave her the silence that she'd asked for and waited, her heart beating so hard she thought maybe Seth could hear it in the front office. After what felt like an ice age, she noticed that Carolyn had grown very still, that she wasn't crying or moving in any way, just sitting with her face hidden in her hands.

It was quiet for so long that Marybeth thought she might have to leave, come back another day, although she didn't know how it would be any different. But Carolyn sat up straight, finally, pulling her shoulders back and facing Marybeth directly.

"I've always known I was adopted, you didn't surprise me about that. I'm years younger than my two brothers for one thing and my parents always said I was their last chance to raise a girl."

She stared at Marybeth. "You look familiar because you look like me, don't you? I'm surprised that Seth didn't comment on it."

She stood up from her desk and moved cautiously back toward Marybeth. "What do you want? Why find me now, when I'm an adult? I'm not anybody's child anymore. And what were you saying about danger? Am I in trouble somehow? I don't understand." She righted the chair and then leaned her hands on the back of it, clearly not ready yet to sit back down with this person, this stranger.

"I'm sorry, the last thing I want to do is frighten you. I know you're an adult and I know it's silly of me to even be here, to be bothering you now that you're grown. For years, I was so scared and worried that I might put you in danger if I came looking for you, but you've always been in my mind. I've thought about you your whole life."

She paused and took another deep breath before continuing. "When I made that decision, all I wanted was for you to be safe, but I was too young to understand what I was giving up, what I would be missing." Marybeth pulled a tissue from her backpack and dabbed at her eyes. "Sorry, I didn't mean to get so teary. Look, I know this is a lot to take in. Would you like to go and get a cup of coffee or something, and talk a little more, maybe sit in real chairs somewhere?" Marybeth motioned toward the little chairs all around her.

Carolyn smiled for the first time since she'd heard the news, and then straightened her back, making her mind up as she went to get her purse from the file cabinet by her desk. "Let's say coffee, I think that's about all I'm up for right now. There's a place close by."

Carolyn closed the door of the classroom and then led them past the front desk and down the worn front steps. This time Seth was so buried in his work that he didn't look up, and Marybeth figured they were both relieved by that.

Like every city, Baltimore was filled with coffee shops, so it was a brief walk around the corner. In the late afternoon, the rush had passed, and a pair of armchairs sat vacant in the corner.

They both ordered and then settled into the corner alcove. The cups with their paper sleeves were way too hot to drink, so they undid the caps and set them on the table. Both women looked up then, startled to see that they'd gone through the exact same motions.

"This is too weird," Carolyn sighed and settled back in the chair. "I have no idea what I'm doing here."

Marybeth broke an enormous cookie into smaller pieces, playing for time rather than eating since her stomach was in a million knots. "I know, I wish there was a way to make this less weird. Could you just tell me a little bit about yourself?"

"I don't know if I want to do that. You're a stranger to me."

"Well, I can tell you a little bit about me. Would that help?"

"Okay, makes sense." Carolyn tested the hot coffee with a sip.

"My name was Sarah Dawes and I grew up in Pittsburgh. I was in my second year at Penn State."

Carolyn looked up. "I went there too."

"It's a beautiful campus, isn't it? Well, I was in my second year, when a boy from my hometown came to take some classes. He'd always been the sexy bad boy back at home, and I was never allowed to have anything to do with him. But I was shy and hadn't made friends very easily at college, so when he arrived, with this familiar face and amazing smile, I fell for him. I ignored all of the warnings that I'd had back at home, and I fell in love." Marybeth slowly spun the sleeve of the coffee cup as she talked. Finally, she looked back at Carolyn. "His name was Jay Warren."

Carolyn's eyes widened. "Wait, I've heard that name. A big court case, right?"

Marybeth nodded. "Back when I was in college, there was also supposed to be a big court case, and I was recruited as a witness, but the case fell apart. Jay and his father were both considered criminals but witnesses started to disappear and the FBI couldn't prove their case. Recently, they were trying again and there's been a lot of publicity, the latest trial of the century."

"Something happened, though, right?"

"Yes, a plane crash in South America. Once I had word from a friend of mine with connections to the FBI that both Jay Warren and his father were dead, I started to think that it might be safe for me to come out of hiding. It happened in mid-May, and I just couldn't get you out of my mind after that. My husband thinks I'm crazy, by the way."

Carolyn leaned forward. "You're married?"

Marybeth reached for her phone. "Yes, my name now is Marybeth Rogers." She brought up a recent photograph. "That's my husband Ken, and our two sons, Grant and Jimmy." Marybeth looked up, handing the phone to Carolyn. "You have two half-brothers."

Carolyn held the phone in her hand and scrolled through the photos. She paused often and enlarged several of them as she went through them. Marybeth waited, giving her all the time she wanted with the collection.

Then Carolyn handed the phone back. "You're not in any of the pictures. Why?"

"Well," Marybeth shrugged. "I was warned about the dangers of being photographed, so I sort of became the family photographer."

"I think I get it, but I don't understand how you found me. Did the FBI give you information about me?"

Marybeth blushed and pushed the phone into the pocket of the backpack. "My friend, the one who sent me the information about the crash, has been helping me. We searched a lot of adoption records."

"Aren't they private?"

Marybeth shifted in her seat. "Yes, some are, but we didn't actually stick to the usual rules."

Carolyn was looking anxious. "What does that mean?" Marybeth hated to tell her about the wake, knowing how they'd probably violated all kinds of laws, as well as simple manners, but somehow, sitting here with her, it seemed important to be honest.

"We found your name in the hospital records and worked from there, I hate to say this, but one clue was the headline about your father's death. I was so sorry to read about that." Carolyn lowered her head, but when she looked up, Marybeth thought that there was as much anger in her look as there was sadness. "I'm embarrassed to tell you, but we actually went to the wake that was held. I was hoping you might be there, but when you weren't, I stole your picture. I'm sorry, I know I had no right to do that, but when I saw it, I knew. I knew we'd found the right person." Marybeth pulled the photograph from her pack and handed it to Carolyn. "My friend thought it looked just like me when I was in college."

Carolyn took the picture, studying the face. Marybeth waited, then commented. "For a college graduate you don't look especially happy in that photo."

Carolyn held the picture against her chest. "No, I wasn't. My dad missed the ceremony that day, something work related. I can't even remember his excuse. My brothers didn't even bother trying to come, and my mother..." She paused. "Well, let's just say she wasn't having a very good day."

"I'm sorry, I'm afraid she didn't look too well when we saw her. Is she ill?"

"Ill, that's an interesting word isn't it, very nonjudgmental." Carolyn set the cup on the low table. "Look, I don't know you, and you don't know my family, so I don't think I want to say anything more about that now. In fact, I should really be getting home."

Marybeth reached to touch her knee, but pulled her hand back and settled it in her lap instead. "Are you married? Do you have any children?"

Carolyn smiled, a broader smile than Marybeth had seen all afternoon. "Married, not anymore, but I do have a son." Marybeth caught her breath as Carolyn pulled out her phone to show her a bright baby's smile that filled the background. "His name is Phillip, but I call him PJ for short. In fact, I'm due at the sitter's in just a few minutes." She rose, pocketing the phone and gathering her purse and messenger bag.

Marybeth stood as well. "Can I give you my number? I don't want to intrude on your life, but I'm here for a few days, and I'd love to talk with you some more." She wrote her number on a napkin and pressed it into Carolyn's hands. Carolyn folded it and tucked it into her pocket while Marybeth watched, her stomach sinking, but Carolyn's face brightened and she held out her hand.

"This has been, I don't know what, amazing, I guess, is the only word I can think of. I need some time to think about all of this."

"Of course." They shook hands gently.

"I'm pretty sure I'll call you, though, if you can give me a little time."

Marybeth followed her out the door. "Thank you, Carolyn, thank you for talking to me." She wanted to say more but felt that she had to let the young woman go. She forced herself to turn away and start the walk back to her hotel. She wanted to skip or yell or tell everyone that she'd just met her daughter, but she held it all in, the city blocks passing quickly as she floated back to her room. Really, what she wanted to do most was call Ken. She headed into the lobby and turned toward the elevator.

Up in her room, Marybeth threw herself onto the bed and wiggled the dance she'd been holding in since she'd walked away from the coffee shop. Her daughter, she'd met her daughter, and she was awesome. Plus, she was a grandmother, and she'd never even known it.

CHAPTER THIRTY-ONE

*C*arolyn walked from the bus stop to Janine's porch in a daze. She knew she was putting one foot in front of the other, but that was about it. She had met her mother. It didn't sound real even when she tried saying it out loud. She held her finger on the buzzer, not realizing how long the ring was blaring until Janine snatched the door open. "What the...Carolyn?"

Carolyn jumped with the shock of Janine's response. "I'm so sorry, so, so sorry, I'm just, I don't know what to say." Suddenly her eyes were filling with tears.

"Hey, hey, don't cry. I didn't mean to snap at you. The buzzer was just going and going, and it was making me crazy. At least the kids weren't sleeping. Come in, what's wrong?" Janine held her daughter April on her left hip and put her arm around Carolyn's shoulder, gently pulling her into the small living room. Two strollers were lined up in the hallway but they managed to squeeze past them and find a seat on the sofa. Immediately the three-year old was off like a shot, singing to herself as she headed away from them. "Sean's in there stealing a snack with PJ. He'll keep an eye on them. Tell me what is going on."

Carolyn pulled a crumpled tissue from her purse and began

dabbing at her eyes, feeling embarrassed by the sudden tears and the unexpected lump in her throat. She willed herself to be calm, but it was a struggle she wasn't sure she could win. If there was anyone to fall apart in front of, though, it was Janine. She was the one other army brat that Carolyn had connected with off and on over the years until they'd ended up roommates at Penn State, a coincidence neither of them could explain. Somehow the universe had brought them together again, and this time they were old enough to make it stick. Their friendship had weathered one bad marriage, Carolyn's, two bad girlfriends, Janine's, until they'd found themselves living down the block from each other in what they hoped was an up-and-coming part of Baltimore. Janine patted Carolyn's shoulder but then became more insistent.

"Come on Carolyn, you're scaring me. You don't look like you're hurt, I know PJ is fine, so what is going on?"

"I met her today, she came to my school."

"Who?"

"My mother, my biological mother."

Janine jumped up from her place on the couch and yelled, "Are you kidding me? Sean, get in here!"

Janine's brother Sean came rushing down the hall, a child in each arm. He handed April to Janine, then set PJ in Carolyn's lap. Frightened by the abrupt maneuver, PJ buried his face in her shoulder.

"Aw, buddy, it's okay," Carolyn cooed, holding him closely and rubbing his back. She didn't even notice the jam that was spreading across her shirtfront.

Janine juggled April on her hip. "Sean, you are not going to believe this. Carolyn met her mom today."

Carolyn snuggled PJ against her and smiled up through her tears. Growing up, she hadn't really noticed Janine's younger brother. He'd tagged along with them a bit, but just as often, was out running around with his own crowd. This past summer, though, he'd come to live with Janine, and Carolyn had slowly but surely been falling in love with him. She didn't let on about it, since she was still worried that he might need to do a little more growing up, but she was patient. Now, though, the wonder on his face made her want to kiss him despite her misgivings. Instead, she handed the calmer PJ back to him while she blew her nose. They all found seats and waited to hear the story.

"You are not going to believe this," she began. "I wondered my whole life what my birth story was and why I was adopted. I mean, I thought about looking, don't get me wrong. Especially before PJ was born, I really wanted to know something about my background. I ordered one of those DNA kits but I never followed through on it. I'm not even sure why. Maybe I figured my family was enough to deal with, right, why look for more trouble, you know? Especially after Tim's death when Mom was so distraught."

Her head dropped and she waited to recover her composure before she went on. "I was angry with her and I was worried to know what might be inside of me, whether depression could be in my future too." She looked up, "Now that I have PJ, I can understand how devastated she was by Tim's death. But back then..." She trailed off. It sounded so selfish to say it out loud. "I'm embarrassed to admit it, but I guess I kind of resented Tim. It felt as though he and Curt had always had a bit more of mom's heart than I did, and when he died, it felt like he took even more. It made me wonder about my biological mother and why she would have let me go as well." She blew her nose and straightened further in her seat, rubbing her hand along PJ's small foot.

"Then today after class ended, this woman came to my room. I felt a little funny when I saw her but I didn't know why. She blurted out this whole story and then I realized, the funny feeling was because she looked so familiar." She looked from Sean to Janine. "She looked like me. We've got the same eyes and hair, even our hands look similar. And, you're not going to believe this, she's a special ed teacher too."

Sean and Janine looked at Carolyn and then each other, unsure what to say. "How can that be?" Janine finally stammered out. "That is amazing."

Then Carolyn laughed. "Oh, no, that is not even the amazing part."

The fits and starts of conversation, the questions and wonderings went on all evening as Sean prepared dinner and the three of them settled down to eat. It circled around and around the table while they sipped a bottle of wine and both children slept.

Finally, Carolyn caught sight of the kitchen clock and covered her mouth as a huge yawn took shape. "Guys, thank you so much for all of this. You're amazing. I don't know what I would have done with myself tonight without you. I think I've finally calmed down enough that I'll be able to call and talk to her tomorrow." She hugged Janine one last time and then Sean helped her carry the stroller with the sleeping baby in it down to the street. Together they walked the few blocks to her door.

"Hey, I forgot to tell you, Clint backed out on buying those soccer tickets from me. I know this sounds a little crazy but do you think your biological mom might like to go with you to see the game? It would be a safe, public place and give you a good amount of time to talk. Besides, Janine's already planning to take PJ and April over to our mom's for a pool party. What do you think?"

Together they lifted the stroller and PJ up the few steps and parked it inside the door. She pulled Sean into a long, unexpected kiss before releasing him. "Thank you, Sean, for dinner and everything tonight. I'll give her a call and see if she's interested."

CHAPTER THIRTY-TWO

*T*he next morning, Marybeth was wishing again that she could just walk down the hallway in her bathrobe and make her own breakfast. Being away from home for so long was really starting to wear on her. She was trying to put together an outfit nice enough to wear in the restaurant downstairs when her phone rang. She was thrilled to hear Carolyn's voice.

"How are you doing, Carolyn?"

"I'm good, but I have an odd sort of question for you. A friend of mine belongs to this soccer group and he can't use his tickets to this big soccer game tomorrow at five. Would you like to go with me? It should be a good game, although I suspect it will be pretty crowded."

"Are you talking about the men's national team, the friendly against Panama?"

"Yes, exactly. Why, do you know soccer?"

"I love soccer. We got interested when our boys were growing up, and now my husband and I watch it on TV all the time. Wait, is your friend one of the American Outlaws?"

"Yes, he is," Carolyn laughed. "But I promise we won't have to dress up or act like idiots. The seats are just on the edge of their section."

"I would love to go Carolyn, that sounds amazing."

"All right, take a cab to the ball park and I'll meet you at the 'will call' office about forty-five minutes before it starts. We can get a bite to eat while we wait."

"And your son, PJ?"

"It's all right, I made arrangements for a sitter."

"Well, then we have a plan. Thank you, Carolyn. I'm really looking forward to it. I'll see you tomorrow."

Marybeth walked over to the window and looked down on the city blocks around her. She was so excited at the thought of seeing Carolyn again, and, truth be told, about the soccer game. She knew Ken was going to be really pissed when he found out she'd gone to this game. She would have to think of something. She tried a quick call but when it didn't go through she decided maybe she could get some sort of gift for him. It wouldn't take away the hurt, but she wanted to do it anyway. In fact, with all of this time on her hands, why not do some shopping?

After breakfast, she stood up straight in front of the mirror and settled her purse strap across her body. She could get something for her grandson, as well as her boys and Ken. She'd head over to the shopping area, look for some gifts and maybe find a book to help fill in the long hours until the game, until she saw her daughter again.

* * *

FOUR HOURS LATER, she was finished shopping and exhausted. She'd found lots of gifts that she liked, as well as a bookstore. She'd gone crazy in there and was now paying the price for it, her shopping bags getting heavier with every step. Finally, she came upon a small restaurant near her hotel, and settled in to a booth. She ordered lunch, then pulled out one of the children's books that she'd chosen and began reading it while she waited for her food. She was smiling to herself, remembering when Ken had read these books over and over to their boys. Many of the lines she knew by heart. She was sipping at her iced tea and trying to remember the next line before turning the page.

"May I join you?" an older gentleman with thick gray hair and a wide belt around his substantial middle stood beside the booth, his hand resting on the far side. It was the passenger in the car that she'd seen from the coffee shop. She had a vague sense now, that he looked familiar. Marybeth nearly spilled her tea as she fumbled to set it down. She wanted to jump up and run from the building but it just wasn't possible. She was surrounded by packages and hadn't even untangled her feet before the man was sitting across from her. "Please don't be afraid my dear. I'm not here to do you any harm."

He had a folded newspaper under his arm and as he set it down on the table, she challenged him. "What do you want? Who are you?" She was panicking even more now, trying to gather her packages up, wondering how to pay for the food she'd ordered but not received.

The gentleman leaned his head back and gestured with his hand, waving away her panic. "Please, Sarah, it's all right. I'm not here to hurt you in any way. I just want to talk with you."

"Sarah," she whispered, unable to gather the breath she needed to speak. "Who are you?"

"My name is Edward Clark. You and I met years and years ago. My sister was Kathryn Clark Warren, Jay's mother."

Marybeth let the packages drop back on to the seat around her as she stared. She remembered him now and he looked like someone she wanted to trust, but hearing him call her by a name she hadn't used in more than twenty years made her mouth go dry and her knees shake beneath the table. The waitress came up and set her plate of food in front of her, then turned to the man.

"May I bring you something, sir?"

He patted the table in front of him. "Could I have a cup of coffee and a slice of pie, please?"

Marybeth just stared at her food, unable to imagine how she could even think about eating.

"My dear, I really don't want to frighten you. I'm an old man, there's nothing threatening about me at all. Could I tell you a story and then let you decide what you think of me?"

Marybeth rested her hands in her lap and tried to force herself to remain calm. He gestured to the children's book still in front of her.

"That was one of my nephew Daniel's favorite books when he was little. May I?" He picked it up and turned the pages. "I loved it so much whenever Kathryn would bring the boys to visit with me and my wife. We weren't able to have any children of our own you see, so we were happy to spoil hers. They were such beautiful babies. You should have seen them. Of course, then Danny got sick and nothing was ever quite the same after that."

Marybeth leaned forward, resting her hands by her plate. "I knew Daniel. I used to volunteer in his classroom in high school. That's how I ended up in special education, actually. He was very sweet."

Edward drew an old-fashioned handkerchief from his pocket and rubbed it in his hands. "I remember you telling me that. Yes, he was a very kind boy. We hated to lose him so young." He wasn't crying, but Marybeth could see the emotion moving across his face.

He pocketed the handkerchief as the waitress returned with his order. "Please eat something, Sarah. I didn't mean to interfere with your meal."

She felt herself relaxing in spite of the bewildering circumstances and picked up her fork to eat. "Tell me more."

Edward sipped at his coffee and tasted the pie before going on. "My sister, Kathryn, was a lovely gal, but I'm afraid she went from living under my father's thumb to living under her husband's. She didn't want for anything, I know, but it never seemed like a truly wholesome place to live and raise a family, if you know what I mean. There were always rumors."

Marybeth nodded as she ate. "I heard the rumors too, growing up."

"But you didn't listen to them, did you?"

Marybeth set her fork down, distress and fear closing her throat again. She managed just a whisper. "How do you know all of this? I don't understand."

"It's important for you to know that once Kathryn passed, I kept a bit of distance from the Warren family. My heart went out to Daniel, so I contributed regularly to a fund for his care but once he was gone, I never really saw a lot of Jay."

He raised a forkful of pie as he gestured toward her. "But many years ago, my friend who worked at Penn State told me about a young woman that he had in class, a wonderful student, I might add, who was struggling at school under odd circumstances. He knew my nephew Jay and had seen them together so he took some steps to look into the situation."

Marybeth lowered her head, embarrassed even after so many years. She looked up finally and saw nothing but kindness on the older man's face. "I had to leave, I had no choice," she whispered.

"No one is judging you, not then, and certainly not now. "

"So why are you here? What is going on?"

"Have you ever heard of Clark Cleaners?"

"Sure, they're all over the place."

"Well, I'm Clark, or what's left of the Clarks. You might say that I have resources. I lost track of you and your baby when you went into hiding. Since the plane crash, I've been more and more curious about you."

"You know about the baby?" She looked up sharply. "How? And why would you care after all of this time?"

"Oh," he waved his hand in the air. "Maybe because I'm old, maybe because I don't have any children or grandchildren of my own." He waggled his head gently. "I have to be honest, over the years I grew more and more unhappy with the way I saw Jay's father living. I didn't see much of Jay but I loved my sister dearly, and she always loved her boys. The Clark family estate was set up to go to both Jay and Daniel. Once Daniel passed, a substantial fund was set up to support programs for those with special needs, the other half was supposed to go to Jay. Since the plane crash, though, I've adjusted my affairs and made your daughter the heir to Jay's portion of the estate. She's all the family I have left now." He took another sip of coffee. "I can tell you, it's a substantial amount."

Marybeth had no idea what to say. She leaned back in the booth, her glass of iced tea stopped halfway to her mouth. It was several moments before she could speak. "I'm dumbfounded, Mr. Clark."

"Oh, please call me Eddie. Do you think Miss Jacobs would be willing to meet me, so that I can tell her about all of this?"

"I don't know. I'm planning to see her tomorrow evening, so I'll certainly ask." She set down her glass and leaned back in her seat, the air rushing out of her a bit. "Wow, I had no idea what I was getting into when I started on this. I'm feeling a little over-whelmed by it all."

"Of course, I can imagine." He smiled. "My friend Charlie and I are planning to do a little sightseeing tomorrow, but I wonder if I could take you both to brunch on Sunday?"

Marybeth put the money down for their bill and a tip, then gathered her packages as she waited for Edward to rise. Together, they walked out, making their way slowly around the other diners. At the curb was the car that Marybeth had been seeing, it's front bumper dented in the center.

"This is your car?"

Beside it, holding the door open was the man she'd seen in Pittsburgh at the coffee shop, the baldhead spattered with age spots. Oversized sunglasses sat atop a bulbous nose and bushy mustache but now there was a real sense of familiarity to the man. "You were in Pittsburgh, at the coffee shop, weren't you?" She looked at Edward. "Is this your driver?"

"Oh no, this is my friend, Charlie. It's his car." He waved at the dent in the front bumper. "Uh, we had a little incident with a pole a few weeks ago, but generally we get along just fine."

"I've been seeing that car." Marybeth said. "It was starting to scare me."

"Oh, I'm so sorry, come and meet my friend. We can give you a ride to your hotel." Marybeth studied the face of the bald man and noticed something familiar once he'd removed the enormous glasses. He gave a short bow as they drew closer.

Edward began "Charlie Wright, please meet..."

Marybeth stepped forward, her hand extended. "Marybeth Rogers. I'm pleased to meet you."

The gentleman winked as he took her hand and leaned toward her. With a whisper of a voice he said, "You are as lovely as ever, Miss Dawes, and I am thrilled to know that you went on to become a teacher. I had such hopes for you."

"Professor Wright?" She pulled her hand back quickly but couldn't help but smile. He handed the seatbelt to Edward and helped him to settle in.

"At your service, my lady, at your service." He said, doffing an imaginary hat. "Can we give you a ride?"

Marybeth shook her head no, gesturing to the hotel behind her. "I'm just right here." Then she leaned down to the window to speak to Edward. "I'll try my best to get Carolyn to come to brunch on Sunday."

"Wonderful, do you know the B&O on North Charles?"

"No, but I'm sure I can find it. Will ten-thirty be all right?"

"Sounds perfect. We'll see you then. Come on Charlie, let's let this lady be on her way." Edward patted the dashboard and waved as they pulled away.

CHAPTER THIRTY-THREE

$\mathcal{B}$y four-thirty in the afternoon, Gregory was checking into the Klimpton Hotel, looking anxiously around the lobby as he signed the paperwork. He grabbed up the plastic key card and bolted for the elevator. He'd barely thrown his bag on the bed before he pulled his new phone out of his pocket. He tried calling Marybeth but it went to voicemail.

Gregory had no idea how Jay had tracked his old phone or who might be following him now. Even more frustrating was the fact that he'd forgotten what hotel Marybeth was staying in. He wanted to find Clark and try to talk to him first, but he had even less of an idea of what to say to him. Hey, talked to your psychopath of a nephew lately, you know, the one who's supposed to be dead?

That evening Gregory stationed himself in the lobby to keep watch. He grabbed a folder off a conference table near a convention room and pretended to be studying its contents. But although the lobby throbbed with tourists moving in and out, there was no sign of Edward Clark. Gregory had already tried two different desk clerks to see if they could give him a telephone number, but he'd hit a dead end there as well. The first was too busy to take more than a cursory look at the register for him, before moving on to other customers. The other had been more willing but still had not found any listing for an Edward Clark. By ten-thirty he figured the old man must have been tucked up in bed and was unlikely to go out so late.

Early the next morning he resumed his vigil, but after a restless night, he was nearly asleep when he finally caught sight of Edward leaving the lobby with another old guy. Gregory shoved the folder back into his bag and followed them out the door. Unfortunately, they were pulling away from the curb in a dented hatchback before he'd even considered the possibility that they'd be in a car. Dammit, no one drives in the city, why were these two old geezers the exception? He knew that by the time he'd brought his own car up from the storage lot, they'd be long gone. Dammit, now what, and who was the old guy with Clark? He dashed inside to the front desk where the more helpful of the two clerks was finishing up on the phone. "Excuse me, I was asking last night about Edward Clark, and I just missed him as he was leaving a minute ago. He was with another older gentleman, and he dropped his phone just outside." Gregory pulled his own new phone out and held it in the air, praying that the clerk would take the bait.

"Oh no, that must be Dr. Wright's cell phone, I can put it in an envelope here at the desk and then return it to him later."

Gregory began putting the phone back in his pocket while trying for a bemused expression on his face. "That's all right." He managed a chuckle. "I'm planning to have dinner with them this evening so I can return it then. You don't happen to know where they're off to now, do you?" The clerk looked mildly offended and Gregory decided he'd gone too far. The tone was now a much more formal one.

"I'm sorry sir, but we do not divulge that sort of information. If you'd like to leave a message, I'd be glad to see that Dr. Wright receives it."

For half a second Gregory considered writing one, something cryptic that would help him to connect without alerting the two men to the dangers involved. But he knew now that the desk clerk would read it as well, so he feigned an indifference he didn't feel and, with a dismissive wave, left the desk and headed for the elevator. There was no way he could sit in the lobby anymore, and he'd have to wait for a different clerk to come on duty before he could ask about Dr. Wright's phone number. He prayed that this clerk would be long gone before the old guys returned.

At three he risked returning to the lobby. Luckily, the desk now had two new clerks, and there was a fairly long line of tourists waiting to check in. He held his key card out in front of him as he waited behind a family of five with twin toddlers that were determined to escape their parents' clutches.

"One moment, sir," the distracted clerk acknowledged him.

Gregory went for an affable response. "No worries, I know you're all busy bees down here."

When it was his turn, he stepped up with feigned embarrassment. "I am so sorry, but I just can't seem to get my key to work. I had it in my wallet with the rest of my cards, but it's just quit working."

"I'm so sorry, sir, that does happen sometimes with these electronic cards. Let me just process a new one for you."

"Oh, thank you so much, it's Wright, Dr. Wright."

The clerk entered the information into the small device and quickly brandished a new key card, slipping it into a paper sleeve before writing the room number on it. "Ah, here you are sir, so sorry for the inconvenience. Oh, I almost forgot, if I could just see some identification please." Gregory began patting at his pockets, pretending to look for his wallet while a large group approached the desk.

"We're here for the Braden wedding," the patriarch announced with pride as the rest of the extended family began crowding forward. The clerk looked impatiently as Gregory continued searching his pockets before waving him off and turning to the big group.

"Welcome to Baltimore, Mr. Braden. Let's get everyone settled in, shall we?"

Gregory was on the elevator within seconds. He listened for a moment, then let himself into the room quietly. He heard nothing, so he eased the door shut and flipped the latch behind him just in case. He hated this. It made his skin crawl to be looking through their things, checking in drawers. He felt like a criminal, not a detective. Finally, on the far nightstand he spotted a half sheet from a hotel notepad. *Sarah, Hampton Inn,* but that had been crossed out and a big question mark was written beside it.

He had no idea what it meant, but at least it was a place to start. He slipped back out the door. The streets were busy, but it was a short cab ride over to the Hampton. He handed the driver a wilted twenty and headed to the main desk. It was deserted, but before long, a young woman arrived with an armful of flowers and set them down behind her on a desk. She turned. "Good afternoon. Are you checking in with us?"

It didn't take long to determine that the Hampton was crossed out because she wasn't staying there. His body sagged, there were so many more hotels he'd have to check. He continued to try her phone but was greeted with the voice mail message each time. Why didn't she have her phone turned on? He used his laptop to search hotels and make calls as he watched the sidewalk empty and fill over and over. He'd had no luck, the sun was going down and he'd started to lose his train of thought. He was trying to decide what to do next when he heard a distinctive click and felt a ring of metal just behind his right ear. He looked up at what had to be at least two hundred fifty pounds of Pittsburgh muscle and felt his stomach clench.

"Tony."

Thank God he hadn't found her.

CHAPTER THIRTY-FOUR

*O*nce she was back in her hotel room, Marybeth dumped the various packages on the bed and collapsed into the nearby chair. "Good lord, what have I started?" She was so relieved to know the story behind the car that had been following her that she felt rather foolish. At any rate, she'd had about enough for one day and decided on a long bath before falling into bed.

The next morning, she wasn't sure what to think. She was excited at the prospect of seeing Carolyn again and guilt-ridden for not having called Ken back. She felt as if she was on some sort of emotional tilt-a-whirl, waiting for everything to right itself. She missed home, a lot.

She knew that was underneath most of what she felt. She missed Ken and her boys. She missed her own bed and her own shower. She wanted to do something simple like get up and go down to her kitchen and make a cup of coffee. She and Ken had rarely spent time apart, she'd taken a few long weekend trips with her girlfriends or gone to a conference, and Ken had gone on a few golf trips, but he rarely traveled for business, and they'd never been apart for this long. How in the world was she going to explain this, and what would he think of her once she had? Suddenly she could picture him at their kitchen table eating his breakfast alone, looking around at the familiar walls, and she ached to be there with him.

The telephone didn't feel like the best choice for breaking all of this news to him so she'd left it turned off. She'd always loved to write letters, she'd written Ken's grandmother for years before she passed away. Maybe writing everything down was the best step to take first. Perhaps it would help her to understand it all as well as explain it to Ken. She dashed down to the coffee shop in the lobby and jogged across the street to an office supply center before returning to her room. She settled down at the desk in her room with her coffee and a fresh pad of notepaper and started writing. It was old fashioned, but there was something comforting in the task.

"Dear Ken, let me start all of this by telling you again how much I love you."

An hour and a half later, she folded the pages into one of the envelopes provided by the hotel. It wasn't perfect, the waste basket was nearly full with the attempts she'd rejected, but in the end, she'd settled on a simple explanation of the time before they met and her recent days of discovery. She hoped it would be enough. They'd both had partners before they got together, so she hadn't hidden that, but she knew there was a huge world between what had happened and what she'd told him about. Marybeth was well aware that she hadn't had a choice in the beginning, but she regretted all of the silence since then and wondered if it would be too much for him. Would he be able to forgive her for the years of lies and welcome her back to their life together? She'd paid such a high price letting Carolyn go, she hated to think that finding her daughter would cost her all that she had gained since then.

She placed the letter in her suitcase then forced herself to put it all aside and get ready to go to the game. She took her time showering and putting on a little makeup. She didn't care if she got there too early. She'd get a cab and be waiting at the will-call window when Carolyn arrived.

* * *

THE CROWD at the stadium was a little bit more than she was prepared for but she found her way to the window and then caught sight of Carolyn. Marybeth noticed her more casual attire, a brightly colored USA jersey and ball cap. Carolyn motioned for Marybeth to follow her and they met at the ramp to the gate. Marybeth was so excited she wanted to grab her in a bear hug but she refrained, and settled for walking along beside her to the concession stand.

"So what would you like? I think the choices are hot dog or nachos, not a huge selection." Marybeth was relieved to hear the light tone in her voice.

"Hot dog for me, please. I think I'd end up wearing half of the nachos, I'm afraid."

"Good choice." Carolyn beamed and ordered two hot dogs with lemonade. Once her order was filled, she handed the hot dog, chips and one of the drinks to Carolyn. She spoke quietly. "I didn't think a beer would feel right, I'm afraid. Is that okay with you?

"Lemonade is just fine with me. I feel strange enough already, I don't need anything more."

"I know just what you mean." Carolyn smiled back at her before leading them up to their seats.

The Outlaws section was filling slowly so they had a little bit of quiet as they ate their dinner. They laughed together at a few of the costumes that were beginning to appear, but Marybeth knew they were both stalling a bit. She decided to be the brave one and go first. "So, I have to ask. How are you feeling about all of this?"

Carolyn took a long sip of her drink and gazed toward the scoreboard before turning to answer. "There really isn't a good word for it, is there? Weird? Stunned? Maybe a little bit happy? It's hard to tell yet, to be honest. Is there more that you can tell me?"

"I appreciate your candor and believe it or not, I feel all of those things too. I actually met someone pretty interesting yesterday."

"Really? Who's that?" Carolyn crumpled the hot dog wrapper and tucked it away under her seat with the other trash to be picked up later.

"I'm afraid it may sound a little bit creepy, but while I was looking for you, it turns out someone else was watching me."

Carolyn looked frightened but Marybeth hastened to continue. "It's nothing scary, trust me. Yesterday I met your great uncle Edward Clark."

"I have an uncle?"

"Yep. Have you ever heard of Clark Cleaners?"

"The dry cleaning company? Sure."

"Well, Edward Clark is the owner of that company and he's your father's uncle."

Carolyn continued to look alarmed. "Didn't you say they were criminals?" She shook her head. "I don't understand."

"Different side of the family entirely. Edward Clark is really nice, I promise you. He told me that he'd always kept his distance from the Warren family. His sister Kathryn, Jay's mother, died some years ago."

"Why would he care about me, then?"

"I got the impression that he loved his sister very much. She had another son. Jay's brother Daniel caught meningitis as a baby and went through school in special needs classes. I met him in high school and it actually got me interested in special education. I got the impression that Mr. Clark kind of doted on him."

"Did something happen to him?"

"He passed away right around the time I went to college, I'm afraid. Mr. Clark says that he gives a fair amount of money to charities in his name." Marybeth stopped short of saying anything more about Clark's fortune as it didn't really feel like her place. Edward wanted to will Carolyn a lot of money. That would take time to soak in.

"I feel like my head's spinning, you know? Here I have half-brothers, a rich uncle, I can't even think."

It was becoming increasingly loud in the stands as the game prepared to start, but Marybeth asked, "Would you like to meet him? He's invited us, including PJ, to brunch on Sunday morning." Marybeth waited as Carolyn seemed to sift through the information and weigh it carefully. She hoped that since it was another public place that Carolyn would agree to come.

Finally Carolyn grinned and threw her hands in the air. "Well, why not, I guess. This all just gets weirder and weirder. Are you sure it's okay to bring PJ? He's usually good in restaurants but I can never be one hundred percent sure."

Now it was Marybeth's turn. "Of course. I can't wait to meet him."

With that, Carolyn pulled out her phone to show her a quick video of the little boy as the game and the fans erupted around them.

CHAPTER THIRTY-FIVE

*T*he beautiful chandeliers hanging over the lobby of the hotel offered a quiet contrast to the noise that accompanied the press conference. Cindy and Ray were only a few of the agents huddled around the crappy TV in the shared break room, watching. They had been getting ready to watch the soccer match when the press conference came on. There he was, Jay fucking Warren, taking off his Ray-Bans and placing them in his pocket as he withdrew a bright white handkerchief. The agents behind them were taking bets on whether or not he would pretend to cry.

"Do you believe this shit?" Ray turned to Cindy, shaking his head.

She nodded and gestured with her chin. "And look at the stack of lawyers he's got lined up."

They watched as the press conference continued. "Learning of my father's death has just been overwhelming," Jay said.

"How did you first hear about his death?"

"My doctor down in Venezuela told me about my father as soon as he felt I was strong enough to hear the news. Dr. Diaz has been attending to my needs since the plane crash." He touched at his eyes with the edge of the monogrammed cloth.

"Will there be a funeral for your father now that you're back?" another reporter yelled out.

Jay looked over his shoulder at one of the black-suited men behind him who shook his head briefly. Then he continued to speak. "Not yet, unfortunately. My father's body has not yet been released for burial. We are waiting to hear from the authorities about that. In the meantime, a memorial service is being organized for him and we will have information on that for you once the details are finalized." Jay looked at another one of the men in his group and gestured for him to step forward. "Now Dr. Diaz will answer any further questions that you may have."

A handsome, older man with dark skin and a thick black mustache stepped up to the microphone as Jay appeared to be helped away by a very large man from their group.

"Look, that's one of the Morellis, can't tell which one." Ray turned to Cindy and the two of them moved back toward her office. As they settled into the chairs Cindy began pulling up reports from news centers around the country.

"He managed to make quite a splash," she offered, skipping from one site to another.

"Do we know anything about this doctor yet? Any reports from people seeing him down there?"

"No, not yet. We've sent agents from the crash site into the city to look around but that whole team seems to be as surprised as we are. I think if they find anything it'll take a while."

Ray stood and paced in the small area behind her desk. "Why Baltimore for the press conference?"

Cindy pulled up her email and gestured toward the screen. "A guy I know from Miami says that they looked into his flight details once the cameras recognized him entering the country. Their records show he was scheduled to fly to Pittsburgh but then changed the ticket in the middle of the night."

Ray scrubbed his hands through his hair in frustration before sitting down again. "So where does that leave us? If this witness, Ms. Rogers, has broken cover, do you think she's in any danger from this guy?"

"I don't know why she would be, but it's hard to say. From what our sources in Pittsburgh say, Jay Warren is all about control. That press conference." She gestured back over her shoulder toward the break room. "That was very well orchestrated. The people, the look on his face, all of it appeared to me to be carefully calculated. Obviously, he has some kind of plan in mind. The problem is that we don't know what it is."

Ray pulled his cell phone from his pocket as he stood to answer it. "Sanchez here." He stepped away as noise burst from the break room and he struggled to hear. As the room quieted he moved back toward Cindy and continued. "I'll be right there."

"Who was that?" Cindy leaned away from her computer as Ray began thumbing through his phone for an application.

He turned the face of it to show Cindy the map route to Chambersburg. "That was Ken Rogers. He just saw his wife Marybeth on television. She's at the soccer game in Baltimore."

"Oh Lord, that does not seem good. Does it worry you that she and Jay Warren ended up in the same place. Does it mean anything?"

"No idea, but I'm going to go see the husband and find out whatever I can. I still can't tell if I think she's in any danger or not, but the fact that they're both there in Baltimore? It makes me nervous."

CHAPTER THIRTY-SIX

*C*oming out of the bathroom, Ken reached for the phone, the towel in his other hand, drying his hair. It was the first time in days that he hadn't taken the phone into the bathroom with him and now, finally, he'd missed her call. He pushed frantically at the buttons, searching for a voice mail or message of some kind, any kind. But there was nothing, just the missed call and her number. He hit redial and listened as it went straight to voice mail, her phone turned off once again. He raised his arm to slam it against the wall, then stopped himself short. God, it was infuriating. Why wouldn't she talk to him? And what was up with her going to Baltimore? Jesus, he was frustrated. It felt as if she was throwing everything away—him, their marriage, their sons, everything. He gave a hard second thought to smashing the damn phone.

* * *

Two days later, Ken closed the car door and juggled his computer bag and dinner while he unlocked the side door. At least there was a game on tonight. It had gotten hard to fill all of the hours in the empty house so he was relieved to have an activity. The men's national soccer team was playing Panama in a match that was supposed to start at 5:00. He didn't know if that meant kick-off or sports chat, but either way he was covered. He'd set it up to record.

Ken had gotten interested in soccer when his boys were little, and the interest had stuck. He'd taken classes and become their coach, then taken a back seat as they moved up to high school and club teams. He'd loved watching them play and still missed it. He'd started playing himself once they were bigger, but an injury had sidelined him. That's why he'd taken up golf. It didn't have the drive and contact that he loved about soccer, but he was trying to learn to enjoy it.

Nowadays the only soccer he experienced was vicariously. He watched a variety of teams but didn't follow any in particular. The exception was the US teams, both men and women. He tried to see all of those matches. Even Marybeth had gotten interested in them, and together they'd travelled to watch a few matches. The memory grabbed at him, and once again he had to take that thought and the anger that came with it and tuck it down out of sight as he turned on the set. Tonight they were playing Panama, and the US was expected to win.

With his dinner on the table beside him, if you could call an overstuffed sandwich and squashed bag of potato chips dinner, Ken settled into his chair. He half closed his eyes when the real time coverage came on since that would spoil his enjoyment of the recording. But there was nothing to worry about. The national anthem was just finishing so his timing had been perfect. He grabbed a huge bite of his sandwich and then pulled up the soccer site on his laptop. He'd stumbled across this website one night when he was trying to look for Marybeth and had quickly gotten addicted. He enjoyed the expert commentary, but even more, he loved it when the posters went after each other, praising their own teams, destroying the others. There was an entire thread devoted to the men's national team, and that was his favorite one to read. He logged on and found that the posters were already at it.

He jumped in his seat, nearly dropping his sandwich when the first goal was scored. The camera panned the crowd, focusing in on the group of fans called the American Outlaws. He knew that a number of these fans posted on the website so it was fun looking at the wild group, their faces painted with bright colors. The camera focused in on one enormous guy who was draped in a flag, his huge belly painted in red, white and blue stripes, screaming his head off. Suddenly, he dropped to his seat, and Ken wondered if he'd had a heart attack. As he went down, two women came into view behind him. He thought he felt his own heart stop. The one on the left looked exactly like Marybeth had when he first met her in college. The other woman looked toward the camera so briefly that he couldn't even be sure he'd seen her.

"What the fuck?" he screamed. "The control, where's the goddamn control?" He found it, finally, wedged under his leg, then bobbled it trying to stop and rewind. He reversed the video back to the goal, then slowed it down to frame by frame as he watched the camera pan the crowd again. There he was, Mr. Heart Attack, and then boom, he's down and there they are. He had no idea who the lookalike was, but the woman on the right was definitely Marybeth. He even recognized her shirt. It looked like they were seated in a row just behind the Outlaws group, not really a part of it, although it was clear that the enthusiasm was contagious. He froze the recording on the clearest image, the nanosecond that she had looked in the direction of the camera.

"I'll be damned. She left me to watch soccer? Goddamn it, I love soccer. She didn't think I'd want to see a game with her? This makes no sense." He set the sandwich and computer aside and just stared at the screen. Where was the game being played, he wondered suddenly? He grabbed the computer and looked at the thread he'd been reading. Baltimore, well damn, Marybeth had said she was going to Baltimore. He looked at the screen again and noticed that one of the fans to their left appeared to be on his phone. The website! Maybe someone from the website was at the game now.

He'd just started typing when he remembered the detective's card. He got up and went searching, then located it finally next to the phone in the kitchen. He punched in the numbers, wondering if anyone would answer in the evening but it was picked up quickly.

"Sanchez here."

"Mr. Sanchez, this is Ken Rogers in Chambersburg, you were here the other day about my wife."

"Yes, have you heard from her?"

"No, well I talked to her briefly one day and then she called and hung up on Thursday, but I couldn't get back through to her. Listen, she's at the soccer game in Baltimore."

"Really, how do you know?"

"She told me she was heading to Baltimore. I didn't know exactly where, but just now, she was on television. She was in the crowd."

Ken was surprised that rather than talking on the telephone, the detective had insisted on coming. There was a tone to his voice now that Ken hadn't noticed before, and he found his old fears returning to him. What in the world could she be involved in? Was she in danger? If only he'd picked up his phone when she called on Thursday.

A few hours later, Ray Sanchez arrived at the house. The doorbell took Ken by surprise and sent an unexpected chill down his back. He'd gotten so used to his kids and their friends all texting when they arrived, he'd forgotten it even worked. He opened the door and ushered the agent in. The earlier look with the Steelers jacket and crisp khakis was gone, replaced by an old Iron City beer T-shirt and worn jeans.

"Come in, come in. I'm surprised you drove all the way down here for this," Ken started.

"Well, your wife's absence has been on my mind this week. Tell me how you know she's watching soccer."

"Sure, I was watching the game on TV, and they panned the crowd after we scored the first time. I'm positive I saw her. Come upstairs, I have it recorded." The agent followed Ken up the stairs, both of them taking the steps two at a time. A screen saver clicked off, and an image on the set was frozen. "I was watching the soccer game and they panned the crowd. Look at this."

Ken backed the recording up to just after the goal and stopped it first on the young woman beside Marybeth. "I have no idea who that is, but I gotta tell you, she looks just like my wife did when I met her back in college." He moved the image forward a few frames until Marybeth was centered in the screen. "That's her. That's my wife." He turned toward the agent, gesturing wildly with the remote. "Can you tell me why in the hell my wife is in Baltimore at a damned soccer game?"

The agent took the remote from him and set it down on the table. "I think we'd better go back downstairs and talk. There's a possibility your wife might be in some danger, Mr. Rogers."

"Danger? What are you talking about? Come on downstairs."

In the kitchen Ken pushed a stack of crusted plates aside and got the coffee started, then sat down at the table across from the agent. He was picturing the scene the day she left, the look on her face. Ken thought it was just determination that he'd seen, but maybe there had been more going on than he realized. He pushed a shaggy bit of hair off his forehead and then leaned on the table. "Maybe here's the first question you can answer for me. It's been bugging the hell out of me since she left. A bunch of our friends and I got in the habit of calling her June or Junie. It started with a joke at someone's cookout a few years ago, and it just stuck. When she was leaving, Marybeth told me to quit calling her that, that she had "chosen" her name and wanted me to use it. What does that mean, she chose it?"

When the machine beeped Ken got up and poured the coffee into two cups, then set the carafe on the table, and settled back down across from the agent. Sanchez spun his cup slowly once, twice, then picked it up and took a sip. It looked to Ken as though he was coming to some kind of decision and he felt his knee bouncing with the tension.

Finally, the agent set the cup down and leaned forward. "Well, I don't know whether it's right or not, but since she seems to have broken cover I'm going to do the same thing. Until she left here, your wife was in witness protection. She did, in fact, pick the name Marybeth when we put her into hiding."

Ken sucked in a breath and leaned back quickly. "Witness protection, are you kidding me? That's crazy, it sounds like something on TV. We're just ordinary people here. She's a school teacher for Christ's sake."

"I know it's hard to believe, but it's true. Your wife started college at Penn State and while she was there, she was dating a particularly dangerous man. The FBI was building a court case against him and his family, and your wife was expected to testify about his whereabouts on half a dozen occasions. Her testimony would have broken a number of his key alibis. Unfortunately, witnesses started to disappear and the court case fell apart. When men came nosing around your wife's apartment looking to tie up loose ends, the agent in charge felt that your wife and her baby were in serious danger. The baby was put up for adoption and your wife was placed in witness protection."

Ken jumped up, his chair crashing into the counter behind him. "A baby? She had a baby, wait, that woman next to her in the stands. She must be Marybeth's. That must be who she was looking for." His mind reeled as so many images from their marriage shuffled themselves and fell, scattered into a new, unfamiliar order. His stomach felt like he'd just hit the bottom floor in a bad elevator and he was struggling to breathe. He didn't know what to say, just stared at the man sitting across from him.

"I think that young woman was the research your wife was talking about."

Ken shook his head. "I don't get it, that woman's an adult. After all this time, why go looking for her now? And why do you say Marybeth's in danger?"

"Do you recognize the name Jay Warren?"

Ken straightened the chair back up and slammed his hands on the table. "My God, of course I know that name. He's a crook, his whole family are crooks. Wait, wait, something happened."

"You're right. A huge case against both the father and the son was getting ready to go to court when they were killed in a plane crash in South America."

"I knew I'd heard something. So, with them dead, Marybeth felt safe enough to go looking for her daughter, is that what you're saying?"

"Exactly."

"So, why is she in danger if they're both dead?"

"That's the issue. Jay Warren isn't dead. He just gave a press conference," he paused and looked at the man with concern. "In Baltimore."

CHAPTER THIRTY-SEVEN

*S*unday morning, Marybeth felt better than she had in several days. She'd had a great time at the game with Carolyn. The team had won, so that was good, and the American Outlaws were a hoot to sit near. But mostly she had enjoyed being in Carolyn's company. They'd both had their phones out trading photographs and baby stories until Marybeth almost felt like she knew little PJ. Now they were coming to breakfast, and she couldn't wait to meet him.

The B&O was a beautiful restaurant filled with dark wood and wrought iron furniture, with soft track lighting and big windows scattered throughout. Edward had made a reservation so she settled in at their quiet booth to wait.

In just a few minutes, the hostess was leading both men back to the table. With a little bit of effort the two of them managed to scoot into the long bench seat across from her. Their faces were as bright and open as she remembered. "How are you two this morning?"

Dr. Wright spoke first. "We always move a little slowly in the morning but we're good. We had a great day looking around the city yesterday, didn't we Eddie?"

"Oh yes, the harbor is looking so beautiful these days, quite different from the last time we were here, wouldn't you say?" He looked toward his friend.

Dr. Wright laughed. "I think you're forgetting just how long ago that was." He turned toward Marybeth. "As young men, we came here with our wives as part of a sailing trip. But the entire waterfront has been redone since then. It's really beautiful."

Edward spoke up then. "But that's enough chit-chat about us. How are you doing, my dear?"

"I'm great. Carolyn and I went to the big soccer game last night and had a terrific time." Just then, she spotted Carolyn pushing a stroller with a small, dark haired boy in it following the hostess to their table. "Here they are."

When she reached the table Carolyn put her hand out, stopping the men from their awkward struggle to stand while seated in the booth. "Oh don't get up, you're fine there. Good morning."

Marybeth slipped out of the seat to stand beside her daughter as she introduced the gentlemen. "Carolyn, this is Mr. Edward Clark and his friend Dr. Charles Wright from Penn State."

Both men laughed and Edward spoke quickly. "Oh my goodness, so formal sounding. Please, we're just Charlie and Eddie and we are so pleased to meet you Carolyn."

Carolyn said, "Okay then, Charlie and Eddie it is."

Marybeth couldn't take her eyes off of PJ as the little boy happily peered back at her. Carolyn began unbuckling the complicated harness. "This is my son Phillip but I call him PJ." She turned toward Marybeth as the waitress moved toward them with a high chair. "Would you like to hold him while I get this stroller out of the way?"

Marybeth reached out without hesitating. He snuggled against her for a second, his head against her cheek as she hugged him gently. She slipped back into the booth then and rested his bottom on the edge of the table so that she could see him better. Charles reached over to tickle a bit of his curling hair as Edward looked on, a broad smile across his face. PJ giggled suddenly and Marybeth didn't think she'd seen anything cuter since her boys were little. She smiled over his head as Carolyn brought the high chair closer. Marybeth kissed his cheek before handing him over to get settled into his seat.

He had grabbed up one of the shiny spoons and was waving it around before whacking it soundly on the tray. Carolyn fished in her oversized diaper bag, traded him some softer toys for the spoon and then settled into the seat beside Marybeth.

Edward spoke up first. "Carolyn, I am so glad you agreed to come today. I have to say, I know you look like Marybeth here," he gestured across the table. "But I also see my sister Kathryn in you. She would have loved to meet you and this little boy."

"I still haven't gotten my head around all of this yet. This has been a crazy few days."

Marybeth laughed as well. "I'm with you there. I had no idea what I was getting into when I started this search." She beamed at her daughter and grandson. "But I'm so glad that I did."

Charles spoke up next. "So Marybeth tells us you're a teacher as well, and you went to Penn State?"

The conversation paused as they all ordered breakfast, then resumed once the last coffee cup had been filled. "That's right. I teach at the Children's Center here in the city. It's an early childhood program that's run in cooperation with the city kindergartens. I'm just finishing my third year with them."

Charles gestured toward Marybeth. "I was her teacher years ago. Now I'm a bit sorry that I retired before you came along."

"Don't listen to him," Edward interjected. "He loves being retired."

"Are you retired as well?" Carolyn asked.

Edward spread his hand flat and wiggled it from side to side. "More or less. I own a dry cleaning business and I have managers for everything now but I still keep my eye on things." He cleared his throat and took a slightly more serious tone. "It's actually an important part of why I wanted to meet you, my dear. I'm getting older now and I'm putting my affairs in order." He paused and Marybeth realized she was holding her breath. "I've just made arrangements to settle the larger portion of my estate on you. I want Clark Cleaners to remain in the family and you and your son are all that's left of my family."

Marybeth watched as the color seemed to drain from Carolyn's face and she dropped her hands to her sides. The young woman looked around the table as if studying each face, trying to understand what sort or bizarre scene she had fallen into. Then she settled her gaze on Marybeth. "Did you know about all of this?"

Marybeth rested her hand on Carolyn's shoulder. "No, I didn't. I just wanted to meet my daughter. I only learned of this the other day."

CHAPTER THIRTY-EIGHT

*G*reg's mouth had stopped bleeding but his head was still throbbing. He remembered that Tony had picked him up late in the day, but he had a sick feeling that hours had passed since he'd been brought here, wherever here was. He studied the space around him but still had no idea where he might be. There was a strong smell of salt water and diesel in the air. The concrete floor was covered with old oil spots, so he assumed he was at the port somewhere, but that was the only information he had to go on.

In addition to having a massive headache, his arms were cramped from being handcuffed to the bench he was on. His legs seemed to be all right, but so far, they hadn't been of any use in breaking free. The bench was welded to the floor, the cuffs hooked through the back of its base. He had tried kicking at the Pittsburgh muscle man, but knew Tony hadn't even felt it. Two blows to the midsection, a quick backhand to his mouth, and then something hard coming from behind had stopped Greg's kicking and left him unconscious.

He had awakened to the smell of salami and ripe cheese, then spotted his assailant in the corner eating an enormous sandwich.

Gregory feigned sleep until the man settled in to snoring after his meal. Damn it, Greg told himself, he had to be smart here, strength wasn't going to be of any use, and he worried about the possibility that Marybeth's safety might be at stake. If only his head would stop pounding so that he could think. He tried shaking it for a second to clear it, but that only made the throbbing worse. A concussion for sure, some loose teeth, he took a careful inventory and stood up slowly.

Suddenly the metal door across from him swung open and a blast of bright sunlight nearly blinded him. Damn, Greg thought, it was the next day. What could have happened in the time he was out? A new man, tall but not as large as his captor, appeared in silhouette, and the door banged shut just as quickly as it had opened.

He was in front of Greg in seconds and plowed a fist into his gut before he'd even spoken a word. "Why the fuck did you tell me the old man was in Pittsburgh, you lying bastard?"

Gregory was bent double, trying to suck air back into his lungs as he scrambled to think of what to say. He continued to gasp until he saw Jay wheeling back to strike again. This time the fist hit him across the mouth, and his split lip began bleeding again.

"I was going by the tracker," Greg finally answered, sucking in air before spitting out a loose tooth. "You were dead. I wasn't watching the old man anymore." He looked up but then quickly dropped his gaze back down, noticing the blood that had splattered on the man's perfect shoes. He didn't know why, but he felt vaguely pleased to see it. He risked looking up again and noticed the sickly familiar face that now accompanied the hated voice. "So, why aren't you dead?"

Jay laughed, a deep bark that sounded more like classic seal than a man. "I wasn't dead, you idiot." He kicked Greg's feet out from under him with a sudden move, and then laughed again as Greg fell and then tried to right himself. "I was just buying myself a little time." He smiled with a look that Greg had seen all too often on the society pages back in Pittsburgh. It seemed so fake, he never could figure out why the reporters hadn't seen through it.

Jay dropped down onto the bench beside him and pulled the sleeves of his shirt neatly over each wrist. "What's the matter, disappointed? Figured you were finally free of me?" He brought his face down right in front of Greg. "You little shit, don't you know by now, you're never going to be free of me? I'm going to be in charge of everything now. The FBI will focus their little investigation on my father, leaving me free to take over operations." Greg tried to reel back, but Jay grabbed him by the shirt collar and held him even closer. "How's your apartment, by the way? Warm enough for you?"

The muscle man, who'd come to attention in the corner, uttered a high-pitched, almost girly sound. "Burned nice, didn't it?" From the corner of his eye, Greg saw the knowing look on the man's face and knew he'd been right about them torching his place.

Jay shoved Greg back against the bench and then turned to the man in the corner. "Where are we? What's this private dick been doing with himself?"

The muscle moved back to the chair and pulled a dark leather satchel up onto the table, then left the room. Gregory's heart stopped. Of course they had his damn computer.

Jay took the computer out of the bag and opened it on the table before turning to taunt him further. "How sweet, a picture of Pittsburgh's skyline as your screen saver. That's just sad, Hanes, really sad. What, no women in your life? Oh wait, I forgot, you and that shit accountant, Arnie, weren't into girls, now were you?" Gregory could see the spittle fly as Jay spat out the name. "What's your password, asshole, something sweet like 'the Penguins rock' maybe?"

Jay began typing. "Aw, access denied, poor me." He reached

into the bag's outer pocket then, drew out a familiar blue USB drive and plugged it into the side of the unit. He leered at Greg again. "You think you're the only one who knows this trick, like you're some sort of fucking secret agent? Get over yourself, Hanes." From his bench Gregory could see the laptop screen change, icons nearly covering the screen. "Geez, you never heard of a fucking folder? What kind of a detective are you?"

Well, Gregory thought, I may be lazy about the icons, but at least I number them rather than give them revealing names. Good luck hunting through all of that mess, he thought, and almost relaxed for a moment. Then Jay looked up as the big man re-entered the room. Jay stood and smoothed out his jacket, then gestured at the muscle man.

"I don't have time for this. Work on him until he tells you what he's been doing and why the hell he's in Baltimore. I'll be back."

"Sure thing, boss." The big man removed his windbreaker and laid it carefully across the back of his chair before facing Gregory, his white T-shirt glowing in the poor light of the room.

* * *

When Gregory came to again, the door was open, and the room was nearly black. A light glowed at the end of the long hall, but he could see almost nothing in the room. He tried to raise his head, but nausea swept over him, and he lowered it quickly before he threw up or passed out again. Instead, he managed to slide his legs up onto the bench and lay almost flat, his arms now numb behind him. As his eyes adjusted he could see the outline of the table and chair, but both were empty. He listened, something seemed to be going on in another room. He heard the big man's girly laugh and realized a card game was in progress. It sounded as though the muscleman was winning.

Greg knew they'd gotten everything from him, and his first

thought was really a prayer. Please God, let her be okay, don't let my fuck-ups hurt her.

When he'd gotten the most recent file open, Jay had yelled, his face dark red with rage. "She had a kid and you never told me?" He'd punched Greg hard across the face. Then Tony, the muscle man had joined in and the blows had come harder and faster after that.

The room around him now was quiet as Gregory blinked, forcing himself to try to wake up. He couldn't tell how much time had passed but the door was still ajar and what seemed like early morning light was streaming in. He shifted and the pain reignited, almost taking him under again. He forced himself to pause and stay calm as a new thought registered, surprise that he was still alive. He struggled to think why it might be, and wondered if it would make things better or worse. What more was Jay going to demand from him?

Finally, the door slammed open once again and the noise reverberated inside Greg's pounding head. "On your feet, let's go." Jay barked and Tony unfastened the handcuffs, grabbed him by his sore shoulder and half marched, half dragged him to the car. "They're at a restaurant on the harbor. We're finishing this, now."

CHAPTER THIRTY-NINE

*R*ay Sanchez waited while Ken left rather vague messages on his sons' phones and then they took off. They arrived in Baltimore long after midnight but by 8:30 the next morning, Ken had already been pacing around Ray's hotel room long enough for the agent to start re-thinking his plan. Sanchez had been on the phone to Cindy and was waiting for files to come through to his computer. He turned to Ken. "Look, I'll let you know as soon as I get something. Why don't you go and pick us up some coffee or something from downstairs?"

Ken pocketed the room key off the dresser and left.

A few minutes later, the information began to load. Ken's phone records came through first, and Ray couldn't find anything unusual. The most recent call from his wife's phone was logged, although it hadn't connected. His wife's phone records indicated it wasn't being used often, but the Pittsburgh number he'd seen earlier had continued to appear regularly, the earliest entry before she left her home. There were a few recent calls to the Baltimore area, but nothing since Thursday. He had begun tracing the different numbers when a larger file came through.

Cindy, God bless her, had gotten someone to release the original Sarah Dawes FBI file, and she'd scanned it for him. He opened the file and began paging through it. The FBI had been interviewing her as the original court case was building, and they'd broken a number of Jay's alibis based on her testimony. Then his breath caught, as a series of stark, black and white photos loaded slowly. In the first, the pretty young woman he'd seen in the earlier photo was sitting behind what looked like a library counter. Her left arm seemed to be in a cast and sling and her face looked haggard. Her hair was long and messy, but didn't quite cover the bruise along her neckline. The room's door opened, and before he could close the screen, Ken was behind him staring at the picture. He put the agent's coffee and pastry on the table and dropped onto the bed beside the desk.

"That's her, that's Marybeth My God, what happened to her?"

Ray gave up any attempt at hiding it, turning the laptop so that Ken could see it clearly.

"Is that why she was put in witness protection?"

Ray had read through enough of the case to know that the injuries preceded the court case. "To be honest with you, no, this happened before the FBI got involved. It was never reported as such, but the clinic at school was suspicious, they thought it looked like domestic violence."

Ray heard Ken's breath catch in his throat. "That son of a bitch hit her?"

Ray didn't answer, unsure of how to meet Ken's growing anger. A second series of photographs began to load, apparently taken in a hospital room. The young woman was wearing just a hospital gown and it was pulled aside in a succession of photos that documented more serious injuries. There was a wide bandage across her forehead, what looked like a two or three inch gash across her shoulder blades and masses of dark bruises that surrounded her lower back and swollen abdomen. Ray suspected that this was the assault that Sam Duffy had told him about, when Jay had tried to kill Marybeth and her unborn child.

Stalling, Ray picked up the coffee cup and blew across the top, unsure of what he could possibly say to this deeply shaken man.

Ken stared at the first photograph and pointed at the dark line under her left eye. "She has just a thin, white scar now she said she'd gotten from a fall."

Ray thought that Ken seemed to sag as he studied her face at the library desk. He pictured the quiet, suburban home they shared and thought that the man had probably never seen her like that, never imagined that she even could look like that. Then as the series from the hospital loaded, he thought Ken had stopped breathing all together. Ray sensed that the anger and frustration that he had been directing at his wife was now shattered.

Ken seemed to slump on the bed in confusion. "My God," was all he could get out. The two of them sat in silence for several minutes. Finally, Ken straightened, took a deep breath and looked at the agent. "So, what's the latest on this fucker who hit her? I'm pretty sure I could take him out myself right about now."

Ray's phone rang and he answered it quickly. "I've got the file, Cindy, anything new?"

"Clark and his friend are registered at the Klimpton Hotel on North Charles Street. The friend's name is Dr. Charles Wright, a retired Penn State professor."

"Got it, Cindy, thanks. I'm heading over there now. Keep me posted."

"Will do." She paused then added, "Keep safe, Ray. Those Warrens are damned dangerous."

He clicked off the phone and turned to Ken who was still sitting, dazed, on the edge of the bed. He looked up. "What was that?"

"C'mon, I'll tell you on the way. We need to go and talk to Jay Warren's uncle and a retired Penn State professor."

Ken didn't ask any questions, just tossed the pastry in the trash and carried his coffee cup out the door.

* * *

AT THE KLIMPTON, Ray showed his badge to the young woman working the desk and asked about Dr. Charles Wright.

"Yes, they're registered here. Let me ring the room." As they waited, Ray's eye caught on a television hanging across the lobby. Its sound was muted but he could see it was broadcasting a news report. The familiar photograph of the plane was being paired with a recent photograph of Jay Warren. Then a video loop from the press conference began. Ray cringed inside but was careful to keep Ken Rogers facing away from the screen. The small group waited but there was no response. Just then, a middle-aged man wearing the uniform of the hotel emerged from the dining area and the young woman turned to him. "Mr. Pierce, this gentleman is from the FBI. He'd like to speak with Mr. Clark and Dr. Wright."

"There was no answer in the room?"

"No, sir." The young woman shook her head.

The man touched his hand to his temple. "Let me think. Friday morning they had me make a reservation for them at the B&O for brunch today." He looked at his watch. "I believe it was for ten-thirty." He looked up and gestured toward the front door. "It's just up on Charles, not far."

"Thank you," Ray responded and nodded at Ken to follow him. As they walked, a siren sounded not far from where they were. They looked at each other questioningly and then quickened their steps.

CHAPTER FORTY

*S*taring at the image on the screen, Jimmy tapped his foot impatiently as he waited for his brother Grant to answer the phone. Finally, he heard him pick up. "Geez, man, why don't you answer your damn phone?"

"What the hell? I had it on do-not-disturb."

"It's eleven o'clock."

"What are you, the fucking phone police? We were out late. Why are you busting my balls on a Sunday morning?"

"Did you get a voicemail from Dad?"

"I don't know, I never listen to that shit. Why can't he just text like everyone else? Even Mom learned how to text." He kept his voice low, and Jimmy figured he was trying not to wake someone.

"Something's wrong, Grant, you gotta get over here to the house. And listen to the damn message on your way over."

* * *

WITHIN TEN MINUTES Grant was at the house, yelling for his

brother as he walked in. "What's going on? Why'd you drag me over here?"

Jimmy came barreling down the stairs. "Did you listen to it?"

"Uh, no. I promised Amy I wouldn't mess with my phone while I'm driving."

"Seriously?" Jimmy started to laugh, but then got a better look at his brother's face and decided to let it go. "Whatever, okay, listen to it now, put it on speaker." Grant pushed the buttons, and then held it in front of him.

"Uh, hi Grant, this is Dad, guess you can tell that from the phone. Okay, uh, so here's the thing. I found your mom in Baltimore, and I'm on my way there now. Nothing to worry about, see you soon."

Grant looked at his brother. "Do we care if he goes to Baltimore?"

"It's not just that. When I got here, there were two coffee cups on the kitchen table."

"So, he had company? I still don't get it."

"I went upstairs to borrow a red T-shirt from him, and the TV was still on." He started back up the stairs, Grant following more slowly. "You gotta see this." One side of the upstairs held their mother and father's bedroom, while the other half held a seating area and the TV. Currently the screen saver was showcasing animals, but when Jimmy hit the button on the remote, the still image came to life. Grant walked over to stand beside his brother, stared at the TV, then looked back at him.

"That's Mom. What is this?" He took the remote and rewound the recording a small bit. Together they watched as the US scored and the American Outlaw cheering section came into view. Grant looked over at Jimmy. "Did you see the game? It was fantastic."

"Yeah, I was watching with some guys from the soccer team over at Joey's."

Grant stilled the screen as the young woman beside their mother came into view. "Who's that? She looks really familiar," he advanced it frame by frame and watched as his mother appeared next to her. Then he reversed it and watched for a second time. He glanced over at the photos on the top of the bookshelf, then went over and picked up the one taken at his parents' wedding. He held it up next to the TV as he and Jimmy took a step closer.

"Damn, she looks just like a young mom, she's got to be some kind of relative."

"I've never met her. Didn't Dad say something about Mom helping a sick relative down in Virginia? She doesn't look sick, and that sure isn't Virginia. Damn, I would love to have been at that game. She's sitting with the Outlaws, how is that even possible?"

The two of them sat down in the easy chairs that faced the TV. They could tell that their dad had been on his own for a while. There were clothes piled on the bench under the window, and a crushed sandwich wrapper was balled up on the table between the seats. "Let's hear your message. Is it the same?"

"Yeah, pretty much." He switched it on.

"Hi, Jimmy. I found that pair of jeans you were looking for, sorry I got them in my basket by mistake. I'll leave them on the dryer. I have to go to Baltimore for a bit. I need to go and check on something about your mom. I'll be in touch."

Grant was raking his fingers through his bed-ragged hair, making various bits stand on end. "I don't get it. In both messages, he sounds surprised that she's in Baltimore. Why wouldn't he know where she was? She's been gone for almost two weeks."

"Have you heard from her?"

"Uh, no, come to think about it," he paused. "That's weird, isn't it? She usually calls or texts or something. I feel bad I didn't notice."

"Yeah, me too. Do you think something's wrong? Should we call Dad? I don't know what to do."

Grant pulled his phone out of his pocket and entered his dad's number. It rang several times before going to voice mail. "Hi, Dad, this is Grant and Jimmy, we're a little freaked out here by your message and seeing Mom on your TV set. Please call us. We're getting worried." He hung up then looked back at Jimmy. "I don't know what else to do, do you?"

"No, I actually tried Mom's phone when you were on your way over, but it went straight to voicemail, didn't even ring. Look, I've got a game to go to if I'm going to keep my spot on the indoor team. Why don't I keep trying Mom's phone, and you keep trying Dad's. If one of us gets an answer, we'll let the other one know."

"Sounds good. Do you work tomorrow?"

"No, you?"

"No. I'm thinking, if we don't hear anything back by tonight, we may want to drive down there. It feels like something really strange may be going on." Grant turned off the set, and they headed back downstairs. They locked up and walked to the cars parked next to each other in the driveway. "Call me by five?"

"Will do."

"Hey, good luck in your game."

CHAPTER FORTY-ONE

The restaurant's meal looked beautiful, but no one seemed to notice the food. In fact, it was several minutes after Edward's announcement before the group slowly resumed their conversation and Carolyn recovered her composure. Studying her daughter, Marybeth thought that she handled herself very well given the strange circumstances. She wasn't sure she could have remained so calm.

As they were finishing the meal Carolyn looked across at her great uncle and smiled. She dabbed her mouth with the napkin before resting it on the table by her plate. "This is an awful lot to take in, but I am very happy I got to meet you."

"Do you visit Pittsburgh often?" he asked.

"PJ and I are actually planning a trip there as soon as classes end. My mother isn't well and I need to check in on her."

"Do you think you could make time to come and see the house?" Edward asked and Marybeth thought she saw Charlie stifling a laugh.

"I'd like that." Carolyn answered as she shifted in her seat. Marybeth scooted the high chair and stroller out of the way so that Carolyn could slide out with the baby. "We'll just be a minute. I want to put a clean diaper on him now in case he falls asleep on the way home." Carolyn settled PJ on one hip, the enormous diaper bag on the other and headed for the ladies' room. The waitress filled Marybeth's coffee cup one more time, then cleared the plates away.

Charles eased himself out also. "I believe I'll head that way too."

Once they were alone at the table, Marybeth saw a change come over Edward's face. "Is something wrong?"

"Marybeth, can I ask you a difficult question?"

Marybeth raised her chin a fraction but tucked her hands under her legs. She nodded rather than risk speaking.

"All those years ago." He paused. "Did my nephew hurt you?"

Marybeth pulled her hands out and rested them on the table beside her. Then she took a steadying breath. "Yes, he did. He nearly killed us both."

"I never got to meet Agent Nowicki but she and I talked on the phone just after Carolyn's birth. She didn't give me any details but I had a sense. I'm so sorry that I didn't take any steps back then." He looked at her squarely. "I feel responsible."

Marybeth cut him off. "No, I was the one who..." She paused and looked at him questioningly. "Wait, you're the one who put Jay's name on the birth certificate, aren't you? Why did you do that? It was a closed adoption. If it wasn't for that crash, neither of us would have gone looking for her or known anything about Carolyn."

Edward shrugged. "I'm not sure really, I guess it just felt like she was a part of my family and I wanted it to say that somewhere."

Just as Edward began to respond further, a deep voice spoke up behind her. "Now isn't this cozy?" Then she saw the tall man and stopped breathing entirely. His body had gone soft, but the eyes were still the same and Marybeth recognized him immediately.

"If it isn't Uncle Edward and the gold digger."

* * *

CAROLYN AND CHARLES chatted easily as they made their way toward the restrooms by the entrance. As they parted ways, Charles thought to himself how much he liked this young woman. But he could no longer suppress a chuckle at the thought of her seeing "the house" as Eddie so blithely put it. Carolyn had no more idea what she was getting ready to inherit than the man in the moon.

It was a small restroom and he didn't notice the other occupant until he was standing next to the man washing his hands. Charles glanced at the next sink and saw the bright red arc of blood swirling toward the drain. Then he looked up and saw the battered face and the torn sleeve with its own pool of blood. The fellow looked as if he could barely stand.

"Son, are you all right?" When the man raised his head completely Charles recognized the face he'd seen in the coffee shop. "Why, you're Marybeth's friend...Gregory isn't it? What's happened to you?"

Gregory shut off the water and looked at the older man. He staggered for a moment, then caught his balance by leaning on the hand dryer next to him. "Do I know you?" he struggled to say, his mouth swollen and thick sounding.

Charles shook his head as he pulled out his cell phone. "I'm calling you an ambulance." The call connected quickly and he gave the name of the restaurant but he saw the man struggling to get to the door.

"Don't, Jay'll finish my..."

"Jay who? Jay Warren? He's alive?" Charles looked at him in shock as he held the bathroom door open.

"He's alive, he's here and he's angry." Gregory spoke slowly, cupping his hand against his swollen jaw.

"He did this to you?"

Gregory steadied himself again and worked to speak clearly. "Yeah, with a buddy of his."

"But why?"

"The short version? He's angry at his uncle for changing his will. He blames me and he blames Marybeth." The faint sound of a siren was slowly growing.

"Listen, help is coming. Let's find you a chair." Charles reached to support his arm and Gregory leaned a bit until he was through the bathroom doorway.

"I'm sorry, I can't stay. She'll never forgive me." Gregory pushed off from the doorframe and staggered to the outer hallway. Charles debated going after him but then thought he'd better get this news back to Eddie. He rushed quickly back toward their table.

* * *

Jay pushed himself into the booth beside his uncle and across from Marybeth. Edward leaned back away from him in the seat, stunned by his nephew's appearance in the restaurant. "You're alive! How did you get here? What's going on?"

"Didn't you see my press conference last night? My doctor explained everything quite clearly. It was a bit of a miracle, really."

"Press conference?" Marybeth hissed out. "What are you talking about? Why aren't you dead?"

Jay smoothed the front of his jacket. "Yeah, reports of my death may be exaggerated." Then he turned toward his uncle, the flippancy gone. "Uncle, I'm not sure what this woman has been telling you, but I want you to know, after I took her to meet you years ago, all she could talk about was your fortune. I can guarantee you that whatever scheme she's got going now, money is behind it."

"I never—" Marybeth started.

"You never what?" Jay cut her off and turned again toward his uncle. "Did she happen to mention the monster mortgage that she and her husband have?" He turned to face Marybeth, an added edge to his tone. "I've been reading up on you Mrs. Rogers. Did a little bit more remodeling than you could really afford now, didn't you? I imagine that you and this supposed 'daughter' have some sort of a finder's fee agreement, is that right? A little package deal so to speak?"

Edward drew himself up to face his nephew. "Jay, you're mistaken. That is not the situation here. I…"

Jay raised his hand toward Edward, his tone now coated with a layer of condescension. "Now Uncle Edward, I'm sure you're not as familiar with these kinds of scams as I am, but we can take care of everything easily enough. We're planning a service for my father this week and I'm sure that once we get back to Pittsburgh, we can have the police look into this little plan they've devised and then the lawyers can correct everything for us."

"Stop, just stop!" Marybeth rose from her seat and stood at the end of the table where the high chair had been. "Carolyn and I never came looking for your uncle or his money. He found us, so you can just back off right now. I'm not some scared sophomore you can push around anymore."

Marybeth turned just as Charles hurried up puffing and out of breath. "I've just seen your friend Gregory. He's hurt."

"What?" Marybeth looked over his shoulder toward the front of the restaurant but saw no one she knew.

Charles was standing beside her, facing the table and gesturing toward Jay. "Eddie, he said Jay's the one who hurt him."

"What?" Edward looked up, shocked at the statement.

"Everyone sit down now, just sit." Jay's voice had tensed and risen half an octave as he struggled to control the situation. "Look, we can take care of all this."

Jay reached into his pocket as Edward tried to slide away

from him on the bench. Charles slid into the booth across from Edward but Marybeth remained where she was.

"I said, sit," Jay repeated, a new edge in his tone, his pocketed hand now resting on the table, the outline of a gun clearly visible.

Edward looked down, horrified. "What is that? What do you mean by all of this?" He gestured around him at the disturbance, the patrons turning their way and Marybeth's defiant stance.

Marybeth spoke quietly. "I'm done being afraid of you, Jay Warren. I've spent too long hiding and waiting. That's over." She held her hand out toward Edward. "We're finished here. Let's go."

Jay pivoted toward her, grabbing her arm hard and pulling the gun from his pocket, all pretense forgotten. "I said, sit. We're done when I say we're done."

Marybeth jerked her arm free and grabbed the nearest water glass, flinging the contents into his face. He reached to deflect it and the gun fired, hitting Marybeth in the shoulder. She staggered back.

At first, it felt like she'd been punched out of the way, then the pain erupted in a way she'd never experienced before. Jay looked up at her in shock just as a bright blue diaper bag came hurtling full force into the side of his head.

His head hit the table hard, the gun falling from his hand as he fell. Marybeth grabbed it and focused it on Jay as he began to rise. "Stay where you are." The gun was shaking as she clasped it in front of her, but she refused to let the pain take her to the floor as well. She spoke slowly and carefully. "You bastard, I'm not some scared college kid you can frighten that way. Sarah Dawes is gone. You killed her. My name is Marybeth Rogers, and I'm not doing another God damned thing you say."

Jay rose and was standing much more quickly than she expected. He waved his hand at her dismissively, his tone dripping with derision. "You're not going to shoot me, so quit pretending."

She could hear a siren, and she sensed the other patrons all edging away from them, but her focus never left Jay's face. What had once been so handsome had been transformed into a cruel, ugly imitation, and she felt sick looking at it. When he lunged toward her she fired and watched him fall backward onto their table. Once his body went still, everything went black.

CHAPTER FORTY-TWO

*C*arolyn retrieved her big bag and quickly pulled a clean diaper out of it to press against Marybeth's shoulder as she lay on the floor beside the table. Carolyn caught sight of several people in uniforms running into the room but she kept her focus on Marybeth and continued to apply pressure to her shoulder. Suddenly, a man with salt and pepper hair knelt beside her and cradled Marybeth's head. He looked panicked, tears in his eyes and fear washing across his face. "Junie, Marybeth, please wake up."

A young paramedic stepped forward and eased the two of them away. "I've got her," she said, opening up and pressing a clean dressing onto the shoulder before attaching a blood pressure cuff.

Carolyn stepped back, pulled some wipes out of her bag, and cleaned off her hands. Then she retrieved PJ from the family at the nearby table and thanked them for calling 911. She held PJ close for a few minutes before setting him in the stroller and pulling it up next to Charlie, who handed him a shiny spoon and reached over to pat him gently.

She could see an officer handcuffing the attacker to a gurney where the other paramedic was treating his wound. Carolyn turned and looked at the man standing beside her and was relieved that he spoke first.

"My God, you look so much like her. You're beautiful." It looked as though the man didn't know whether to hug her or shake her hand as he stood there awkwardly, his eyes returning to Marybeth's face.

Carolyn offered her hand. "I'm Carolyn Jacobs." There was the tiniest pause. "Her daughter." He was clearly puzzled but a slow smile eased her fears.

He took her hand and held it for a moment. "I'm her husband, Ken." Then they both turned as the paramedics lifted Marybeth onto the stretcher. She was stirring, and he reached for her hand, moving along with the gurney. "I'm here, Marybeth, I'm going wherever you go now, so don't even try to shake me off."

She smiled up at him. "That sounds terrific." She looked over at Carolyn then and spoke softly. "I'm sorry Carolyn, but that jackass over there is your dad. Thank you for saving us all."

"No, Marybeth, you did it. I'll make sure that Edward and Charlie are all right, and then PJ and I'll catch up with you." Ken clasped her hand again briefly and then looked over at the agent.

"I have to go."

"Of course." He leaned toward Marybeth. "I'm Ray Sanchez by the way, FBI, and I'm looking forward to talking to you." Carolyn watched as the agent leaned over the gurney and introduced himself but Marybeth's pain seemed to rise again and take her under.

CHAPTER FORTY-THREE

*K*en was surprised that the ambulance was cold, as well as loud, the jump seat under him bouncing, the siren blaring as they drove through the city. The trip was short, with Marybeth drifting in and out of consciousness. The paramedic ignored him, only speaking to her, telling her what she was doing as she started the IV and continued monitoring her pulse. On the radio, she let the ER know what was coming. "Single gunshot wound, blood loss." Ken gripped Marybeth's free hand even tighter. He could feel his phone buzzing in his pocket but ignored it, not wanting to take his eyes off her.

It was so odd, he felt almost sick to his stomach. She was his wife in every way that she had been before she left, but he couldn't change the fact that suddenly all of the pictures of their life together were altered. It was as if a camera filter had been lifted or a familiar soundtrack switched from folk to techno. Nothing felt quite the same. His head was swimming.

They arrived at the hospital, and Ken jumped down out of the way. He tried to hold onto her as they sped toward the operating room, but inside, a nurse put up her hands to stop him, the wide doors opening and shutting, swallowing the gurney with a hydraulic whoosh. "Sir, they've got her, they're doing everything they can. Please, help me get some details on her, let's get a quick medical history, so that I can inform the doctors."

Ken raked his hands through his hair and let his shoulders fall, leaning back against the wall. He wondered if he knew anything at all that might be helpful.

When he'd finished getting her registered, Ken fell into the plastic seat in the closest waiting room he could find. The television was blaring one of those stupid Tiny House shows that Marybeth loved to watch, so rather than punch the screen out, he moved to a more distant seat where he could put his back to it. His phone buzzed again, and he pulled it out, looking at the number of texts and missed calls he'd had from his boys. He hesitated, unsure what in the world he could possibly say to them. He sat there feeling bewildered for a while before slowly typing in Grant's number. He walked out to find a quiet area before connecting the call.

"Hey, Grant, how's it going?" Ken tried to make his voice sound casual but was pretty sure it wasn't working.

"Dad, what's going on? Jimmy and I are freaked out. Who was on the TV? Why was Mom at a soccer game?"

Ken rubbed his hand against his pantleg, struggling with how to sum up everything that had been going on. "It's a pretty wild story, Grant, I have to be honest. Your mom is in surgery now, so I'm waiting for them to tell me more."

"Surgery? What for?"

He paused, unsure what to say. "Uh, Grant, she was shot this morning."

"What? How?"

"It's a long story, a big story, I guess you'd say, but I'd rather she tell it to you herself."

"Dad, Jimmy and I are on our way. What hospital?"

"Mercy on Saint Paul, but you don't have—"

"We'll be there as quick as we can, Dad." Grant hung up before Ken could talk him out of it. He prayed they'd be careful driving.

An hour into the surgery Ken had gotten up to pace when he saw Agent Sanchez at the nurses' station. He waited while the agent spoke with the nurse in charge, and then walked up. Ken looked at both the nurse and the FBI agent. "Is there news?"

Agent Sanchez shook his head. "Not really, they're both still in surgery but she said that Marybeth is nearly finished."

Ken leaned in and under his breath asked, "and the rat bastard that did this?" Agent Sanchez took Ken by the arm and led the two of them back down the hall to the small waiting room. "They're still working on him but the prognosis is good."

"So she didn't kill him? I wish she had."

Agent Sanchez spoke in very measured tones. "No, you don't. It would be a hard thing to have on her conscience, believe me."

Ken sagged back against the hard, plastic sofa. "I guess you're right about that. Did you find out anything more about what happened at the restaurant?"

"I did." He flipped open a small notebook. "Once the police finished taking her statement, I was able to speak with Carolyn Jacobs, that's Marybeth's daughter. Apparently she had her son in the ladies' room when Jay got there. She came out of the bathroom and saw the disturbance at the table. She said that from where she was, she could tell that the man was threatening Marybeth. She handed her son to a family at a nearby table and asked them to call 911. The gun went off just as she got to the table, and she walloped Warren in the head with her big diaper bag."

"Really?"

"Yep, it knocked the gun loose and Marybeth picked it up. Apparently, Warren was taunting her, saying she'd never shoot it and then lunged at her. That's when she fired, hit him in the chest." He flipped the notebook shut. "Carolyn said after that, the two of them fell over in opposite directions. She got pressure on

Marybeth's wound right away and held on until the EMTs got there."

Ken blew out a long breath. "My God, these women."

Agent Sanchez smiled back. "They're pretty amazing, I'll give you that."

CHAPTER FORTY-FOUR

*G*rant didn't want to waste time trying to get Jimmy on the phone, so he drove directly to the indoor soccer center. He left the car running in the driveway and jumped out, then had to make his way through what looked like hundreds of 8-year-olds in a sea of blue and green jerseys. Jimmy's game was on the back field, and Grant hollered as soon as he got close to it. Jimmy was driving the ball down the field, planning to shoot, when he began yelling to him. It looked to Grant like his first reaction was fury at being interrupted, but he passed the ball off quickly after he caught a glance at Grant's face.

Jimmy ran toward the bench and jumped over the low wall, motioning for his friend Chris to take his place. He shoved his stuff in his backpack and hurried around the field to where Grant was waiting. "C'mon," Grant started for the car. "Mom's been shot, she's in a hospital in Baltimore."

"Shot, are you kidding me? What the hell?" The two of them began running.

"Dad finally called just a few minutes ago. He said it's a long story, wait no, he said it's a big story, something he thinks Mom will want to tell us herself."

"Is she gonna be okay? What kind of surgery?"

"I guess to take out the bullet? I don't know anything more. We can call him back on our way. Do you need to go home first?"

"No, let's go. I've got my wallet and a clean shirt in my bag. What's the address?"

"Here, it's on my phone." He tossed his phone over, and Jimmy plugged the information into the map system. They were on the highway within a few minutes.

More than an hour into the drive, they were getting on each other's nerves, speculating and arguing about what might or might not have happened. Grant's phone rang, and Jimmy answered it quickly, putting it on speaker.

"Dad, this is Jimmy, we're in the car. How's mom?"

"She's out of surgery, and they're moving her to recovery. I should be able to see her in just a few minutes. She lost some blood, but they think she's going to be all right. They're going to watch her for a while and then get her checked into a room."

"Thank God, Dad," Grant answered. "Jimmy, how much farther?"

"Dad, we're still more than an hour out, according to the GPS. We'll come to the recovery area but if they move her before then just text us her room number."Jimmy paused, looking at Grant. "Dad, are you okay? What's going on?"

There was a long pause, and Jimmy was starting to check if they'd been disconnected when he heard his father again. Grant thought his voice made him sound so old.

"I'm fine, there's just no way to explain everything on the phone. Be extra careful driving here."

"We will Dad, you take care of Mom. We'll be there as soon as we can." Grant and Jimmy exchanged glances, but neither of them seemed to know what to say. They both stared ahead at the highway, waiting for the next set of instructions from the GPS. After several minutes had passed, Jimmy looked over at Grant again.

"Weird weekend, huh?"
"You got that right."

CHAPTER FORTY-FIVE

$\mathcal{T}$he recovery room had a row of beds, white curtains hanging down between them. The nurse led Ken to where Marybeth was lying, touched him on the shoulder and gestured behind her before stepping away. "I'll be at that desk right over there, if you need anything. She'll be asleep for a little while though."

He nodded distractedly and pulled up a chair next to the head of the bed. Marybeth's arms were laid out straight beside her, in a way that made her look dead.

Marybeth always slept on her stomach, one arm under her pillow, the other hand often resting on his shoulder. He had missed that so much. He could feel tears running down his cheeks. He brushed at them with his sleeve and reached for her hand. He'd forgotten how small it was as he rubbed it gently, tracing the length of each finger with his thumb. She was so still, it was scaring him. "Marybeth, I'm here, I'm not going anywhere. The boys are on their way too, I couldn't stop them. I didn't tell them much. I know you're going to want to tell them the whole story in your own way. Honestly, I want to hear it, too. I'm just so glad to be here next to you, please don't take off like that again, ever." He felt a gentle squeeze on his hand and he saw her eyes open briefly before falling asleep again. He smiled and held onto her. "Take your time and rest, it's going to be all right."

After about twenty minutes, her eyes began to flutter and Ken leaned a little closer to the bed. "Marybeth, can you hear me?"

Slowly she seemed to regain her focus and she looked at him clearly, tears falling down onto her pillow. "Are you angry at me? You've every right," she whispered out and then hesitated.

"Marybeth, Jesus, I thought I'd lost you when you took off and then you get shot? My God. I'm not angry, I'm still in shock." He was shaking his head as he held her hand once more.

"Me too, but I'm so glad you're here. I've missed you so much."

Ken couldn't help but pull his hands back then. "What's going on? All of this secrecy? A daughter? Witness protection for God's sake? Why couldn't you have told me all of that?" He straightened in his seat. "Why didn't you trust me?"

Marybeth struggled to get a little more upright, wincing at the pain. Ken reached over to help adjust the pillow behind her and she reached up to touch the lobe of his ear before settling her hand back in her lap. "You have no idea how often I wanted to tell you, especially in the beginning. I wanted to pour everything out to you but I was afraid. Each time it felt like I'd get my nerve up and then there'd be something in the news and I'd close back down." She reached for his hand again and he closed his around it. "What I did was wrong, I know that, but it was never about trust, Ken. I've always trusted you."

Ken took a deep breath before he spoke again. "He hurt you. I saw the pictures." He traced a finger along the scar that ran under her eye.

Marybeth lowered her head. "I'm sorry you had to see those. I was so ashamed of what happened." She raised her head again. "I felt like a fool, Ken, embarrassed at what an idiot I'd been for having stayed in that situation as long as I did." She squeezed his hand. "Once we settled into our life at home I really did start to forget most of it. I was so glad that I wasn't living in that constant fear anymore, I suppose it seemed easier to let it all stay hidden."

"Until the crash?" He waited a moment, watching her face. "I've known something was up for a little while, really. I wish now I'd said something when I first noticed it."

Marybeth agreed. "I'm sorry, I wish I'd said something too. I should have. I was wrong not to. It was just that the more I thought about it, the more I thought about her, I couldn't let it go." She looked up at him again, a more certain look on her face now. "I'll tell you whatever you want to know, answer any questions that you have, but Ken, I need to know what you think of all of this, of my having a daughter."

Ken leaned back in his seat. "I'm pretty blown away by it, I have to say, by all of it really. It's going to take me some time, I'm sure." He stood and took a step away from the bed, looking around him at the hospital room, the variety of lights and beeps creating an odd soundtrack to their conversation. Then he turned back to her, settled on the edge of the bed and couldn't help but smile. "She looks so much like you did when I first met you that it's hard not to like her."

Marybeth grinned. "I'm a grandmother. Can you believe that?"

"My God, I'm not sure I'm ready to live with a grandmother." He laughed as Marybeth tried to give him a weak punch on the arm.

She sobered then. "What do you think the boys will say?"

"I don't know, but they're going to be here soon so I guess we'll find out."

$\mathcal{M}$arybeth was awake in her room upstairs when the boys arrived. The bed was angled so that she could sit up, and Ken was perched on the side of it giving her a sip of water. Their boys, men, really, she had to remind herself, stopped at the door and for a second, looked like they were afraid to come in, but she smiled at them and they hurried toward her. Ken stood up and gestured to them. "Come on around to this side, so you can get close. We don't want to bump her other arm."

Marybeth looked at her boys and couldn't stop crying. "I've missed you two so much." She reached up to touch each of their faces as they leaned in to kiss her, barely touching her cheek as though they were afraid of hurting her.

Grant spoke first. "Mom, what's been going on? Why in the world were you shot?"

"Where have you been?" Jimmy asked.

Marybeth looked at her boys and knew she didn't have the strength to tell them the whole story now. She was exhausted. But she knew they needed something, all of them did, including Ken. "You three, you're my family, and you know I love you more than anything else in the world."

She paused. "But you need to know, I'm not quite who I always said I was. Before I met your father I was someone else with a different name and everything. I was in danger and the FBI gave me a new identity." She looked at Ken. "A new identity, a whole new life really." She looked from one face to the other and then saw Carolyn hesitating at the door.

Marybeth gestured to her to come in. The young woman was holding PJ in her arms, a shiny restaurant spoon still clutched in his hand. Marybeth laughed and winced, then turned back to them. "Grant, Jimmy, Ken, I want you to meet my daughter, Carolyn Jacobs, and my grandson PJ." Ken walked toward the young woman and rested his hand gently on her shoulder.

"Hi, Carolyn, it's nice to meet you." Then he looked at PJ as he waved the spoon around.

Carolyn laughed. "We left the restaurant in such confusion, I didn't even realize he had it."

"I can't imagine they'll miss it," Ken said.

At a knock on the door, Ken moved forward. "Agent Sanchez." Ken led him into the room and introduced him to their sons.

They shook hands all around and Agent Sanchez made his way to the end of Marybeth's bed. "Well, you look a little better than the last time I saw you. How are you feeling?"

Marybeth reached her good hand forward and Agent Sanchez leaned in to shake it gently. "I'm feeling a lot better actually." Then her face stilled. "Is there any word on Jay?"

"I just spoke with the charge nurse. He's out of surgery now. They're moving him into recovery." He looked around the room. "He'll be under guard until he's well enough to be moved to lockup."

Marybeth leaned back in relief. "Will I have to face any charges?"

"No," he smiled easily. "Ms. Rogers, you and Ms. Jacobs were just protecting yourselves. We have a restaurant full of diners eager to step up and tell us what happened."

Marybeth could see the confusion on her sons' faces. "What did happen?" Jimmy asked.

Agent Sanchez looked at the family spread out in front of him and then at Marybeth. "Okay if I tell them?"

She nodded and Agent Sanchez struck a more serious tone, taking his time as he told them the story. "I want you all to know how brave Ms. Jacobs and your mom were today. They stood up to a dangerous man and because of them, he's now in custody. His name is Jay Warren, I don't know if you've heard of him or not. He was from your mom's hometown of Pittsburgh, and she knew him when she started college at Penn State. Jay Warren and your mom were together back then, and the FBI was investigating him and his dad. That spring, his dad called him back to Pittsburgh, and the FBI began interviewing your mom. She was going to testify to the fact that many of his alibis weren't true. In fact, her testimony was going to be one of the keys to our putting Jay away along with other members of that family." He paused and looked over at Marybeth before continuing. She was relieved that he hadn't mentioned all of the details. "Unfortunately, though, the FBI's case fell apart that summer and we were worried for your mom's life. So, we took steps to put her under protection."

Ray looked around him and then tucked his hands in his pockets. "I know everyone's heard of the witness protection service, but you have to know that in reality, it's pretty rare. The FBI wouldn't have gone to the trouble of hiding your mom if her life hadn't been in danger. Believe me, she was as brave then as she was today."

Marybeth heard a faint buzz and Agent Sanchez pulled his phone out of his pocket and pulled his glasses back down on his nose, then looked up. "I'm going to leave you folks in peace for the moment. I won't lie, there are going to be some busy days ahead for all of us, but I'll leave you to it for now. Take good care of each other." He left the room, dialing his phone as he went out.

Marybeth saw Grant look around the room and then back at his dad's face. "This is unbelievable." He looked at Carolyn and then at Jimmy. "Can you believe we have a sister and we're uncles?" The group couldn't help but laugh, his enthusiasm catching.

Marybeth watched as Ken gestured toward Carolyn and asked, "May I?" He reached toward the baby, lifting him carefully. Ken held him close for a minute studying his small face and then carried him over to the side of the bed where the boys were standing. Marybeth couldn't help but smile as she watched the interaction. He held PJ so that he could stand next to her, waving his spoon around, before letting it fly across the room. Jimmy grabbed it out of the air and walked toward Carolyn to hand it to her.

"I'm Jimmy, it's, I don't know, a little bit weird to meet you, I guess." Marybeth watched as her shy younger son met her daughter and wondered, as usual, what in the world he was thinking. Jimmy always took in everything at once without seeming to, then ideas and perceptions would come out later, in slow but interesting ways.

Grant stepped forward also, smiling as he held out his hand. "And I'm Grant." She knew Grant was just the opposite, his heart on his sleeve ever since he'd been PJ's age. She was overwhelmed at how much she loved them, how deeply she had missed them these past few weeks, and she couldn't keep the tears from pooling in her eyes. Then she looked again, paused and really studied the faces around her. They were all here. All of the pieces of her life were together in one room. Her breath caught in her throat as she reached for a tissue.

Ken handed it to her and with a kindness that she was so afraid might have been lost, he asked quietly "Should we go and let you rest?"

Marybeth shifted and winced as the pain reminded her of its presence. She looked around the room at all of the faces that she loved. "I don't want anyone to go, but I'm afraid I am pretty tired."

Her boys kissed her again and everyone began to file out. She couldn't stop her eyes from closing then, until Ken kissed her on the lips and touched his forehead to hers.

"I'll be back before you wake up," he assured her as he pulled the cover up.

She looked up and whispered, "I promise I'll be here."

CHAPTER FORTY-SEVEN

$\mathcal{T}$he hall outside of the hospital room was empty but Ray Sanchez waited until he'd reached the other end of it to connect the call. "Cindy, it's Ray."

He could hear the relief in her voice. "We've got him, and everyone else is safe."

"I'm so relieved to hear that. Guess the case of the century is back on?"

"You better believe it is, and I need our chief analyst here on the scene. How soon can you get here?" When she answered, he could hear that extra note in her voice, and he knew it wasn't going to be soon enough.

"I'm on my way," she answered.

"Hey Cindy, pack something nice to wear. I'm making us a reservation at this beautiful restaurant I saw this morning." He laughed. "They'll probably have the blood cleaned up by the time you get here."

"What a charmer you are, Sanchez." He was still smiling when he got to the elevator and headed downstairs.

CHAPTER FORTY-EIGHT

*T*hey settled around tables and extra seats in the library, Marybeth joining her fellow special education teachers at the round table near the checkout counter. Gerald had finally gotten the microphone to work.

"Welcome back, everyone, have a seat and let's get started. I've put some paper out on the tables and I'd like to begin by having everyone write a quick, little 'what I did on my summer vacation' essay. Then we'll share them at our tables."

Marybeth looked up in horror, nearly choking on her cup of coffee.

"Just kidding, everyone, didn't you hate doing those when you were in elementary school?" The room filled with laughter. "Welcome back. I know we're going to have a wonderful new school year, and I just hope everyone had a good, relaxing summer break."

Marybeth could feel the cool wood against her healing shoulder as she leaned back and let the breath she'd been holding go.

ACKNOWLEDGMENTS

I left my home in Pennsylvania to go to college at seventeen. I glanced back the first summer after I'd left, but after that, home was wherever my husband and I were. We carried the feeling of home with us and planted the flag where we slept. Luckily for us, where we ended up was Ann Arbor, Michigan and that is where we remain. It is a place I had never imagined myself living with its flat terrain, frequently awful weather and truly wonderful people. From a shared bus stop grew a family of friends, and with my loving husband they, too, have helped to form the sweet base on which I've been able to build an amazing life. I hope they know how grateful I am to all of them.

I would especially like to thank my first readers: my sisters-in-law Karen Brawn and Nancy Tusa and my colleague and friend Suzanne Biermann. Many other friends were early, supportive readers and I would like to thank all of them as well.

Finally, I would like to thank the Ann Arbor District Library and Fifth Avenue Press for all of their support and encouragement.

The press provided me with an opportunity that is a dream come true and for that I am especially grateful.

ABOUT THE AUTHOR

Linda Cotton Jeffries grew up in Carlisle, Pennsylvania. She's a graduate of the University of North Carolina at Chapel Hill and was a special education teacher for more than 30 years. Linda lives in Ann Arbor, Michigan with her husband, and is surrounded by close family.